THE HUNTER

J.G.TEE

Paperback: 978-1-968667-20-7
eBook: 978-1-968667-21-4
Library of Congress Control Number: 2025914110

This is a work of fiction.

Ordering Information:

Prime Seven Media
518 Landmann St.
Tomah City, WI 54660

Printed in the United States of America

TABLE OF CONTENTS

CHAPTER ONE

YOU SAID YOU WOULD LET THEM GO.

"Oh! Yes, Ahrrr Ohh fill me Ron" Laura cried.

A deep sigh and a long exhale of breath came from the lips of Ron as he withdrew his penis from Laura, then rolled of her body, the bed to stand on the floor, with a wet towel washed his body.

The naked Laura lay on the bed and watched as her lover Ron hurriedly dressed.

"You know what you have to do at eleven o'clock" Ron asked.

"Yes, I know what to do, you promised me that no one will get hurt" Laura stated.

"No one will get hurt" Ron assured her.

As Ron left the room, Laura climbed out of the bed and stood and looked at her body in the mirror Laura was not bad looking, going to the bowl and taking a wet towel, she washed herself all over, dried off, then dressed putting on shirt and jeans ready for riding, she proceeded to pack a saddlebag with items she wanted to take with her.

Laura was not happy by the way Ron was so cold, and in such a hurry that their love in was cut short, the way he did after putting his seed into her, quickly deserting her, Laura put this behind her as the two of them were going away at eleven o'clock.

Leaving the room Laura proceeded to the livery stable to tend to her horse making sure it was fed and watered, walked to the café for breakfast, Laura worked for Wells Fargo in a town called JAYTON north Texas, on completion of her breakfast she returned to the livery stable, saddled up, rode to work tying the horse to the hitch rail outside the rear door of the office walked around the building and entered, at eleven o'clock she released the catch on the rear door of the premises.

Ronald Bates is going to rob the Wells Fargo office of a payroll expected that day, Laura knows this and is in fact his accomplice, poor Laura did not know that the good looking , smooth talking man Ron who had just seduced her, has done this a few times before, but this is the way the man operates, he finds a nice looking woman who works at a bank, general store or like in the present case the Wells Fargo office or anywhere there is money that can be stolen, as Ron is good looking and has a silver tongue and appeals to females so recruits them by seducing them to enable him to rob there employers.

Five minutes after Laura took the catch of the rear door, a Wells Fargo stagecoach pulled up outside the front entrance of the building the guard on the coach passed the one hundred-thousand-dollar payroll to the office manager, left the office climbed on the box (Seat) of the stagecoach and drove away, the guard in the office closed the front door and locked it.

In the office was the manager and two guards as the guard locked the door Ron Bates and his four henchmen burst into the room, shot the manager and guards grabbed the payroll turned to go out the rear door where they had just entered.

Laura came running from the back room.

"NO! NO! you said no one would get hurt" Laura cried.

"Laura, they pulled their guns on us we shot in self-defence" Bates lied to her.

Ron Bates grabbed her arm and directed her to the rear door to the waiting horses, an unfortunate young couple were passing the entrance to the gap where the Wells Fargo back door could be seen.

"Get them" Bates yelled.

"No" Laura called.

"Shut up and mount up, NOW" Bates said the last word loudly.

The gang of robbers turned their horses with Laura and the two young captives and rode away from the town, the gang of thieves were lucky as they had been able to get away quickly the only persons who could indemnify them are the persons they had with them, the sheriff and people of the town were slow to respond getting to the scene.

On his arrival at the scene the sheriff after scouting around found that the sign showed him the tracks of the robbers, left the rear of the Wells Fargo building going straight across a piece of rough open land which puts the robbers into a grove of trees about three hundred yards in a straight line from the building.

"Johnny" the sheriff yelled.

A young man separated himself from the crowd of spectators and approached the sheriff.

"You want me sheriff" the young man said.

"Yeh! Johnny get your horse and follow those tracks" the sheriff ordered.

"OK" came the reply.

The sheriff turned and addressed the crowd.

"You men get your horses I want a posse to meet me outside the sheriff's office" then strode of to get his own horse.

By the time the posse had been assembled and ready to move, an hour had passed by which gave the robbers more than an hour start, meanwhile Johnny had found it easy to pick up the robbers sign mainly because the thieves only immediate intension is to make as much distance from the town as possible after a few miles Laura said to Ron.

"Ron, we have managed to get away from anyone pursuing us let the young couple go"

"I will let them go when I think it is safe not before" Bates announced.

"Ron, we are well ahead now" Laura stated.

"Laura, I am boss here and I will decide when to let them go so shut up now" Bates told her.

Laura for the first time, started to have second thoughts about her actions, it was all right when it was only the robbery but the killing of the three Wells Fargo agents she did not like, as she had been promised that no one will get hurt, now the kidnap of the young couple to Laura it was all wrong, she decided to remain quiet for the time being as Ron was getting angry she thought for the time it would be wise to be silent until Ron calmed down.

Meanwhile Johnny is still finding it easy to follow the gang, as he now knew what sign to follow as he knew the pattern of the horses hoofs, that the robbers have left behind, also mainly because one of the party chain smoked, leaving a continuous trail of strong smelling discarded cigarette ends.

The thieves carried on until just before it became dark, when they were forced to rest for the night, a few miles back down the trail Johnny was also forced to sleep as it was getting to dark to follow sign.

"Ron it's been a full day now surely it is best to let the young couple go" Laura asked again.

Ron did not get mad like before and had done previously but did explain to Laura.

"Laura, we have a tracker coming up behind us, this will help them to catch up to us, if I leave these two behind too early, they can give the sheriff our descriptions and of the help you have given me, we must put some distance between us before allowing them to be questioned" Ron explained.

Laura remained quiet but the thought in her head was different (It does not matter if they are set free today or tomorrow the two-young people could still give the law a description of all of them) the more she thought, the more distressed she was becoming, (What have I done) then thought (What is going to happen, can I do anything) looking around she realised it would be impossible, as one of the men was constantly on guard.

Laura had thought of two things she might do but discarded them, her first idea was to release the young couple as the guard stayed so close to them and seemed to be alert and keeping near them, the second idea was for her to slip away but Ron held her close to him all night and then thought if she did get away, (What could she do) Laura reluctantly forced herself to go to sleep.

At dawn the next morning the party had breakfast loaded up, broke camp the party rode out Laura noticed only three of the men rode out with them she asked Ron about it.

"Ron why is a man being left behind"

"He is going to clean up the camp area and disguise the sign we have left to confuse any tracker following us" Ron explained.

"Oh! I see" Laura said.

The man who stayed behind was called Dutchy by the other members of the gang, this man was overweight stocky type of man with a foreign accent, the man cleared away the remains of the fire they had lit the night before and covered the remains with a piece of turf, then scouted around the camp area to clear up any sign left by the party, with a branch from a nearby tree he wiped all sign that was left of the camp site and their tracks when leaving.

Johnny the man tracking them woke up before first light and was ready to proceed as soon as it was light enough to see and follow sign, once more the young man started to follow sign, and this was his undoing, as Duchy's orders from Ron was to clear camp hide as much sign as possible, to go back down the track a hundred yards wait for the tracker and take him out.

Johnny without thought was following sign and rode into a clear area his head down checking sign and did not find anything unusual to warn him, too late the loud sound of a rifle being fired as the heavy bullet hit him, in the shoulder just above the heart, falling from the saddle hitting his head on a large rock knocking him unconscious , Dutchy believing Johnny was dead moved out hiding his own sign as riding to catch up with the rest of the gang of thieves.

Laura like everyone else heard the loud shot, as Dutchy used a rifle and because it is a heavy weapon it also makes a very loud bang when fired, Laura looked at Ron a question on her face, Ron explained.

"Dutchy has wiped any sign possible that we left behind, then waited for the man that was tracking and killed him"

Ron smiled when seeing the concerned look on Laura's face, Laura being naive had known, plus expected the robbery, but did not expect the amount of death that followed because of the cold-hearted way Ron informed her she became more and more worried.

Two hours later the sheriff found the unconscious Johnny and was happy to find him alive, the sheriff told two of the posse members to detached from the posse and look after Johnny, while the sheriff and the remainder of the posse searched to find sign but to no avail as dutchy had done a good job, the trail had been lost which forced the posse to return to JAYTON.

The band of robbers, killers rode through the next day, camping once more that night the second night. The following day they rode most of the day until they reached the foothills of a mountain range in the afternoon. Entering a large cave, they made camp, the cave was large like a caisson at the rear it had a couple of tunnels.

"Ron let the young couple go" Laura asked.

"Don't worry we don't need them anymore" Ron told her.

For a time, everything settled down as they went through the routine making camp, building a fire, putting food on to cook, they lit a couple of torches as the cave became darker due to it being sunset, the five robbers gathered in a group, getting the money out they started dividing it out between them each of them getting twenty thousand dollars.

When the gang left the cave, it was there intension to split up and go their separate ways, they congratulated themselves on a job well done and carried out successfully and had previously agree d they would split up and do their own things after splitting the money.

Now that they had distributed the money, and each man had twenty thousand dollars in their saddlebags and now sat around the fire excitedly talking about how they intended to spend their plunder.

"What are you going to do with your money Dutchy" the dandy asked.

"I'm going to buy a livery stable and maybe a small bit of land" Dutchy replied.

"What about you Carl" Dutchy enquired.

"That is easy I'm going to live it up lots of drink and plenty of female company and just enjoy myself" the dandy told them.

"Well Billy what about you, drink and cards" Wes Arnold asked.

"You know I have always wanted to wear new smart clothes, a black gun belt and a pearl handled forty–five then maybe I'll get my girl back after that I will live it up" Billy bragged to them.

"How about you Wes" Dutchy asked.

"Now I have a little money, I would like to travel but I really have not made up my mind I'm going to have to think a bit about it" Wes replied.

"Ron what have you decided to do with your share" Wes asked.

"I have seen a piece of land up north near the northern border of Texas, I think I will buy it and start ranching it puts my money where it will be useful and possibly make me more money" Ron Bates explained.

After talking Ron sat back a quick thought came to him, he looked at the other four men.

"Fellows we now have a problem since we have all told each other what we are going to do, and where we intend to go, we now have another task to do we have to get rid of them" pointing to the young couple

"No" Laura almost screamed at Ron.

"Laura, they have heard too much" Ron told her.

"Ron, you promised me" Laura reminded him.

"That was before they heard our plans," Ron said.

"You said you would let them go" Laura said in an angry voice.

"Things have changed, kill them" his last two words directed at the four men.

Laura ran at Ron fists flying, Laura swung a fist at Ron punching him full in the face and Ron felt it, Ron hit Laura hard it broke her nose she went down hard which made her hit the ground enough to stun her.

The men advanced on the young couple, the young man showed bravery by standing in front of the girl with his fists up ready to fight, not having a gun the boy intended to stand up to the four men, Wes Arnold drew his gun and shot the boy killing him, the four men went towards the young girl.

The four men grabbed the girl and started stripping her, it was obvious the men's intentions even though Ron had only told them to kill her the other four were intent on rape it didn't matter that the girl was a seventeen-year-old virgin they showed no respect as normal men would do, Laura came to her senses as she heard the terrible screams of the girl being raped.

Laura ran at Ron intending to hit him with a rock, Ron drew his revolver and pistol whipped her, hitting her hard enough on the head to knock her out she fell unconscious to the cave floor.

Meanwhile the other men kept up their relentless attack on the young lady she went through torture until one of the men realised, she was dead, the men were callous as they went back to the fire laughing, at this time the unfortunate Laura groaned as she started to revive.

"Dutchy, Carl takes her over the back of the cave and kill her" Bates ordered indicating Laura.

The two men grabbed the dazed Laura, roughly dragging her body towards the back of the cave, Laura is a nice looking women and Dutchy and Carl had already decided to rape her before killing her, while she was still drowsy the two rapists starting to undress her, almost naked with only her small pants on she came to her senses, it did not take a genius to understand what they intended to do and Laura is a smart young lady and saw straight away their intentions, taking the two men by surprise she pushed Carl into Dutchy, while they were of balance, she ran down the shaft.

Dutchy jumped to his feet drew his revolver and shot the running Laura in the back, Carl followed Duchy's lead and fired into the back of the running girl, Laura felt the impact of the bullets as she fell forward knocking her head on the mine floor rending her unconscious. The two killers laughed out loud as they went back to the other members of the gang around the fire.

"She's dead Ron" Carl said.

"I know I heard the shots; I think it is time we moved on, let's get all the gear together" Ron said to the others.

For the next twenty minutes, they brought canteens of water what food they had left checked their horses.

"Ron everything is ready" Billy informed him

"OK, split the water equality in five canteens also make out an equal amount of food to each of us" Ron told the others.

"All ready to move" the dandy spoke for the first time.

"Right saddle up, let's get out of here I think we have been here long enough don't you agree" Ron ordered.

The other four did agree, in fact they were eager to leave the cave. After riding around twenty yards from the entrance Ron called them to a halt.

"Dutchy do you still have that stick of dynamite you pretend is a cigar" Ron asked.

"Sure, do Ron" came the reply.

"OK you ride back and place the stick in the rocks above the entrance to the cave that should cover the cave, right" Ron stated.

"OK Ron, I'll meet you further down the trail on completion" Dutchy informed them.

Moving a short distance from the cave the four men watched and waited, after hearing the explosion Dutchy joined them the five men laughed about it.

"Right you four I am riding north, but first was thinking of stopping of at Turkey to celebrate our good fortune, I intend to have a drink, as we have eliminated all the persons who know us we should have no more problems, anyone of you who would like a final drink together before going our separate ways can join me, of course if you have other places you want to carry on to I understand if so good luck" Bates told them. As it happens a couple of the other men had also thought of going to Turkey for a drink, they all thought it was a good idea, the whole gang therefore proceeded to the town called Turkey.

Meanwhile back in the cave Laura became conscious but still lay crying with the pain she was going through, Duchy's shot had hit her in the shoulder the bullet still lodged in it, Carl's bullet also hit her and because of the distance the pair fired from the projectiles did not have the power to go through the body, the bullet from Carl's gun was jammed against the hip bone.

Laura lay for quite a while crying until sense came to her and she began to think of her situation, the thing that finally drove her was the built-up anger which turned to hate for Ronald Bates the man who seduced her then ordered her execution.

Even though Laura was still a young lady she had a good head on her shoulders so started to think of what she should do, first realising she was almost naked so must find her clothes and therefore started to drag and crawl back up the tunnel, reaching the place the two men stripped her she felt the cloths as it was too dark to see them.

Laura after a bit of thought new she was breathing fresh air, but how ?, she needed to know to find out where the air was coming from, but she was knackered, using her head she looked at the abandoned camp sight, luck seemed to be on her side the fire had not been extinguished properly and there was enough fuel for to keep her warm, it also meant she could have some light, the good thing is that she had air, light and heat but the downside is there is no food or water, because of her very tired state she found a place to lie comfortable and went to sleep.

Waking up Laura winced at the pain of her wounds, partly dragging and staggering herself across the cave, first to the bodies of the young couples, beside the naked body of the girl was her clothes she kept the petticoat aside then using the rest of her clothes to cover the body, she tore the petticoat and made pads out of it to cover her wounds.

What Ron did not know is that Laura was normally a level headed young woman she is a thinker, the fact that Ron had seduced her and she had fell for him was the first time she had lost her head over a man, when she found out that the gang had taken all the food and water she did weep for a moment or two but thinking of her survival gave her the added strength to carry on, this made her think of what she needed to do.

Laura's thoughts.

1) I have air where is it coming from could she get out.
2) What can I do about thirst.
3) Food, she could only think of one possibility but put it from her mind.

Partly staggering, hopping, crawling and dragging herself around the cave she looked for the source of the air she was breathing. Laura could not find where the air came from until a few hours later she saw a sunbeam come through the roof of the cave, she sighed as she knew even if she was not wounded, she would not be able to get to the hole in the roof, and now knew the only way out was to dig.

Laura had tired herself out by moving all over looking for a way out so once more had to rest, after drifting off to sleep for a couple of hours woke up, her first task was to attend her wounds, making a couple of pads, using spit she cleaned the shoulder wound the best she could then use her bra strap to keep the pad in place, she did the same routine for the hip wound holding the pad into place with her jeans.

"Dad! Your wonderful" she exclaimed to herself loudly.

While cleaning the wounds Laura remembered something her father had once told her. (darling if your mouth is dry find a smooth round stone clean it then suck it for a brief period) then carried on and told her to use the method sparingly wet your mouth and that is all then take it out of your mouth until the mouth is dry again as long as your body has moisture it will help.

Every possible moment she could Laura with her bare hands clawed at the muck, shale, stones and rocks by lying on the side of her body that did not have bullets in it she slowly made progress the hatred for the five men in particular Ron Bates spurred her on.

After four days Laura new she had to eat and had put her only source of food out of her mind but now knew she would have to go ahead and do it, finding a piece of stone with a razor sharp edge she crawled to the body of the young girl she removed the clothes from the arm then with tears running down her face and repeatedly saying "I'm Sorry, I'm sorry, I'm sorry" she hacked the girls arm until it separated from the body then she tried to suck any blood left in the arm to get as much moisture from it before putting the arm on the fire to cook.

Laura had stopped worrying about her wounds and learned to live with it as she found it harder to reach the wounds she just concentrated on digging, therefore at first dust got into the wound then Laura knew because she felt them bugs and beetles were eating around the wounds.

Now the start of the seventh day Laura realised she had little left in her body she was getting weaker by the moment, her tongue was swelling through lack of moisture and she could not eat the wounds were hurting bad the shoulder wound turning green on the verge of giving up she pushed a small rock her arm went through and air rushed in through the hole she had made, this development gave her the strength to enlarge the hole enough to squeeze her thin frail body through it, but too late as she lost all her strength as she collapsed unconscious just outside the caves entrance she Knew she was dying, Laura's body lay there for two hours the life draining from her.

Two young men on the box of a light wagon were driving through the hills.

"Alex, I like Julia in the general store, I think I'll ask her to go to the towns dance next month" Vince stated.

"It's funny you should bring that up, I have been thinking of asking Victoria about the same thing" Alex replied.

"I have had Julia on my mind for a while, I think I love her, that lovely face and the long dark hair, makes me think of her a lot she is beautiful" Vince explained to Alex.

"Yeh! I know what you mean" Alex agreed

"Let's get back to town, the dust out here makes me crave for a beautiful cool beer" Vince said liking his lips.

"This haulage job is good I enjoy it, but sometimes the heat is unbearable out here in the open" Vince complained.

"Yes! But we just must take the good with the bad" Alex pointed out.

"Yeh! I guess you are right" Vince acknowledged.

"Well as soon as we deliver the cargo at Jayton, we can relax before the next job" Alex told Vince.

"Yes, as I have said I am looking forward to holding a nice cool glass of beer in my hand in fact I can taste it" Alex said

Both men Laughed out loud happily.

"I do like the idea of a cool beer, but I admit the thing I am looking forward to the most is seeing Victoria those cool blue eyes and long blonde hair gives me a picture of her continuously in my mind" Vince omitted.

"Yeh! I know what you mean" Alex said with a sigh.

"Alex pull up quick"

"Why"

"Does that look like a body in those rocks ahead of us to the right" Vince asked.

"I think you are right, whoa! let's go see" Alex said as he brought the team to a halt.

Both men rushed to where Laura's body lay.

"I think there is a pulse, but it is very slow she is nearly dead" Alex said.

"Alex back the wagon up as near as you can, put up the canopy then bring a sheet and a canteen" Vince instructed him.

Alex carried out Vince's instructions.

Vince could see the swollen tongue in the open mouth, wetting a cloth he squeezed a couple of drops of water into her mouth then placed the wet cloth onto her forehead, they cannot give Laura a drink with a swollen tongue as she could drowned the young men knew it had to be a couple of drops on the tongue the wait and do it again, the wet cloth cooled her.

"OK Vince, we will carefully put her on the blanket then move her into the wagon under the shade" Alex advised.

"Yes, very slow and carefully, If I remember right about half a mile from here there is a grassy area and a stream, get on the box drive very, very slowly I will get in the back and hold her still" Vince said.

As they moved Laura, they found the two bullet holes in her back.

Getting Laura into the wagon they moved off knowing there is not much they could do about the wounds until they could stabilise Laura, about every few minutes they put a couple of drops of water on her tongue until the swelling went down and she started to breath properly the two young men washed and covered her wounds.

"Vince the shoulder wound is coloured green and smells" Alex said.

"Look Alex the lady will take a long time to get back to health she is now breathing so let's start moving very slow one of us will drive while the other stays with the lady" Vince said.

"I agree, the sooner we get her to a doctor the better" Alex summarised.

"Your right we will move slowly to town" Vince admitted.

Three days later they pulled up the wagon outside the doctors in Jayton. The doctor Vince Alex and the sheriff carefully took Laura into the doctors and laid her on the bed, Alex and Vince told the doctor about Laura's condition, they were quizzed by the sheriff, before going to the saloon for that lovely cool beer.

The doctor with the aid of his wife who acts as his nurse, slowly began to peel the clothes from her body, as the clothes were stuck to her body except around the two wounds where the two young men had washed them, her body was in one hell of a mess, it was dirty, grazed and black and blue all over, as she could not look after the bullet holes in her back, these two holes looked bad the one in the hip was red with a black rim around it, but the doctor was more concerned with the shoulder wound as it being green which indicated gangrene.

Laura was near death, her body was thin and gaunt being malnourish nearly a Skelton all bony little flesh on her body, her once beautiful face drained, the doctor surprised she still lived, after an examination of the wounds decided not to operate as it would kill her, his examination revealed the gangrene in her shoulder slowly spreading towards her heart which means Laura did not have long to live, with care she may last a month if she is lucky, the doctor told his wife his intention is to keep her alive as long as possible, using drugs, painkillers and fluids plus washing her body.

After three days of intensive care the doctor was pleased with the result when her eyes slowly opened then closed again, two days later Laura had a tinge of colour and opened her eyes, she was still weak unable to talk the doctor whispered into her ear calming her. A couple of days later still weak lying on her bed she could now talk her first sentence was to ask the doctor.

"Doctor get the sheriff for me please" Laura requested.

"OK Laura" the doctor replied then sent his wife, no way was the doc. Going to leave his patient and decided to let Laura Know the situation.

"Laura please listen, I must tell you the truth" Doc started to talk when Laura cut in.

"You're going to tell me I am dying" she told him.

"Who told you"The doctor demanded.

"Nobody told me I just know; I have forced myself to stay alive until I put something right, I have done wrong" Laura explained.

"I see" once again Laura broke in.

"Well doctor what is wrong with me"

"The bullet in your shoulder is infected with gangrene and it is slowly spreading to your heart, when it reaches it you will have minutes to live" doc explained

"How long have I got" Laura asked.

"With care two weeks to a month" doc told her

"Oh! Good I thought I didn't have long" Laura said.

"Laura, you are very brave" doc told her.

"Oh! No doctor I am mad, there is five evil men out there I hate them and want them caught" Laura said.

The house door opened, and his wife stepped in.

"This way sheriff" the doctor called out.

"Your wife told me you need my help is everything OK" the sheriff asked.

"Jack, this is Laura she needs your help" doc introduced them.

"Hello, miss Laura sorry you are ill, I hope you get better soon" Jack Brent the sheriff said.

"Thanks sheriff there is not much chance of that, can you get paper and pencil I need to give you some details" Laura informed him.

"I will get you some" doc said

"OK Laura I am ready" the sheriff told her.

"Doctor, could I have a glass of water please" Laura asked.

"Yes of course" doc replied.

"Thank you"

"Sheriff about three weeks ago at the Wells Fargo you had a robbery, and three men were gunned down, that was my fault" Laura stated.

"No Laura" the sheriff said.

"Yes sheriff, listen and take anything you think is irrelevant down"

"OK Laura" the sheriff returned.

"Sheriff I was seduced by a smooth, handsome, good looking, smooth talking man, I fell in love with this man and thought he loved me, and this man told me of his intention to rob the Wells Fargo office All I had to do is at eleven o'clock, is take the latch of the rear door and promised no one would get hurt, I believed him and stupidly did what was asked of me," Laura talked for over half an hour with the help of taking frequent sips of water, but could not carry on as she drifted off to sleep.

"Jack, could you come back in the morning, she needs sleep she is too exhausted to carry on" the doctor said.

"Right doc let her sleep make her comfortable I will be back in the morning" the sheriff told doc.

Mid-morning the next day the sheriff knocked on the doc's door.

"Hi! How is she this morning" the sheriff asked.

"Jack, she is weak and fretting, because she was unable to give you all the information, she wanted to tell you, so you coming here will be a tonic to her" the doc explained.

"Morning Laura" the sheriff greeted. Laura sighed

"Thank you for returning, I am sorry about yesterday" Laura told the sheriff.

"I understand, look Laura you do not have to make this statement today, we can do it another day" the sheriff suggested.

"Sheriff, I take it the doc. Has not told you about my condition" Laura said.

"The doc has told me you are very ill and needs lots of rest" the sheriff replied.

Laura looked straight at him. Jack saw in the gaunt pale face, what looked like an attempt to smile.

"Sheriff I am determent to tell you everything I can to assist the law to capture or kill the five evil men, what the doctor has not told you is I have gangrene in my shoulder where they shot me, the gangrene is slowly travelling towards my heart, nothing can be done about it, it is terminal, I am dying" Laura informed the sheriff.

"You are a very brave lady" the sheriff said.

"Sheriff I am angry with myself, I hate the five killers but most of all I hate the man who seduced me then ordered his men to kill me, and I am determined to do the right thing and correct the wrong I have caused the best I can before I die. The hate for these animals and the idea of putting things right kept me alive in that cave so before I do die, I want to give the law as much information I can" Laura explained

"Has doc told you how long you have left" the sheriff asked.

"I could die tomorrow I am so weak, but the doc blesses his soul has told me his intention is to keep me alive as long as possible" Laura stated.

"Well, I can tell you there has been a ten-thousand-dollar bounty dead or alive on the heads of this gang of men, now do you feel like continuing" the sheriff asked.

"Good" Laura acknowledged. Then gave the rest of the information.

CHAPTER TWO

I'LL GET THEM LAURA

L ying in some long grass on the Brough of a hill the young man patiently surveyed the land ahead of him, looking from end to end of the small valley with a pair of glasses (binoculars), being patient not rushing things or taking anything for granted, his interest focused on a small tree covered patch where a stream ran through which burst into life as a group of birds flew into the air, flying up like a cloud, the young man knew this was unusual this meant the birds had been disturbed by something or somebody.

Suddenly a horse and rider burst from trees, the man bent low along the horse's neck going fast as applying spurs to get away moving in the direction of the south of the valley, the young man smiled and said to himself.

"Thank you! Thank you!"

Now the young man knew that the man being hunted knew someone was hunting him, something the hunter did not know of until now, this action meant the young man from now on will have to be extra vigilant, because now his quarry is aware of the hunter there is various things the man being hunted could consider doing laying traps being one of them.

At a leisurely pace the young man stood up obviously in no hurry, calmly taking out the makings began rolling a cigarette walked over to the big horse and patted his neck before mounting up, once again in no hurry, directed the big horse to the tree covered area the hunted man had rode from, his intention is to check the area for any sign the man had left behind, there was no need to hurry as to track properly you must have patience and take your time, there was quite a few things to look out for when tracking a person, the obvious part is hoof prints left by the horse.

There is a few different things you can find about sign, there is obviously sign from the horses shoes, If when you look at the shoe print it has clean edges the shoes are new, on the other hand if the edges are rounded the shoes are worn, If the shoe is damaged you can see the crack or missing nail, by the depth of the print you can tell if the rider is a big man or the horse is carrying some weight, you can also by the tracks tell if the horse is walking, cantering or at the gallop, horse hairs are often on bushes enabling you to see the colour of the horse, the horse shoes also make scratches on rocks and stones, you also can see the direction a horse travelled by the way the grass is laying or the indents in shale or sand.

As for the signs often given by men are often easy to follow, If the man smokes there is frequently cigarette end which take time to decompose, shirts and jeans leave threads on brush chaps leave scrapes on trees and break twigs and small branches, If the man lies down and imprint of his belt or gun belt, when dismounting his boots will leave there mark, the man could have worn boots, or new boots or expensive made to measure boots .

Once more the man doing the hunting stopped his horse to let it blow while extracting the wanted dodger from his pocket, looking at the picture of the man and the words below stating, (wanted for robbery and murder Dead or Alive) this man killed two men while robbing a general store, the man hunting him always tries to take his quarry alive if possible, but finds it is not always possible.

The man doing the tracking followed the sign for a further two days, the quarry being followed tried every trick that he could think of to throw the man following him.

Once out of the valley the man being followed took a branch from a tree, tied a rope to it and dragged it behind the horse to wipe away his tracks, after a couple of miles left the main trail rode through a small forest with lots of brush then re-joined the main trail further down in the direction of his choice, out in the wilds where they were riding there really is no such thing as a trail, but when talking about the main trail it usually means the easiest way to travel.

The stunt the hunted man carried out was one of the oldest tricks in the book, the man coming up behind him might be young but he had seen this trick performed many times before, in fact each time a man has been hunted by him most of them try this trick first, but because the man did carry out this action it did cause him to slow down as it made the hunter more vigilant due to the possibility there could be a hidden reason, (like the chance for the hunted man to lay other traps for him,) but this time the man didn't, and the hunter was not concerned, there was no need to hurry as long as his prey did not get away from him, when reaching the main trail again there was a smile on his face, the reason being without any incident just losing a little time the trail still look fresh telling him there was little time lost he knew he was still on track.

Coming across a stream the hunted man moved into the water turned left walking the horse through the water until out of sight of the spot of his entry leaving the stream, riding in a large half circle and re-entered the stream further upstream after riding another half mile in the water, left the stream and started heading back south once again.

Once again this caused the hunter to lose a little time but finding the trail the horses prints, that was all that was needed, because this man is a dogged pursuer who did not give up easy, any sign is enough to keep him hunting.

The running man tried every trick in the book, or at least everything that he could think off, every trick like covering his horse's hoofs to leave no tracks for a couple of miles, then tried every trap and trip wires, but to no avail the man hunting him kept on coming.

Henry Walker the hunted man on the run admitted running out of ideas to stop this man and more than once said to himself (who is this man) Walker came to the conclusion that the only way of stopping this man is to find a place where it was possible to bushwhack him, riding on keeping his eyes open, looking for a favourable spot to carry out his thoughts.

Riding south keeping up a steady pace Walker looked for a place which it was able to ambush the man hunting him, Walker had no remorse about the men he killed, they were in his way when trying to steal the money, having no regrets also meant there was no regrets about killing the man hunting him.

Unknown to Walker the young man hunting him had come to the same conclusion and knew Walker would eventually come to think (how can I get this man of my tail) because of these thoughts his vigilance increased every foot taken with extra care.

Riding between two hills Walker came across a large expanse of open grass land it stretched for at least a mile or more but visible at the other side of this open land is a small mountain area, as the man hunting him was a few miles behind him, it came to him that it would be possible to get to the rocks in time to find a place in which to set up his assassination attack before the man behind him came into view.

Using his spurs, kicking the horse into a gallop it covered the expanse of land in a short time, Walker realised the sooner the horse got him there the more time would be available to find an appropriate place to set up the ambush, when arriving at the base of the rock wall in front of him and finding a place to leave the horse, climbing up a slope at the side of the rock Walker found what looked like the ideal place a flat rock to lie on with a good view of the trail below. With a smile on his face looking at the terrain gave him a sense of satisfaction, settling down into a comfortable position waiting for his prey levelling his rifle a couple of times to practice and check his sights estimating the distance when the man hunting him will come into range taking in the distance because of the height of his position.

The young bounty hunter was not fooled, and had also spotted the rock formation ahead and had the same thoughts of the man being hunted, it is a place a man can set up an ambush, If as the hunter suspects Walker would be waiting for him, the young man doing the hunting thought (how can he make the killer uncomfortable) the longer it took him to arrive at the scene the man would be sitting on hot rocks waiting for him.

Now about to enter the plain (the large expanse of grass approaching the rock formation) the young hunter kept his horse to a walk, advancing slowly imagining the man in the rocks waiting in the sun, sweat running over his face and trickling down his spine, becoming more and more unsteady.

Meanwhile the young man on the big black horse stopped before the rocks just out of rifle range, taking the making from his pocket started rolling a cigarette hooking his leg over the saddle horn, lighting the cigarette, drawing deeply and studying the rock formation ahead of him looking for any sign, not being certain but the man on the horse was almost positive that the sun reflected of a rifle barrel and mentally marked that spot.

The hunter was right in his assumption of the situation the man lying on the flat rock had the sun burning down on his back, being very uncomfortable sweat running down his face, unthinkingly wiping the sweat of the face with his hand made it awkward when holding the rifle.

Coming to the end of his smoke the young bounty hunter unhooked the leg from the saddle horn bent forward, unsheathing his rifle with a slight pressure of his heels the big horse moved forward.

Walker wiped the sweat from his brow, seeing the actions of the hunter telling him the man below expected to be ambushed, picking up and levelling the rifle sighting along the barrel, once again sweat ran down his face drops of sweat dripping from his eye brows on the verge of pulling the trigger a wasp attracted by the moisture flew across his eyes causing him to jerk and premastering pulling the trigger making him miss widely (Most men in the west carry a sheathed rifle, but also a lot of men who carry a rifle did little practise, and few men could hit a target at maximum range) It is more than likely Walker would have missed anyway.

The reaction of most men who knew someone was shooting at them would normally turn around and ride out of range or dive for cover, the young man did neither nudging the horse with his heels (the young man did not use spurs) but the big horse reacted to the rider's nudge and went from walk to Gallup in a second going forward to the shelter of the large rock formation. Getting close into the rocks deprived Walker of a target.

Dismounting the young hunter looked for a place where it was possible to climb, finding what he was looking for a place to climb between two large rocks, the young man started to climb the hunter due to Walkers shot knew roughly Walkers position so slowly advanced in that direction taking one step at a time very slowly and carefully, the one thing the young man had learnt never take your adversary for granted therefore his ears strained to register every noise knowing his quarry would not stay in the same position, therefore must move it would be stupid remaining in the same place and the young man knew Walker is not stupid.

Standing under an overhanging rock, there was a slight sound then a trickle of shale starting to drop down in front of him, it was obvious the man's position is directly above him, which gave him two choices of action. One, to drop back down to the ground, climb up behind the man, two, to carry on going up as intended. Before making the decision, the young man heard Walker moving, it sounded like the man was moving away to his left, which made the decision for him to carry on as intended in the first place moving to the right.

Climbing to level ground the young man found out why the noise and shale came from above Walker had been shuffling along a narrow shelf ignoring the shelf the young man climbed further up and turning left, suddenly Walker still on the shale covered area came into view about four yards apart.

"Raise your hands you're under arrest for murder" the young man called loudly.

Walker on hearing the voice grabbed the rifle with both hands and swung round fast, forgetting the shale under his feet, his fast movement made him slide over the edge, at this time they were a hundred feet up, Walkers body bounced of a rock fifty feet below before crashing to the ground, falling out of sight the young man who made his way down to ground level and walked towards Walkers body gun ready but after a few steps relaxed as just by looking at the man could see Walker was dead, the body lay across a edge of a large rock by the angle of the body his spine was broken, half way down the unfortunate man had hit a protruding rock with his face which was a red blotch.

Straightening the body out the hunter rolled Walker in his tarp (large heavy rain coat) put the body across his horse and lashed him down, mounting up the young man holding the reins of the other horse rode back over the expanse of green grass and entered the small valley, looking at the sky and estimated it would be about an hour to sunset, and made the decision to camp for the night.

After setting up camp, making coffee, sitting with his back against a rock took the dodger from his shirt pocket and read it, noticing Walkers body was worth $750 at the sheriff's office in Jayton because of the time it had taken him to catch this murderer it will take three days to get to town, there was no hurry as the job has been completed taking the makings from his pocket rolled a cigarette settling down for the night.

Scott Burrows is twenty five years old, and stands five foot eight tall in his stocking feet, slim built with dark hair and cool blue eyes, the girls say Scott is ruggedly handsome, when on the trail doing a job his choice of shirt is a dark blue dungaree type that matches his jeans, the jeans were held up by a two inch wide leather belt, his boots and gun belt are black leather, the gun belt stretched across his body from the left hip to the right upper leg ready for a straight draw, the holster tied down with a short barrelled colt forty five police special in the holster, the last item of clothing was his wide brimmed low crown Stetson, as a young boy his mother and father was gunned down in cold blood, that night made him take his father's gun swearing to kill every man who turned out to be a killer, (murderer), that is why Scott is not only a bounty hunter but now has a reputation of being the best bounty hunter, when sheriffs have problems they hire Scott, criminals steer clear of him, lots of people tread softly when Scott is around.

The job just completed had taken quite a time to complete because Walker was also good at ways to evade capture, doing well because of his knowledge of ways to frustrate anyone trailing him by throwing every trick possible at the man pursuing him but unfortunate for him is the fact that one of the best was on his tail.

Scott was looking forward to getting back to Jayton, it meant a bath and shave a good meal of a steak dinner followed by a trip to the saloon where a large cool glass of beer waited for him then last of all sleeping in a comfortable bed for the night being in the job that takes him out in the open most of the time makes you appreciate the fine things in life, needless to say a happy and satisfaction feeling came over him as eventually Scott rode down main street in Jayton stopping outside the sheriff's office.

The people of Jayton had seen Scott ride into town before with bodies over a horse but it still fascinated everybody when he rode into town they took a lot of interest in him wondering who the man across the horse is, pulling Blacky his big black horse to a stop outside the sheriff's office tying the horses to the hitch rail walked into the sheriff's office.

"Howdy sheriff" Scott greeted.

"Hi Scott, you been busy" the sheriff replied.

Scott walked to the wall where a stack of dodgers hung, searched and pulled out the wanted notice for Walker giving it to the sheriff.

"You can pull these dodgers in the man is across a horse outside" Scott told him.

"Right Scott" the sheriff said.

The sheriff looked at the dodger of Henry Walker wanted for murder $750 Dead or Alive.

"Did you kill him Scott"

"You mean did I kill him in cold blood, look at the body then you can apologize"

"I didn't mean anything by it" the sheriff said hastily.

"I'll trouble you for $750 then if you want me, I'll be at the hotel" Scott demanded.

"Yes! Yes! You earned it" the sheriff walked to the safe in the corner extracted the cash for the bounty which he gave to Scott.

"As I said the body his horse and all his belongings are outside at the hitch rail, they are all yours" Scott turned and walked out.

At the hitch rail Scott climbed on Blackys back and rode to the livery stable, the young boy attending the stable and horses,

"Hi! Sir how can I help you" the boy asked.

"Come here boy" Scott said.

"Yes sir, what do you want" the boy asked.

"Now boy my name is Scott, and this is Blacky, I'm going to introduce you to him, he is a one-man horse now I have introduced you to him you can attend him, but do not try to ride him" Scott explained.

"Scott, I am Danny I will look after him for you"

"Good now give him a bag of oats and water give him a clean stall and let him sleep, lately this boy has done a lot of work" Scott told him.

"OK here is ten dollars for you to take care of my pal, and here is five for yourself let me know when you need more" Scott gave him the money and left.

Leaving the stable Scott proceeded to the hotel where after acquiring a room, ordered a bath to be put in his room, after the bath and a shave and dressed in a clean set of clothes, leaving the room his next destination was the local café, eating a substantial meal of steak, double veg, potatoes and gravy, plus thick apple pie and cream also a large mug of coffee, Scott gave out a contented sigh called the waitress and paid the bill, strolling down to the saloon looking forward to the lovely cool beer.

Standing at the bar Scott just started on his second beer, when a man dressed in a suit came and stood beside him ordering a whisky.

"Mr Burrows, could I have a word with you please" the man asked.

"Mister" Scott said.

"Alex Morrison, Mr Burrows I am a Wells Fargo Agent" the man stated.

"Mr Morrison, I am not interested in finding your cash for you" Scott told him.

"I have heard a lot about you, one of the things I did hear was that you would always listen to a request and this one is a lot more serious than stolen money" Morrison said.

"OK shoot I'll listen" Scott assured him.

"Mr Burrows" Scott stopped him.

"The name is Scott"

"Mine is Alex"

"Now Alex how can I help you" Scott asked.

"Scott, I have heard you are a bounty hunter, the sheriff and others around here say you are the best and Wells Fargo needs the best right now" Alex told him.

"Tell me the circumstance of the job you have in mind" Scott asked.

"Just under three weeks ago five men robbed the Wells Fargo in Jayton of a payroll of one hundred thousand dollars, they killed three men in the office then kidnapped a young couple of around eighteen years old, when they were clear they killed them also as they did not want to leave any witnesses, this town is grieving for that young couple" Alex explained.

Since the mention of the killings, Scott showed a lot more interest in the case being described to him, his jaw tightened at the mention of the killings specially the young couple.

"What happened" Scott asked.

Alex spent the next half hour going through the attack on the Wells Fargo robbery explaining as much as possible.

"Do you have any detailed information like the description of these killers" Scott asked.

"Would you come with me; we have a witness I would like you to meet" Alex asked

"Sure, let's go" Scott agreed.

Alex directed Scott down the main street to the doctor's office, knocking on the door the doctor opened it.

"Doc, could we see Laura please." Alex asked

"I don't know Alex she is tired" Doc said.

"Doc tell her I have Scott Burrows with me" Alex told him

"Oh! Hold on I will ask her" Doc replied.

The two men heard a croaking voice say,

"Bring him in, bring him in"

"Mr Burrows! Mr Burrows! I am glad to meet you please sit down you are my last hope and I have heard you are the best bounty hunter in the territory, the law cannot help me I need the best" Laura croaked out, the doctor looked worried.

"Laura Scott Burrows" Alex introduced.

"Scott Laura Gibbs our witness"

"Ha! Ha! Ha! Is that what I am" Laura tried to laugh.

"You did witness the robbery" Scott asked.

"Witness the robbery, it was my fault, I was part of the robbery Mr Burrows" Laura stated.

"Miss Laura, hold it start from the beginning and don't call me Mr Burrows I am Scott" Scott said to her.

"OK I am Laura"

"Scott, I need you, mainly because the law cannot help in any way, anyway this is what happened"

"OK Laura I am sorry you are so ill I hope you get better soon" Scott said.

"Scott that's not going to happen I am dying it may be tomorrow, next week or longer the doc says it's possible it may be longer because Doc intends to keep me alive as long as possible" Laura explained.

"I'm sorry Laura"

"Scott that is why I need you to hear my story, I need to get it off my chest" Laura stated.

"OK let's hear your story" Scott said.

"Thank you Scott needless to say the story is about the Wells Fargo office robbery where three men died and I am to blame, it was all my fault, and I take the blame for it, Laura went on explaining about Ron Bates and how she was seduced by him, she told him how it was her who unlocked the back door to the office, Laura told Scott everything that happened and only stopped after telling him how she escaped from the cave," by the time she completed her story she was very weak, you could see the effort it took on her face, she was drained of energy so the doc stepped in.

"Right hold it, enough for the moment" Doc said.

"Stop it doctor" Laura said weakly.

"NO, I am the doctor, and you must have some rest before you go on"

"Laura Shhhhh! The doctor is right how about you go to sleep for a couple of hours anyway it is lunch time, and I am hungry, I am going to check on my horse I'm going to lunch, I will be back in a couple of hours now get some rest a couple of hours will not make any difference" Scott explained.

"Thank you, Scott," she said weakly, she understood what Scott was doing and drifted off to sleep before Scott left the room.

Scott and Alex arrived back at the doctors two hours later, the doc informed them that Laura was still asleep, so the three men sat with a cup of coffee and jawed a bit.

"She is quite a brave lady getting out of that cave the way she did" Scott said.

"Yes, she is, also by the way she has accepted the fact she is dying" Doc acknowledged.

"Yeh! She has guts owning up and taking the blame, I'd like to get my hands on this man Bates" Alex reflected.

About an hour and a half later Laura woke up she invited them in.

"Doc, could I have a damp cloth a hand towel and a cup of coffee please" Laura said.

"What did your last slave die of miss" the doc said a smile on his face.

After rubbing her face drying it and taking a slurp of the coffee.

"Now I feel much better" Laura announced.

"I'm happy you are now refreshed Laura" Scott told her.

"Yes, I feel great, thank you for letting me lie a bit longer" Laura replied.

"You have told me you are dying, but you did not tell me what is wrong with you" Scott asked.

Laura saw the doc about to protest but Laura put her hand up to silence him "it's alright doc" she said.

"Sorry is it OK for me to ask" Scott said.

"Yeh! It is OK, doc is just being overprotective" Laura explained.

"When telling you earlier about what happened in the cave I was trapped in and told you about the two men who shot me in the back" Laura reminded him.

"I remember" Scott said.

"There was two men Dutchy and the Dandy who shot me in the back, well one bullet hit me in the hip and the bullet is still in there and it hurts like hell sometimes when I move, the main problem is the second bullet which is lodged beside my shoulder blade, once again the bullet is still in there and doc has told me to try to extract it would almost certainly kill me, while in the cave I could not tend to it as there was no water anyway so first a lot of dust and muck got into the wound, then a little later I felt bugs crawling all over the open wound, I could not do anything to stop them, being a bit delirious at the time, anyway the wound has become infected, I have gangrene, and the gangrene is slowly travelling towards my heart. I know I am going to die but cannot tell you when. What will be will be, but that is why I must get all the information out, I have told you my story and I have some information that could help you and I must get out before I die" Laura explained.

"I am sorry" Scott almost whispered.

"No, Scott do not be sorry for me, this was all my fault I deserve to die, if I had not unlocked that door people would not have died" Laura told him.

Scott walked over to the bed and sat on the edge, reaching over he took Laura's hands in his then looked into her eyes.

"Laura, we all have feelings and there is always someone who will take advantage of you for it, you did not think of unlocking that door until Bates asked you to, but on the other hand Bates had it planned, so you are not to blame, I am still sorry but you are right you must still get everything of your chest, so tell me all you know" Scott asked.

"You might need a piece of paper and a pen or pencil" Laura advised.

"Don't worry Laura, I have a good memory, I will remember everything you tell me" Scott assured her.

"OK, Scott the first man and leader of the group is that bastard Ronald Bates, sorry for the languish "she paused to apologise.

"That's OK Laura I would have done the same now what about Bates" Scott asked.

"Bates as I said was the leader, handsome, good looking and a very smooth talker and appeals to people mainly women, you already know about him seducing me and persuade me to open the rear door of the Wells Fargo office, this man mainly dresses in a suit with a shirt and tie, I did notice his gun but never saw him used it, and if Bates wanted to get rid of someone, he gave the other orders to do so, What I did hear Bates say in the cave it is his intention to go north near the Texas border and buy a ranch, it sounded like a specific ranch." Laura stopped to take a sip of water.

"The second man I thought was the most brutal, a big man they called Dutchy this man spoke with a foreign accent so I guess being called Dutchy means the man is a Dutchman, I am certain this man was the first to rape the girl I heard her scream and the sound will be in my head till I die, Dutchy was the person who went back and killed the deputy following us and wipe out any sign that had been left, the big man was a burly, stocky, unshaven brute a brawler who thinks with his fists and says, with his fists no one can beat him, I don't know his destination but did tell the other members of the gang the intention of buying a livery stable with his share of the money this is one of the men who shot me in the back" Laura announced.

"I suppose you would call the third man a dandy his real name being Carl Tim's who dressed mainly in black with pearl like buttons on his shirt and silver bits attached to his clothes this man is rash and impulsive, plus thinks that all women were his slaves him being a gift to all females to give them pleasure, is always dusting himself of and spraying himself with smelly sprays, this is the man who put the second bullet in my back, when asked by the others what his intentions were now having a lode of money

He answered by saying the first thing on his mind was to buy a fancy tailored suit black leather fitted boots, a black leather gunbelt with a pearl handled gun, I don't know if it was a joke or not but I am certain his intention was to buy a brothel so there was always a supply of girls for his own personal use" her face grimaced at the thought.

"The youngest member of the five men the others called him Billy boy, this is the fourth man, this young man was naive, young, brash with a big head, who loves gambling and cheats most of the time, as he cannot really play and has a gun, plays with it most of the time but is not very good with it, during their conversations I don't think his intentions came out except to live it up get drunk and enjoy himself" once more Laura stopped for a sip of water.

"The last member of the gang is called Wes Arnold "Laura stated, Scott broke in.

"Wes Arnold this man has a reputation of being good with a gun"

"All I know about this man is that this man is a murderer and that is a fact, the young man taken with the young girl they raped stood in front of the girl with his fists up to I think protect her, the boy had no gun or knife to defend himself but Arnold drew his gun and shot him it was a cold blooded act the boy had no chance, there is little I can tell you about him, when asked what his intensions were now there was money in his jeans said the intension was to buy a saloon, the only sign I could see about the rep of being a gunfighter was his hand continuously brushed the gun in the holster as the man walked." Laura ended her head flopped back onto the pillow.

The doctor moved quickly to check her.

"Oh! Stop fusing doc I am OK" but they could all see she was weak.

"Thank you, Laura, get some rest" Scott said to her in a low soothing voice.

"Look Scott, I don't know how long I have, I know I have little time left, if you can bring these men to justice, I will die happy" Laura told Scott.

"I'm sorry you will not see it, but I promise you I will do my best to get these men I don't like killers" Scott assured her.

"The doc keeps given me painkillers, I hope when the time comes, I will die peacefully but whatever happens I know I will die happy known you are out there getting these men thank you" Laura told him her voice very low.

"Get some rest (I'll get them Laura)" she smiled.

CHAPTER THREE

MAKE ME HAPPY

"**A**lex lets visit the sheriff" Scot said.

"Why" Alex asked.

"I need to know what they want done with the two bodies in the cave that is the place I will have to start my search from" Scott explained.

"I see" Alex returned.

As they entered the sheriff's office, the sheriff looked up from what article in the local paper that had caught his eye.

"Hi, how can I be of assistance to you" the sheriff asked.

"Sheriff I am about to pursue the gang that robbed the Wells Fargo office and stole the payroll three weeks ago. What I want to know is do you want me to bury the remains of the young couple the gang kidnapped and murdered in the cave or do you know if there folk want the remains to be returned to Jayton" Scott asked.

"I will find out from the families then let you know" the sheriff told him.

"I want to move out at first light in the morning, sheriff find out and let me know as soon as possible so I can organise thing its important" Scott emphasized.

"OK I'll get straight on it" the sheriff informed him.

"Good, thank you" Scott said.

Round about an hour later the sheriff found Scott and Alex having a beer so joined them.

"Hi! Sheriff what's the verdict" Scott asked.

"Scott the families wont the bodies brought home so they can put there remains in their own plots of land" the sheriff said.

"OK Sheriff, I want you to get permission from the council to employ the two young men with the wagon who found Laura to go with me and having to coffins to return with the bodies" Scott explained.

"I'll go see the mayor now about employing the lads and the wagon I'll be back soon" the sheriff departed. But returned in fleeting time.

"It's fixed Scott" the sheriff informed him.

As Scott and Alex sat at a table for about fifteen minutes, the two young men Scott was about to go looking for came through the batwings, Scott called the two young men over to the table.

"Alex, will you get four beers please, right boys sit down I want to talk to you" Scott said

"OK! Scott" Alex replied

"How can we help you" Vince asked.

"Boys I have arranged for you to be paid by the sheriff for you to assist me" Scott said

"What would we have to do and why us" Vince asked.

"You two found Laura so you know where the cave is, I want you to take me out there with a couple of coffins to bring the remains of the two young people dead in that cave, will you do it" Scott asked as Alex arrived with the beers.

"Why are you wanting to go there" the boys asked.

"I suppose you know about the Wells Fargo robbery and the killing of the three guards about three weeks ago" Scott asked them.

"Sure, we know"

"My name is Scott Burrows, I am a bounty hunter I am going out after them in the morning, the families of the two dead people in that cave wants their bodies brought back to Jayton, I need someone to help me to get into the cave, the cave is where I have to start my investigations, then of course we have the grizzly task of putting the two unfortunate peoples bodies into the coffins, I also want you to be prepared as animals and bugs will have been at the bodies and there is the chance there will be little left of them, so you will need masks and gloves with you, are you in" Scott asked them

"Yes, we will be ready in the morning" Vince replied.

"Well good luck in the morning, I am bushed so its bed for me" Alex said holding his hand out, Scott shook it.

As arranged the two young men were out in front of the hotel all loaded up ready to roll.

"Come on boy's breakfast we will charge it to the sheriff's office" Scott said.

"Yeh! that's a clever idea" Vince replied. The three men entered the café.

Scott ordered three full breakfasts and coffee to follow then told the staff to charge it to the sheriff's office tab, the trio mounted up and headed north waving to the sheriff as they rode passed him.

"How long do you think this job will take Scott" young Alex asked.

"No longer than five days, why are you in a hurry" Scott asked.

"It means we get back in time for the town dance. "Vince told Scott.

"Ah! I see girls" Scott said.

"Yes, I will be back in time to take Victoria to the dance" Alex stated.

"And I will see Julia" Vince announced.

"If we have no hold ups or problems you should be back in time, it will take roughly two days to get there we will save a little time if we camp late and start moving early in the morning" Scott explained.

"OK Scott we will cut down the time as much as we can" Vince agreed.

As Scott had predicted it took them Two days to reach the mouth of the cave as it was dusk when they arrived there was not much that could be done before morning in the morning the main heavy work began removing as much of the rocks that covered the entrance, they needed enough room to carry a couple of coffins in and out without killing themselves, once the mouth of the cave was cleared enough Vince and Alex watched with interest as Scott removed his boots and replaced them with a pair of moccasins.

"Why" Alex asked.

"Alex moccasins do not spoil sign, they do not leave prints, and if there is any small object lying around, I can feel them through the soles" Scott explained.

"Are you going in by yourself" Vince asked.

"Yes, I need to scout around first to see if I can pick up any sign, I'll have a look first before we trample over everything as the might be something there that could be of some help to me" Scott told them.

Walking through the opening Scott moved in about three yards with a lantern then stopped to allow his eyes to get used to the cave before starting his search, even though Scott carried a lantern the first task was to light as many torches to light to give him all the light possible, it was still not easy with the shadows but Scott was good at his job still managed to pick up a bit of sign (things of interest) like one of the men smoked almost continuously there was numinous cigarette ends left lying around and as Scott himself smoked it helped, Scott broke open the faded papers the tobacco was a light colour but there was very little smell it was pungent which could have been because of the length of time it had been lying there, but if that was its normal smell it will be easy to recognise, Scott suddenly saw something flash on the floor of the cave picking the object up after losing it with his boot then putting it to the light.

Rubbing it could see it was a coin, could one of the gang have a hole in his pocket therefore dropping coins as the man walked or rode along or is it a coin that had been accidentally dropped, Scott did find lots of boot marks and since the men left the place has not been disturbed, scouting around the cave gave him the chance to examine where the horses had been, the remains of the fire, until seeing the remains of the young couple, as they had lay therefore, a little time they were not pleasant to look at but part of their task was to move them gently.

Laura had explained with her injuries she could not redress the girl, but did cover the body with her clothes, not finding anything else Scott decided to terminate his search so returned to the entrance of the cave.

"Right boys put on your masks and gloves and bring in the first box (coffin)" Scott asked them.

The nearest body belonged to the young man moving the first coffin as near to the body as possible, Scott directed them to lift the boy's body very gently keeping it all in one piece, putting the lid on nailed it down then scratched a letter "B" on the lid, then the grizzly task of doing the same with the girl's body, after completing the task the two coffins were loaded gently onto the wagon bed, as the job had taken all day they moved away from the mouth of the cave and made camp for the night.

"Right boys at first light we will rise, have breakfast then you can start back to town and thanks for your assistance" Scott informed them.

"What are you going to do Scott" Vince asked.

"Well with the information I have gathered I hope to find some sign, if I can get into their minds, I may be able to work out where the gang went to" Scott explained.

"Good luck Scott" Alex said.

"From what Laura told me the men had planned to go north from here and that is a start, the gang thought they have eliminated everyone that knew about them so I hope they become complacent so I think it's possible the gang will go to the nearest town to celebrate, I will look at the map and make a decision" Scott explained.

"Good luck" the two young men chorused.

"Thanks boys" Scott whistled the big horse came to him.

Scott did not have to go far before coming across his first sign, cigarette ends even though they were weather beaten there was enough of them to match the other cigarette ends in the cave, the cigarette ends were stained, split and what tobacco that is left is dry and flaky but it still had a little bit of the pungent smell, this small piece of sign made Scott smile as his decision was the right one, being out in the wild country where very few people go and finding a trail of cigarette ends puts him on the right track.

Even though Scott had made up his mind what to do, he did not, take anything for granted therefore stayed vigilant still looking for sign by the time Scott rode out of the hills, quite a bit of information had been gathered like they rode a grey, brown and black horses one of them has a broken shoe.

Just after leaving the hills Scott decided to stop the horse and let it blow for a moment, hooking his leg over the saddle horn, removing the makings from his shirt pocket rolled a cigarette, began to smoke it, pulling the map out of the saddlebags studied it.

"Now if I had done a job and I thought there was no one who would be able to recognise me what would I do" Scott talked to himself. After pausing for a moment looking at the map, "Turkey" came from his lips, "Yes Turkey being the nearest place on the map I would go there and celebrate" Scott told himself, like most men who spends a lot of time alone so often talks to himself.

On his way to Turkey a lot of signs was found matching the sign from the cave and trail so far hoof print and lots of cigarette ends, during his journey Scott found a cold camp and with the prints and discarded cigarette ends, this could not be a coincident they must come from the gang.

Riding on for a few miles it started to get duller, this made him make up camp for the evening, but woke up early the next morning had breakfast cleared up the area, rode out arriving at Turkey around ten am in the morning, Scott knew it was not necessary to rush things, the robbery happened three weeks ago so thought it would be to his advantage to allow the robbers to get complacent this gave him the decision to sleep in a bed tonight.

Scott pulled up at the livery stable.

"Hi! Sir can I be of assistance" a female voice asked.

"Howdy Marm is the owner here" Scott asked.

"I am the owner see that sign up there, it says (JACKIES LIVERY STABLE owner Jackie Barton) that's me" the young lady said.

"You are a bit young to own a livery stable aren't you Marm" Scott inquired.

"STOP calling me Marm I am Jackie, WHAT do you want" she asked

"Ma Jackie this is Blacky I want a stall for him and a bag of oats" Scott requested.

"OK I can do that" Jackie informed him.

"No Blacky is a one-man horse Jackie, just point out the stall and I will see to him" Scott informed her.

"Right mister the last stall on the right" Jackie said.

"Skip the mister my name is Scott"

"Scott, do you need anything else" Jackie asked

"Maybe you can, three weeks ago five men came to this town on their way through do you remember it, were you here" Scott asked.

"Well, everyone in town remembers that night but I was not here one of my staff looked after the place, but the story circulated the everywhere, I cannot tell you anything about that night the best person to see is the sheriff" Jackie told him.

"Thanks Jackie" Scott left.

As Jackie had said the best place for any information is nearly always the sheriff's office, bar tenders or barbers, Scott made his way to the sheriff's office to see if it was possible to pick up any information, Turkey is a small sleepy town so if anything happened in town everyone would know if anything unusual happened it would circulate the town like wildfire.

"Hi! Sheriff" Scott greeted.

"How can I help you" the sheriff asked.

"I'm Scott Burrows sheriff" Scott introduced himself.

"I've heard of you, Scott" then stuck his hand out to shake it.

"Three weeks ago, five men robbed the Wells Fargo office in Jayton and killed three men, I have tracked these men and I believe they passed through your town about two weeks ago do you remember them" Scott asked.

"Remember them that was a night no one in this town will forget" the sheriff said.

"That bad eh!" Scott said.

"First off you can see the size of Turkey, it is what's known as a one-horse town up until that night I was a part time lawman, that night I was at home on my homestead outside town so did not get to know about the events until the men had left the town, but this is what happened. The five men arrived in town in the afternoon, the group of men first stopped at the saloon, but only stopped for one drink then left, from reports of the citizens they went to the hotel and when they next arrived on the street it looked like they had all bathed and shaved and were all dressed in clean clothes, there next destination was the local café, where they all had a large meal the only unsavoury act was when one of them molested the owners daughter, she did avoid them so this gang of men made their way back to the saloon, the five men started drinking and enjoying themselves, for a couple of hours apart from them being boisterous everything seemed normal, after having a few drinks the booze took over.

That is when the trouble started, I'm afraid that night turned out to be a night we wish we could forget, the trouble seemed to start because of the youngest member of the gang I believe this lad was called Billy, there was not very many men in the saloon but there happened to be a card game going on in the corner of the room, this young man managed to get a seat in the game, for two or three games it looked normal at about nine o'clock one of the players a member of the town's population accused this young man Billy of cheating, the young man stood up drew his gun shot his accuser and the man next to him, this caused a protest from the local people of the town, the other four members of the gang drew their weapons and supported Billy by threatening to kill people who went against them.

As a part-time lawman, I spent time in town as designated by the town council, that night I was at home with my wife who is expecting our second child, now you know all towns as small as Turkey are so quiet we have no problems its normally very, very quiet not a lot to be done, so the council will not pay anyone to work full time to save money. These five men caused mayhem this night and they took over the town and terrorised the town, they walked the street and shot at anything that moved, people dived into indoors drew their blinds, the five men were laughing loudly as they came back into the saloon and began drinking again.

Another member of the gang called Carl Tim's the dandy of the gang, told Mandy the only saloon girl to get upstairs saying let's go to bed, and became angry as she refused, the dandy backhanded Mandy across the face, she fell face down on the floor.

"We are not good enough for you eh!" Tim's yelled.

"Her refusal was her down fall two of the men grabbed her arms lifted her to her feet then through her face down across a table lifted her skirts and ripped of her underwear, the Dutchman dropped his trousers and brutally raped Mandy, one of the barmen tried to stop them and was pistol whipped to the floor and the other members of the gang covered the other people with their weapons while each took there turn to rape the poor girl there was no way anyone can stop these men after this attack on the girl they threw her across the room, the gang then pistol whipped the remaining barmen they each took a bottle of whisky then walked along the main street shooting there gun discriminably shooting at anything, I don't think they meant to but one of them shot and killed a young boy only six years old, the mob of monsters ended their night of terror when they arrived outside the house with the red light outside the door at the edge of town. They each took a girl and refused to pay for them, they had their way with the girls at dawn they rode north out of town. I had no idea what had taken place in town until I arrived back in town to do the morning rounds," the sheriff finally coming to an end to his version of the incidents.

"Thanks for telling me sheriff" Scott said.

"I tried to get a posse together, but no one was interested, or they were a little apprehensive "the sheriff told him.

"Would it be OK to ask the people of the town about that night" Scott asked.

"Sure, now there has been a period of cooling of you may get a bit more help than I did, Scott I did try to track the gang, but you could put my tracking skills in a coffee cup so I'm afraid I did not get far sorry" the sheriff stated.

"Thanks sheriff" Scott said then proceeded to the saloon.

"Hi! Barman, my name is Scott"

"How can I help you" the barman asked.

"A beer and some information" Scott said.

"Beer that's OK but I am a little short on info" the barman returned.

"Were you in the bar the day the five men terrorised the town killing and raping" Scott asked.

"You say you are Scott, but really who are you" the barman asked.

"Stand still Burrows" a voice came from the batwings. Scott saw the reflection of the man in the mirror behind the bar.

"Ahrr! Grant Carter"

"Yeh! So, Scott Burrows bounty hunter you're not getting my scalp"

"Carter, you raped then killed a fourteen-year-old girl" Scott said loud enough for all present to hear him.

"RAPE ", a female voice called out accompanied by the sound of a cocking revolver.

"No Mandy" a concerned male voice called out.

Grant Carter was caught off guard, when hearing the pistol being cocked turned to change his aim, to confront the problem behind him, which gave Scott the chance to draw and shoot his quick shot hit Carter in the wrist causing him to drop his weapon Scott then called out to the young lady.

"STOP MISS"

The young lady froze, Scott took the gun from her slowly lowering the hammer.

At that moment, the sheriff burst through the batwings his gun in hand.

"Everyone hands above your head" the sheriff called out.

"It's all in hand Sheriff, this man is Grant Carter, tie his hands, arrest him, put him in the cells and call the doctor. I'll be over to see you presently" Scott informed him.

"OK Scott" came the sheriffs reply.

"Please miss come this way, sit down, barman two coffee's please" Scott ordered.

"Whisky" Mandy uttered.

"And two whiskies barman"

"Hello, miss, thank you" Scott greeted.

"Did that man really rape and kill a fourteen-year-old girl" Mandy asked.

"Yes"

"I should have killed him, pulled the trigger"

"Believe me miss you did the right thing, the torture he will go through in his mind before the big drop, the wait for the hanging will make him scared out of his pants" Scott told her.

"Mandy"

"OK Mandy, I understand you were here the night the five men came to town" Scott told her.

"Yes, I was, why do you ask" the young lady said uncertainly.

"Would it be OK if I came back this evening and have a talk with you about that night" Scott asked.

"I don't know, what would it be about" she said hesitantly.

"Miss, it would be observation questions, I am trying to get as much information as I can about the men who terrorised the town" Scott explained.

"Why" she asked

"Because I am after them"

"Wait a minute, that man Carter said you were a bounty hunter is the true" she asked

"Yes"

"If Carter knew you, I take it you have a reputation" she said.

"Let's say people who know me, hire me because I get the job done" Scott told her.

"The name is Mandy and yes I will answer your questions" she said.

"OK Mandy, I'll see you later" then walked over to the bar.

"Excuse me barman my name is Scott; I want to pick the brains of anyone that was here when the five men came to the town and killed that young boy were you here that night" Scott asked.

"Yes, Scott I was here, the name is Jake" the barman said.

"Jake when you have a quiet moment tonight could I have a word with you"

"Sure"

"See you later" Jake retired to serve another customer; Scott proceeded to the sheriff's office.

"Hi! Sheriff how is the prisoner"

"The Doc is with him in the cell right now" sheriff replied.

"Good I'll relieve you of five hundred dollars" Scott said.

"I thought you would be, I have it ready for you" the sheriff acknowledged.

"Thanks"

"Where to now Scott" the sheriff asked.

"Next stop the cathouse" Scott said.

"Good luck" the sheriff said a big smile on his face.

Scott made his way to the edge of town to the big house at the end of main street with the red light outside the door, Scott walked straight in, the woman who was obviously the madam approached him.

"How can I help you" her voice boomed out loud.

"Just over two weeks ago five men terrorised the town, and from what I have heard your house was appropriated" Scott said.

"Yes, that is right those horrible men came here and took my girls" she replied.

"Could you get your girls who are not busy at the moment to come down here I would like to have a word with them" Scott asked.

"Sure mister" then rang bell three girls arrived. Chatting loudly.

"Ladies, Ladies two weeks ago five men invaded this house. Took what they wanted, I would like any of you to give me any information you could about these men, anything you can that will help me to catch them." Scott asked them.

"The young member of the gang they called Billy boy has a little cock does that help you." the girls laughed.

Scott smiled.

"What is your name miss" Scott asked.

"Anna" she told him.

"Well Anna since you are observant enough to see (Billy has a little willy) I'll talk to you first" Scott said.

All the girls had a good laugh, Scott talked to all the girls one by one, during the conversation they gave him quite a bit to think about, like tattoo's, body hair, scars and unusual habits. Scott enjoyed the investigation because the girls were happy, jovial and joked a lot, because of the enjoyment time slipped by and realised it had taken most of the day, as it was later than expected Scott made his way to the livery stable to check Blacky his horse, on his arrival at the stable Jackie was putting a nose bag on Blacky.

"Thanks for looking after my pal Jackie" Scott said.

"It's been a pleasure Scott; that's a good horse you have there" Jackie commented.

"See you later" Scott said then made his way to the town café.

After eating a substantial meal, once again asked questions about that night in general, but received little information as the owner saw what was happening in town so shut the café and sent the staff home. It was now time to interview Mandy turning down the street headed for the saloon.

"Hi! Mandy how do you feel" Scott asked.

"Hello Mr Burrows at this time I want to die" Mandy replied.

"Mandy the name is Scott hear me out first"

"OK Scott what do you want to know" she said a bit reluctantly.

"It's a bit busy in here tonight, is there any place we can talk in private" Scott asked.

"Sure, your room" she hesitantly said.

"OK If that is the only place lets go"

"Oh! OK" she seemed uncertain about it.

"Are you alright Mandy"

"As far as I know the rooms upstairs are the only place, we can have peace and quiet let's go" Mandy agreed.

The two of them rose and then walked to where Scott's room was. Mandy cautiously looked around the room.

"Now what do you want to ask me"

"Mandy, you helped me earlier, so I want to give you this" Scott handed her a pile of money.

"What is this for" she asked.

"As I have just told you, it's for helping me earlier"

"Helped you"

"Yes, when you pulled a cocked gun on Carter, it gave me the chance to overcome him, this man is a bad man, there was a $500 dollar bounty on his head, I have just given you your share $250 dollars" Scott said.

"Thank you is this what you wanted to see me about" she asked.

"No Mandy I want to ask you some questions about the night the five men terrorised the town and raped you" Scott said softly.

There was a period of silence then Mandy started crying, she cried for around ten minutes, she started to speak brokenly.

"Why do you want to know" Mandy asked.

"Mandy, you know I am a bounty hunter, the five men who caused the trouble here in town killed six people in the town called JAYTON as they committed a robbery one of the people they killed was a seventeen year old young lady who they raped to death, I have been given the job of tracking them down" Scott explained.

"Oh! I see I'll try to help in any way I can" she still crying said.

"She was a virgin just like you were" Scott sat down on the bed beside her.

"I feel dirty, and I have thought of killing myself" Mandy stated.

Scott took her hand

"Mandy take it from me you are not dirty and don't even think of killing yourself I know you went through a horrible ordeal, but these so-called men are not men at all, you have to know that most men are not like them, most men never think of rape, we men want to make love to our ladies, we want to make them happy" Scott explained.

Mandy sat quiet for a few moments looking at Scott, she leaned over and kissed him

"Scott make me happy" Mandy asked him, pleading in her eyes, Scott understood.

Putting an arm around her, drew her to him and kissed her, his hand caressed her body, you are beautiful then kissed her lips neck and nibbled her ears, because she is a saloon girl she wore a low strapless dress, Scott placed his hand to cover her breast, she tensed but calmed down as she heard his soothing words in her ear, (Shh my darling you are wonderful) the hand behind her back undid the dress, his hand slid the front of the dress down to reveal a lovely pair of breasts, still kissing his hand caressed the breasts his thumb gently rubbing the nipples, a low moan came from her lips.

Scott had been ready to stop if she wanted him to, but no complaint came from Mandy, standing up, putting his hand out she took it came into his arms as the dress dropped to the floor, still kissing whispering in her ear his hand on her breasts, his clothes were quickly removed Mandy felt the erection touch her body and started pulling back but once again Scott assured her it will be alright as Mandy was lowered gently onto the bed Scott removed her pants she saw the erection and looked uncertain Scott lay beside her once again continued kissing and cuddling her whispering soothing words of love in her ear, his hand gently moved over her belly to her crotch , touching the lips of her vagina and slowly rubbing between her legs which slowly opened as she became aroused, doing this gently for a while taking his time, she gasped a little as the finger invaded her body and started to wriggle a little but you could see she enjoyed the feeling she was experiencing as her body produced the juices of love and the invading finger swirled around inside her brushing her chitinous she was lost to the normal world and was now in a world of her own, she gasped loudly as the erection entered her body, putting her arms around Scott holding him as she felt the penetration, (God it's in me) she said, as it did not hurt her and felt the penis probe into her body she was happy as Scott's seed entered her body then the erection leaving her body, the two sweat covered bodies lay side by side breathing heavy after a moment Scott took her in his arms and smiled at her and was over the moon to see a smile on her face, Scott then kissed her tenderly.

"Thank you, Mandy," he whispered in her ear.

"No Scott, you have made me happy"

"You are beautiful, and nice to make love to"

"Scott the pain I experienced when I was raped, I did not ever think I would go to bed with a man again and as I said I wanted to die but you have shown me love and happiness, and I am ready to answer your questions" Mandy said.

"Good"

"Scott give me a kiss and cuddle but not make love, then let's get dressed then I'll answer your questions" Mandy said.

"I understand" Scott assured her.

"Now what would you like to know" Mandy asked.

"OK I would like you to recall anything you might have seen that might help to identify these animals" he asked her,

"The big man called Dutchy was the worst man and hurt me the most, the thing I observed about him is the fact that this man is very hairy all over, the tattoo on his left arm I think is unusual, the skull and crossbones with the one-word (mother) underneath."

"That is unusual to associate your mother with some skull and crossbones" Scott thought

"Tim's the one that is a dandy, has a tattoo on his right arm the words (I love sex) so I don't know but I would say the man is insecure or thinks a lot of himself"

"Yeh! That sounds like him" Scott said.

"The one called Ron who seems to be their leader and told the other men to rape me, held my arms down saw the pain on my face then threw kisses at me, this man has a deep scar on his left forearm, this man is a nasty piece of work"

"You are right this man is the leader Laura told me that".

"Who is Laura"

Scott told Mandy about Laura.

"The only thing I can tell you about the one called Billy, is there is a birthmark on his shoulder like a half star shaped and he gets over excited.

"Billy is brash which could be made to my advantage" Scott replied.

"As you can see, all these observations are on the upper part of their bodies, because each one of them held me down over the table, the last man the one they called Wes has a tattoo on each arm, one was a horse's head with the word (Blue) under it, the other tattoo was the Confederate flag" Mandy explained.

"Thank you, Mandy, I know this must have been hard for you to do after what you have been through sorry" Scott said to her gently.

"If we had come up to your room, and you had asked me straight away about what happened to me, I don't think I could have told you as every word would have reminded me of the pain I endured, the shame I felt, I wanted to commit suicide but believe it or not through your tenderness and understanding, the pain has gone away and left me with the desire to get those responsible, I am still a little ashamed because I know quite a few people saw it happen, most of all I want to live and put the experience behind me, don't be sorry, thank you, you have made me happy again" Mandy said and kissed him.

"What do you intend to do now" Scott asked.

"When I came up here, I felt dirty, I felt no man would want me, you have changed the way I feel, I feel loved and want to change my life" she told him.

"How do you mean to do that" Scott asked.

"I am going to stop working in a saloon, hopefully meet a nice guy, get married have a life maybe a couple of kids, and settle down, I know you are a bounty hunter and I could not marry a man like you, even though we have made love, I know I don't love you, but I am grateful thank you again" Mandy told him.

"Do you have a man in mind"

"No but the man will be an ordinary man" she said.

"A barman maybe" Scott said then knew she did not know.

"A barman, storekeeper, I don't know but someone who will love me" she said.

"Do you know Jake the barman downstairs" Scott asked

"Yes, I like him, each day I talk with him" she said.

"Well settling down is a promising idea" and smiled.

"Wait a minute, you said barman why" she asked.

"I think Jake loves you, I see the way the man looks at you, plus there is a couple of things you should know about him, the night you were attacked by those men Jake stepped forward to help you and they pistol whipped him, did you hear someone call out NO MANDY when you levelled the gun at Carter, if you did it was him with a concerned look on his face" Scott explained.

"Oh! I did not know, thank you Scott, give me a cuddle but I do not want to make love" she told him

"I understand and good luck to you I hope all goes well"

"Thank you again, I cannot thank you enough" she threw herself into his arms they kissed and cuddled before they left the room.

"Jake, can we talk" Jake looked around the room.

"Sure, it's quiet at the moment, there is a table in the corner" he said.

"Scott how can I help you" Jake asked.

"I would like you to tell me what you saw on the night the five men terrorised the town, Any information you can give me would be appreciated, I have just asked Mandy about that night, she did break down but I consoled her and she gave me lots of signs to look out for, Look Jake you know I am a bounty hunter and I have been hired by Wells Fargo with the backing of the law, I have been employed to track down and either capture or kill these animals" Scott explained.

For the next half an hour Jake talked, and told all about what went on that night, explaining that it was all possible to see because they had pistol whipped him knocking him unconscious.

"Scott, I hope you were kind to Mandy, and you did not upset or hurt her" Jake said.

"You are in love with her" Scott asked.

"Yes, I am, and she has had a tough time" Jake said, Scott smiled.

"When Mandy and I went upstairs to talk she was upset and said she wanted to kill herself, but I calmed her down and talked her out of that idea, told her I will get those men, and she could help by giving me what information she could tell me, she then told me everything she could, and after getting all she could of her chest she felt fine. I think when you next talk to her you will find she is much happier" Scott assured him.

"Thank you, Scott," they shook hands and parted happily.

After drinking one beer Scott went to his room and turned in for the night. Before dawn Scott opened his eyes, lying still for a moment or two, then rose washed and shaved, packing all his gear, went to the livery stable checked fed and watered Blacky, walking down the boardwalk getting to the café just as they opened the doors, after eating a substantial breakfast, saddled up packed the big black horse rode north out of town.

CHAPTER FOUR

THAT'S THE DANDY

Riding north out of town, Scott after giving Blacky a chance to run for about a mile to get the kinks out of him, bringing the horse down to a amble, rolling a cigarette then had a smoke, there was no need to hurry and at a walking pace it would enable him to see any sign available.

It often takes a long time for certain items to decompose thing can remain on the ground for years, then some items take different lengths of time to decompose, one of these items are cigarette ends it also depends on where they land, if it is dropped in water it will not take long to break up, if it is dropped on grass or soil they will take couple of weeks to go to pieces, if it lands on rocky or dry land it could take months to go away depending on the weather, so as a tracker Scott knew it was very important to be vigilant, keep his eyes open.

Putting himself in the minds of the criminals as they rode north, (what would they do) then started to talk to himself as men by themselves often do.

"If I had just left a town after causing trouble I would carry on at a reasonable speed to put as much distance I could for at least half of the day or even longer, this means I could travel the whole day before seeing any change of direction, I'll have to keep my eyes open for the time being, but as there is no need to hurry Ill take my time"

After travelling for most of the day, approximately six thirty Scott came across the remains of a camp the sign was old, there was quite a few fag ends were lying about and the tobacco smelt the same as the earlier fag ends, plus Scott did find an old hoof print which looked familiar, the shoe print had a bar across it, this is when Scott left the main trail and followed the horse with the bar across the shoe moving on to the right from the trail.

Scott hooked his leg over the saddle horn, took out the makings and rolled a cigarette lighting it he drew deeply, during this operation Scott was thinking continuously reaching back to his saddlebag pulled a map and unfolded it, Scanning the map (now what would this man do) was his thoughts, the man going off to the right gave him two choices, studying the map the trail split about a day's ride from his present position the hunted man would have a choice of going straight up to the town of Wheeler or turn right and cross the border into Oklahoma to a town called Hollis. The best idea was to just follow the sign and see where it leads him.

After a further scrutiny of the map, it came to him that the man would at some time must leave the trail if going to Hollis the sign should tell him when.

Tracking a man is not always easy, you cannot just look at the map and assume the person has taken the easiest route, you must have patience and look for sign and follow any sign you can no matter how old it is, plus each person that is on the run must camp sometimes, stop to eat, stop to visit the loo, this means there quite a few things you can look out for when following or hunting someone.

Coming across the remains of a camp site, accessing straight away the man was getting complacent as had made a shoddy camp, this is an unexpected bonus the man is hurrying which was not necessary but this made his quarry easier to follow, the camp gave Scott lots of sign, because the camp had been made in a secure place no one had been there to disturb any sign, there was faded hoof prints that had not been touched, deuterating horse droppings, the remains of a fire the ash telling him the man had not extinguished the fire which is dangerous but also a sign the man was in a hurry the remains of a rabbit had not been disposed of, after camping anywhere it is the edicate of the west to clear the camp space and burry any remains or rubbish, there was also some scuffed boot marks all of these thing plus lots of other thing gave Scott enough items to build up a picture of the man (he is lazy), all these item Scott found helps when coming across the next camp where the man stops, looking at the sky his assessment was that there was still about three hours to sunset so carried on following sign.

Two and a half hours later Scott found a place to camp for the night, following his normal routine the camp was set up automatically, after putting water on to make coffee, there was enough time for him to go over and digest what information had been collected.

Coming quickly to his feet his hand reached for the revolver, flicking the loop of the hammer about to draw when a voice rang out.

"Hello, the camp" relaxing slightly but leaving the loop of the hammer then called.

"Come ahead friend".

Two people rode into the camp area a man and a woman, Scott smile as the loop was put back on the hammer.

"Now what are you two doing here" Scott greeted Jake and Mandy.

"We are going to Oklahoma" Mandy blurted out.

"OK, I have just taken out bacon and beans, the water is boiling for coffee so see to your horses and we can eat" Scott said.

"Scott forget about the bacon and beans we have ham sandwiches and roast chicken, so Jake can unsaddle the horses and I'll make the coffee" Mandy told him.

"OK, I'll give Jake a hand with the horses" taking the reins of Mandy's horse.

As they sat on their bedrolls and ate their meal Scott opened the conversation.

"Why Oklahoma".

"The other night in your room you stopped me from killing myself and gave me faith, you made me happy and gave me the strength to carry on, leaving your room I went down stairs and sat at a table, most people were leaving the saloon going home, Jake was left clearing up, after shutting the doors Jake came over with a drink gave it to me and asked if I was OK, I invited him to sit and talk" Mandy told him.

"Scott, Mandy told me what happened between you in your room, I must thank you." Jake butted in and held his hand out, they shook.

"Then I bought Jake a drink, after a couple of drinks Jake said to me, (Mandy, I love you)" Mandy said.

"And I do" Jake broke in again.

"Scott we sat and talked for a while needless to say I found I liked Jake, found that Jake was sincere, I took his hand and we went to bed and made love which I enjoyed, we lay and talked it was during the conversation, Jake told me about his family who ran a large haulage business in North Oklahoma, also during the talk I told Jake because of what happened to me I was uncomfortable staying in this town and thought of leaving in the morning, next thing I knew Jake proposed to me in his words (Marry me, in the morning we go get a couple of horses and ride for Oklahoma, what do you say)" Mandy explained.

"She said yes, and we intend to marry in Oklahoma" Jake said a big smile on his face. Leaning over to Mandy they kissed

"Because of the money you gave to me, we could afford to get all the supplies we needed plus horse's saddles and everything we needed then rode out of town, Scott, I owe you we have a good chance of happiness and a good life together, Jake loves me and want kids the same as me thank you" Mandy ended.

"I must thank you also, Mandy told me how you told her I had feelings for her, I know we will be happy thanks to you" Jake said.

"Since you two are going to get married let me be the first to congratulate you" Scott replied.

"Thank you" Mandy said.

"It's getting late, I'll wash up, let's get some sleep" Scott told them.

Just before dawn Scott's eyes opened his body remain still a smile came to his face as his ears tuned into the sounds of the dawn chorus, getting onto his feet his first task was to put a pot of water on the fire to boil for coffee while the water heated Scott put a little water in a pot and washed his hands and face. Making the coffee, putting beans in the pot, the skillet on the fire, cutting thick rashers of bacon, with the smell and the sound of sizzling bacon a sleepy female voice could be heard.

"Oh! That smells good" Mandy said

"If you two want to wash, it will be ready in a moment coffee is already made help yourselves" Scott told them.

They ate and cleared up the camp ready to ride.

"Scott where are you going" Jake asked.

"South of here there is a town called JAYTON the five men who attacked you Robbed the Wells Fargo office then killed three men" (Scott continued the story Laura told him). In Turkey, I interviewed a lot of people and that included the girls in the Cathouse part of their information was that the five men rode north out of town in a hurry. I therefore took the north trail myself looking for sign of a bunch of horses for quite a long time I could not work out there tracks because being a main trail out of town their tracks were lost, but luck came my way as the group of men left the main trail about five miles out of town, due to the information I required in town I was able to find a little but enough sign that matched some of the items I did pick up in town.

There are things that take longer to decompose, about a day out of Turkey I found a camp where five men had camped, when breaking camp one of them detached himself from the others and came this way, getting my map out I studied it and realised this man's destination could only be one of two places Wheeler in Texas or Hollis over the Oklahoma border, I intend to go to the nearest town of the two which happens to be Hollis, what I am going to do is go to Hollis and if I don't find anything in Hollis I will double back and go north to Wheeler. If I do find one of the men, I am hunting I will take him alive and extract the destination of one of the other men" Scott ended.

"Scott you're doing a lot of work to catch these men for money" Jake queried.

"No, the job is not about the money, I would not be doing it if it was"

"Then why do you do it" Mandy asked.

"As a boy I lived in a small town with my mother and father, my folks ran a small store which barely made eating money, two men came into the store pistols drawn my father told them to take what they wanted, I was hiding, one of the men went to the till there was only $10 ten dollars in the till, they asked for more money, my father told them there was no more, the men shot him this left my mother vulnerable so they raped her then shot her, even though I was very young I made a vow to get every murderer and rapist and bring them to justice" Scott told them, his face bland.

"I see" Jake said

"I now understand" Mandy replied, tears in her eyes.

"Now where are you two of to" Scott enquired.

Eventually we are going to Fairview, north Oklahoma, it will take us about a week to get there but our next stop is Hollis to pick up some supplies" Jake explained.

"In that case I will ride along with you" Scott said.

"OK it will be good to have company" Mandy stated.

Even though the trio, had set of early in between noon and 1pm they entered the town of Hollis Oklahoma slowly riding down the main street taking in the sights, looking at the shops, Suddenly Scott saw Mandy stiffen in the saddle and the change to her face.

"What is wrong Mandy" Scott asked.

"Quickly stop at hitch rail" Mandy returned. They stopped.

"Why" Jake asked

"Scott across the street outside the General store, the man in the dark red shirt its Carl Tim's the one they call the dandy" Mandy told him.

"Are you sure Mandy" Jake asked.

"Jake darling when a man holds you down so you can be raped his face two foot from you smiling and making lurid remarks you remember him" Mandy said.

"I'll kill him" Jake said through gritted teeth.

"No, you won't Jake, I want him alive, don't worry I'll make sure the law will deal with him, now I don't want him to recognise you or Mandy specially you Mandy a man never forgets a pretty woman, and Mandy you are very attractive, this man thinks all good-looking woman are his, this man will be attracted to you like a moth to a flame" Scott told her. Mandy and Jake smiled. Mandy kissed Scott.

"Thank you, Scott, you always make me, feel good" Mandy said, Jake shook hands

"Thank you, Scott, Mandy and I will pick up what we require from the general store, carry on with the journey we were hoping to sleep in a bed tonight, but we can do that at the next place we stop at, so we will say goodbye" Jake told him.

"Mandy, Jake it's been nice known you, I am sure you will have a happy married life, look after each other goodbye" Scott said then rode to the livery stable.

"Hi!" a young jubilant holster greeted him.

"Howdy" Scott replied

"Can I take your horse I'll look after him" the boy said.

"My name is Scott, Blacky is a one-man horse, I will look after him myself I would like a stall a bag of oats and freshwater OK"

"I'm called Art "

"Art as I have said Blacky is a one-man horse and is weary of strangers, I want him to rest don't let anyone near him" Scott explained.

"Right Scott, I'll see no one goes near him" Art said.

"My intension is to leave either late tonight or dawn tomorrow, so how much do I owe you" Scott asked.

"$5 dollars Scott" Art said

"Well here is $10 dollars OK"

"OK Scott" Art answered.

"Thanks" Scott left the stable deep in thought.

(I could maybe get this part of the job done later tonight) were his thoughts, (All I have to do is to wait for the opportunity moment).

Making his way to the hotel, booked a room and paid for one night only, as Mandy had pointed the dandy out to him, the only thing left to do is to watch the man and take him when possible. As it was still afternoon Scott decided to get a few hours' sleep, known the dandy the man would be in the saloon or the towns cathouse meaning it will be easy to find him, turning over on his side his pistol under the pillow Scott slept.

Four hours later Scott's eyes opened his body remained still for a few seconds before rising, it was about seven in the evening and felt refreshed, using the bowl and jug on the dresser washed and shaved, with a fresh set of cloths on, the taste and dryness told him it was time for scran (food) and being hungry made his feet take him to the local café, on his approach to the café the painted sign over the door read PATSIES PAD. The café obviously belonged to a woman and like most towns you go to in the west it was kept clean, brightly coloured with tablecloths and condiments on the tables, the waitress approached his table.

"Can I take your order please sir"

"Could I have a tee bone steak, potatoes and veg. apple pie with cream and coffee please" Scott ordered.

The door of the café opened and to Scott's surprise the dandy walked in.

"Oh no" the waitress uttered.

The dandy took a seat at a table and started banging on the table demanding service loudly, anyone could see the two waitresses were reluctant to serve him, after a few moments one of the young ladies slowly went to the table, the young woman took his order, but as the dandy ordered the girl did everything to avoid the hands that tried to molest her, the dandy laughed as she evaded his hands.

Scott stayed at the café drinking coffee on purpose until the dandy left, Scott asked for the bill.

"Not a very good customer miss" Scott indicated the leaving dandy.

"Oh! That man is horrible, there is not a woman in the whole town that has anything good to say about him, in fact all the females of the town give him a wide berth" the waitress told him.

"You would not miss him if the man left town" Scott hinted.

"Mister I will tell you quietly no one in the whole town would not miss him, I'll tell you mister the women of the town would put the flags out, have a street party, the bastard is only welcome in the red-light house at the end of the street, but that is only because of his money which there seems to be lots of and throws it around freely" the young lady informed him.

"That is nice to know" Scott was elated by this news but did not show it, all the girls had told him was music to his ears.

It did not take long to find where the dandy had gone in fact the dandy was where Scott thought the man would be, playing cards at one of the tables in the saloon, time passed by as Scott stood at the bar drinking watching the dandy then realising the time left and walked to the stable, saddling up Blacky and another horse after receiving some information from Art. Going back to the saloon Scott tied the horses to the hitch rail and was happy to see the dandy still at the saloon.

The dandy at about midnight left the saloon, turned towards the north of town, the dandy only left the saloon as the two girls did not want anything to do with him when trying to get one of the girls to go upstairs with him they both made it quite clear they wanted nothing to do with him, that is why the dandy headed for the cathouse, Scott discreetly followed watching him enter, when the dandy took money from his pocket and pay the madam of the house proceeded with a pretty slim blonde they climbed up the stairs, Scott kept his eyes on the building.

At the front of the building there is a veranda, on the first floor you could climb out onto the top of the veranda, As Scott watched the cathouse a light came on, shinning from the window of the room at the far end of the building.

Walking back to the saloon, Scott mounted Blacky took the reins of the dandy's horse, Art had told Scott which horse was the dandy's riding back to the cathouse, dismounted and tied the reins to a rail out of the lanterns light, around the corner at the far end of the building not far from the room the light came on.

Praising of his boots and replacing them with moccasins he climbed up the drain board (drainpipe) to the veranda, (Thank god) Scott whispered to himself when spotting the window was open because of the warm weather most people at this time of the year opened there window a little, creeping silently towards the window, Scott removed the loop of the hammer of his colt, reaching into his pocket his hand pulled out a cosh.

The lamp in the room still shone, in the glow of the light Scott could see the dandy was busy while the girl lay back showing no interest as the dandy pounded her body, bit by bit the window was raised until fully open, holding the club firmly in his hand Scott stepped swiftly through the window clubbed the dandy hard over his head, then quickly put his hand over the girls mouth, looking into her eyes and putting his finger over his lips, she nodded so took the hand from her mouth, rolled the motionless body off her onto the floor, getting all of the dandy's clothes and belongings together into a bundle, next lowered all his belongings down to where the horses stood.

"Right miss, I am going to tie you up, I will make you comfortable" Scott told her.

"Mister I'm open for business and its all paid for so it's free" the young lady said.

"Not tonight miss, I'm here to do a job of depriving you of a customer" Scott said.

"Oh! You can have him" she told him.

"I can see you don't like him much miss" Scot observed.

"Mister none of the girls like him, this man is only here because of all the cash the man has, so we are told to entertain him, that man is a bastard and gets his kicks by being rough with the girls" she explained.

Taking a spare sheet, Scott ripped it into long strips getting the young ladies' right wrist and tied it to the bed , then repeating the process with the left arm, telling her to put her feet together and lashed her legs together also, with a long strip of the sheet, tied her legs to the bottom of the bed.

"Miss, I Have a job to do, I am going to gag you softly, I want you to go to sleep until morning OK You understand" Scott said

"Yes mister" she replied.

Lifting the tied-up body Scott kissed her then gently before gagging her.

"Is that comfortable" she nodded. Placing a sheet over her, Scott said.

"Go to sleep".

Getting the dandy's naked body across the balcony and lowered him to the horses, tying the dandy's body over the saddle and the bundle to the saddle horn mounting up they rode out a couple of hours later they rode over the border into Texas but kept riding making as much distance as possible.

Just after dawn back in Hollis they found the girl tied to the bed, she was so excited she told the story over and over again, the story travelled around town, the men of the town were happy, but the ladies were elated and could not help laughing at the dandy's extinguishment.

Meanwhile the dandy was waking up coming back to life, Scott ignored his yells until midday where there was a good place to make camp and have lunch.

Scott pulled the naked dandy from the horse roughly putting him on the ground beside a tree and secured him a little tight on purpose.

"Ah! Mister Tim's how are you" Scott asked.

"Give me my clothes" the dandy demanded.

"Well, it's like this, you and your four friends robbed the Wells Fargo office in Jayton killing three guards I want to know where your friends are" Scott said.

"What four friends" Tim's said.

"Like that Eh!"

Scott left Tim's and poured a cup of coffee, drank it as Tim's looked on.

"Hey, you give me my clothes" Tim's called out. Scott ignored him.

Tim's kept calling for his clothes, but Scott took no notice of him for half an hour when he stood in front of the dandy who once again asked for his clothes.

"Where is your friends hanging out" Scott asked.

"I don't know what you are talking about" Tim's yelled getting up tight.

Scott once more walked away getting the brushes out and gave Blacky a good brushing before returning to confront the dandy.

"I'm asking you again where are your friends" Scott asked.

"I don't have any friends" Tim's said.

"Oh! I believe that, so I will put it another way where are your partners in crime you will tell me eventually, so I would tell me now" Scott told him

"I don't know what you are talking about" the dandy said.

"Maybe a little pain will help" Scott said.

"Ha! Ha! Ha! That won't make me say anything I do not want to say" Tim's laughed.

"Oh! I wonder how long it will take for you to talk" Scott said.

"I won't talk ever" the dandy yelled.

"Let me tell you what I have in mind then you can let me know whether you want me to carry on, I am going to finish my lunch, we are going to ride as I have wasted too much time and need to get going, you are going to ride naked the way you are but tied down tight you will be exposed to the hot sun, as we ride along your naked balls will bang hard against the saddle, bouncing of the saddle horn, now after half a mile your balls will be itchy and you will be unable to scratch them, after an hour your body will burn your balls will be red raw and painful a further hour on they will be bleeding and very, very, very sore and painful it will feel like your balls are hanging of but they won't it will increase the pain think about it, I need a leek" Scott told him.

Scott walked into the brush, when coming back sat on a nearby rock and rolled a cigarette and had a smoke before going back to confront Tim's.

"You cannot do what you said it's against the law" the dandy said.

"I am not a lawman"

"Who are you" Tim's asked.

"The name is Burrows, Scott Burrows"

"I've heard of you, you, are a bounty hunter" Tim's said.

"You heard right, now I have a dodger in my pocket which says DEAD or ALIVE, so it is up to you how I deliver you" Mister Tim's.

"You cannot just kill me"

"Why not we are miles away from anyone, who is going to know, now are you ready to talk" Scott told him

Tim's went quiet and Scott moved away for a few moments to give him a minute to think, then confronted him again.

"Right Tim's are you ready to tell me where your friends are" Scott asked.

"I don't know" Tim's said.

"You're a liar, I know you and the rest of the gang were in a cave, each of you talked and told each other your plans, where you were going what you were going to spend the money on talk now" Scott ordered him

"H H How do you know that" Tim's asked.

"Laura told me"

"Laura"

"Yes, Laura the girl you shot in the back"

"Can't be she was dead"

"She was not, and it took her a week to crawl her way out but she did do, and the main reason she succeeded was because she did not want to leave five monsters like you getting away with your crimes and the murder of more innocent people, she asked me to get you and after what she told me I agreed". Scott told him.

"What makes you think she told you the truth" the dandy said.

"She was dying. Look Tim's this is your last chance, I have a job to do and as you have heard of me you know my rep, (reputation) I always get the job done, I have a job to do and come hell and high water I am going to get it done, so to save yourself discomfort and pain, I want to know what information you can tell me about your friends, then you can have your clothes back" Scott told him.

"All right I will tell you what I know, Billy said his destination is Wheeler I think some of his relations live there, as for the other three I can only give you a rough idea, Wes Arnold was heading east, there is a woman who owns a saloon, his intention is to go into partnership with her, the other two headed north Dutchy intends to own a livery stable but I did not hear where, but Ron Bates said up near Texas northern border with Oklahoma there is a ranch for sale, I understand this ranch is already his as a down payment for it has already been paid, that's all the information I can give you now give me my clothes" the dandy asked.

Going to the bundle of clothes Scott first picked out the underwear checked it for hidden knives then threw them at him Tim's put them on one handed as still tied to the tree, picking out the gun belt out he placed it to the side, when finding a money belt checking it, the belt had $15.000 dollars in it, this was also put to the side, (going through the pockets of the shirt and trousers looking at the boots and the waist band of the Stetson making them into a bundle) dropping the clothes beside Tim's Scott untied him then stepped back.

"Get dressed" Scott also gave him a sandwich and a cup of coffee.

Clearing up the camp checking everything was packed including the money after which the prisoner was helped to mount then tied him in place, mounting up taking the reins of the dandy's horse they rode out.

For the rest of the day Scott kept them moving only stopping to allow the horses to blow, chew some jerky meat and drink of water and a smoke they camped overnight, at approximately eleven am on the next day they rode down main street, to the sheriff's office in Turkey, releasing the dandy's legs Scott dragged him from the saddle and frog marched him into the office.

From the time Scott entered the Main Street to the short distance to the sheriff's office quite a crowd had gathered some of them recognised the dandy, one or two of the citizens called out but otherwise it was OK. If the town had been really hostile to the prisoner, it would have been Scott's duty to take him elsewhere for his safety.

"Howdy sheriff" Scott greeted.

"Hi! Scott how are you" came the reply.

"I have a present for you" then marched the dandy into the cells.

"I suppose this is one of the men who terrorised the town and raped the saloon girl" the sheriff enquired.

"Sure"

"What you going to do with him" the sheriff asked.

"This is Carl Tim's known as the dandy and this man is wanted for robbery, murder and rape and is your guest for about two days" Scott informed him.

"How? Why?" the sheriff asked.

"It will take that long for a couple of deputies to get here from Jayton to get here and pick him up" Scott explained

"I see"

"What's your name sheriff"

"Andy Becks, why do you want to know my name" the sheriff asked.

"When I leave here, I am sending a wire to Jayton telling them of the capture of the dandy and the money I have retrieved and that I have left the dandy with you and for them to send deputies to take him of your hands" Scott instructed him.

"What money"

"I also managed to get $15000 dollars of the stolen money back" reaching into his shirt"

"After leaving here the money goes into the bank with instructions to return it to Wells Fargo Jayton" Scott told him.

The tasks that had been outlined to the sheriff were carried out, getting the money to the bank, and send for a couple of deputies to pick up the prisoner after sending them of the teller asked if the return messages should be delivered to him.

"No, I will be back later"

Going to the hotel Scott booked a room, paying for twenty-four hours taking his bags and rifle to the room, rode Blacky to the livery stable, making sure the big horse was settled, patting the horse neck.

"See you in the morning boy" Scott said. Going back to the telegraph office and received the return messages then retraced his steps to the sheriff 's office

"OK Sheriff I have contacted the sheriff's office in Jayton there is a deputy on the way already to pick up Tim's, I have also told Wells Fargo about the transfer of the money from the bank to the bank in Jayton" Scott informed him.

"I will be leaving at dawn to chase the next man the one called Billy boy, so I will have a meal at the café, a beer at the saloon then I'm of to bed ". Scott informed him.

As the first crack of light, gave a beautiful ribbon of light silhouetting the hills east of the small sleepy town, Scott's eyes opened, lying for a minute or two stretched before climbing to his feet, pouring water into the bowl on the dresser his next action was to splash his face taking the sleep out of his eyes, while washing and shaving his mind came to the task that had to be done that day trailing (Billy boy).

On completion of his ablutions Scott packed his bags, left them in the room ready to pick up later leaving the hotel turning left out the door heading for the café. Scott new the day was going to be long so a good hearty breakfast before riding out is a good idea, taking a table in the corner of the room called the waitress.

"Good morning sir how can I help you" the waitress enquired

"Morning miss could I have a full breakfast and coffee, could you all so put some cold chicken and sandwiches in a bag to take away" Scott ordered.

"Yes sir" she replied.

Scott knew there is jerky meat in his saddle bags and some cold chicken, and the sandwiches would see him to Wellington three and a half days away, there will be no need for him to look for sign until passing the Hollis turn off, if Tim's has told him the truth and Billy has travelled to Wheeler. (From the Hollis turn off and Wheeler there is two towns the first one being Wellington.

As Tim's had told him that Billy boy had definitely gone to Wheeler that is the place to go to next, and there is no way he could have lied under the circumstances and because of the information given to Scott, but it does mean that there is no need to stop so can move faster which is good news.

Not pushing Blacky but still moving at a reasonable pace, at the end of the second day Scott passed the turn off for Hollis in Oklahoma, travelling all the next day they arrived at Wellington the following morning, his first stop was the livery stable to settle Blacky into a stall, when Blacky had been taken care of Scott headed for the café looking forward to a hearty breakfast on his arrival at the café it had just opened so it was at that time quiet. The waitress came across to him.

"Howdy miss full breakfast please" after riding for three days Scott was looking forward to a decent meal.

Sitting at the table relishing his coffee realising the café will be full very soon, catching the eye of the waitress.

"Miss before it gets busy could you spare me a moment"

"How can I help you" she asked.

"I am looking for a young man called Billy Watts who may have come through this town about two weeks ago, the young man I am looking for has hair like a mop and is trouble" Scott asked.

"Wait" the waitress said went into the café kitchen.

About six to seven moments later the sheriff entered with his gun drawn pointing at Scott.

"Talk mister"

"Talk about what sheriff"

"Billy Watts known as Billy boy" came the reply.

"Do you know his where about"

"Believe me mister, If I knew where that bastard is, I'd make sure that the sod would be in my cells or dead" the sheriff said.

"Billy has been naughty again I take it, that boy cannot stay out of trouble" Scott said.

"Mister I am losing my patience talk"

"OK sheriff, calm down I am Scott Burrows Billy has had a hand in killing seven people that I know of, and I have been hired to get him and the four other members of the gang, after Billy there is only three of the gang left, I have already taken care of one of them" Scott explained.

"Scott Burrows am I supposed to know you" the sheriff asked.

"Sheriff send, a wire to the sheriff's office in Jayton, they will explain about me meanwhile put that gun away, there is no dodger out for me, I have not caused any trouble or committed any crime in your town, so you have no reason to hold me in fact you are depriving me of my rights" Scott explained.

"Mister don't go anywhere, I don't trust a smart arse, I'm not finished with you" the sheriff told Scott.

"Sheriff if I wanted to leave I would but my horse needs his rest before I carry on, the other reason is you are going to send that wire, and I am quite happy to wait until you get the reply then you will tell me what went on in this town with Billy boy" Scott informed him.

Scott stood up adjusted his gun belt tied the holster down by fastening the thong around his leg, once happy threw a dollar on the table and walked out of the café.

The sheriff did not deter him, making a tourer around the town calling into every business asking about Billy Watts and came up against a town sworn to silence nobody wanted to talk to Scot as if the people of the town did not trust him a stranger amongst them.

After walking and trying almost every place in town, Scott decided to go to the saloon and have a beer and cool down as the walk around the town had made him hot and thirsty, when the barman returned with his beer Scott decided to try one more time.

"Excuse me barman do you know what went on in this town the night Billy Watts stopped here"

"Excuse me I will get the boss sir" the barman replied.

His boss turned out to be an attractive middle-aged woman, as she approached Scott saw the small nod, she gave to the head barman, who slipped out the door.

"How can I help you stranger" the lady asked.

"I have spent a week trying to catch a man called Billy Watts I know by the actions of the people of this town that Billy has been here but all I get is doors slammed in my face can you tell me anything" Scott asked. At that time, the barman returned with the sheriff.

"Burrows what have you been up to" the sheriff bellowed.

"I have done nothing but ask questions" Scott admitted.

"Listen no one wants to talk to you so why don't you get out of town"

"Sheriff I will leave town when you or one of the good folk start talking.

"Burrows" the sheriff was about to carry on, but a voice called out.

"Burrows! did you say Burrows?" a man dressed as a cowhand said.

"Yes, I said Burrows why do you know him" the sheriff said

"Scott Burrows" the cowhand enquired

"Sure" Scott said.

"I'm happy to meet you I have heard about you" the man held out his hand Scott shook it.

"Who the hell is Scott Burrows" the sheriff asked angrily.

"Scott Burrows is a bounty hunter who normally works down south of here and is well known for getting the job done, by reputation this man is the best" the cowhand explained.

"What reputation" the sheriff demanded.

"Look sheriff, what I have heard, is when a sheriff or Wells Fargo have a problem, they cannot solve they call Scott Burrows" the cowhand explained.

"Burrows finish that beer then come to my office" the sheriff said.

"Sure sheriff" Scott finished his beer then went to the sheriff's office.

"All right Burrows talk, I don't like bounty hunters, so you had better have a good explanation why you are here" the sheriff asked.

"OK Sheriff" Scott told the sheriff everything, from the robbery to the present day.

"So, you were told by the one called the dandy that Billy is heading for Wheeler, and this is one of the towns on the way to Wheeler, how do you know this man the dandy told you the truth" the sheriff asked.

"Sheriff I am good at my job, I get results, I am not a lawman so I have no restrictions in what I do, believe me the dandy was telling the truth I made sure of that, the biggest part of my job is reading people and sign, by the way this is, there is enough sign for me to tell this town has a problem they shut up every time I ask a question this town has the jitters, then go running to you, the funny thing is when I say the word Billy, would you like to enlighten me" Scott asked.

"OK Burrows"

"Scott sheriff"

"Are you sure Billy will be in Wheeler" the sheriff asked.

"No! I do not know if Billy will be in Wheeler, but I know the dandy told the truth and was told Billy will be in Wheeler, that means I go to Wheeler, this town and the next town north called Shamrock are the only places on route to Wheeler and that is why I am here, now sheriff I have not had a straight answer since I arrived, now tell me what happened in this town." Scott requested.

"Basically Scott it was murder, because it was special and hard to believe such a thing could happen, everyone in town is scared to answer question and believe you could be a friend of Billy's and therefore a possible killer to, needless to say the people of this town will not answer your question until they know who's side you are on, me being the sheriff they have elected me to ask the questions" the sheriff told him.

"Sheriff you now know I am here to either kill or capture Billy, to bring him to face justice, I have a dodger in my pocket which states dead or alive, now tell me about this special murder Billy committed." Scott asked.

"When Billy arrived in town it was a pleasant afternoon, sunny and warm everyone in town was happy billy rode in wearing shabby clothes raggy shirt and jeans, but by night fall, Billy had changed, when next seen Billy wore new clothes, a new gunboat and a new pearl handled revolver, that night the first murder happened of course we could not say it was Billy who done it, later we found it could not have been anyone else. The following night the main incident occurred along with the good clothes somehow Billy had money to burn, and it went to his head" the sheriff paused.

"It was a Saturday night and every Saturday there is a special table laid out for the town council to play cards and discuss town matters, and the rule is only council members or people with council business can attend that table of course everybody in town knows about it ". the sheriff explained.

Billy approached the table, then it went like this: –

"Have you a place at the table" Billy asked.

"Sorry son this is a private game" the doctor explained.

"I don't see why it is private, I'll sit in"

"Look son we have already told you this is a private game, son there are three other tables where games are taking place why not join one of them"

One of the men at the table was the Mayor, who could see this man causing trouble to avoid trouble the doctor suggested they break up the game and play another night the other players agreed, what happened next nobody could have foreseen, Billy stepped back facing the table, and yelled (I am not good enough for you Eh!) drew his pistol and shot the five men sitting at the table, this of course was not just any murder, the people at the table were the most prominent men of the town and none of them carried a gun, at the table was the Mayor of the town, the town's only doctor, the owner of the general store, the Wells Fargo manager and the head man of the cattleman association, All of this might not mean anything to an outsider of this town, but as an example, one of the group was the only doctor for miles the next doctor is in shamrock and a lot of the ladies in town depended on him.

"I take it Billy stole a horse and rode out of town," Scott said.

"Yes, I did get a posse together even though it was dark we rode and searched for hours everywhere we could think of, we did not find him" the sheriff.

"Sheriff, I have been here all day, the town and yourself has stalled me, as this incident happened about two weeks ago no harm taken I will carry on with the search in the morning" Scott replied, as Scott was about to step of the boardwalk outside the sheriff's office when a buggy stopped beside them a young man and woman on the seat.

"Hello folks could you tell me where the doctor's office is please" the man asked.

"Sorry we do not have a doctor" the sheriff told him.

"I know I am the new doctor; this is my wife and nurse" the man said.

"Oh! I see, I am the sheriff, Scott good luck, if you come this way doctor" the sheriff replied.

DOC HE IS DOING IT

Scott left Wellington during the afternoon the next day, looking at the map, Scott calculated it would take one and a half days to get there, once again there was no need to hurry, sitting on his horse on the Brough of a hill looking at the country ahead.

"Ah! I wish it could be like this every day" talking to himself, hooking his leg over the saddle horn, taking out the makings, rolled and smoked a cigarette.

Riding for the rest of the day until sunset, camped overnight, then rode the last of the way getting into Shamrock late the next day, Scott saw Blacky was comfortable, found a room at the hotel, As Wheeler is only a day's ride from Shamrock his estimated leaving at dawn should put him in Wheeler before sunset, Making sure that Blacky was settled for the night, Scott decided to put the nosebag on himself so made for the local café.

While waiting for his meal Scott spotted an article in the local rag, the Shamrock Times, the article in the paper told the folk of the town that the sheriff used his authority to eject an undesirable from the town, the article read.

UNWANTED KICKED OUT OF TOWN.

PEOPLE OF SHAMROCK, I AM HAPPY TO TELL YOU OF THE EXCELLENT WORK, CARRIED OUT BY THE TOWN LAW, USING HIS POWERS OF SHERIFF, A DRUNKEN UNDESIREABLE WHO CAUSED TROUBLE IN THE TOWN HAS BEEN EJECTED, HIS NAME WAS BILLY WATTS I'M HAPPY TO SAY THIS MAN WILL CAUSE NO MORE TROUBLE.

Now that Scott knows that Billy is no longer in the town it was not necessary for him to stay any longer than it is necessary, it means there is the possibility to get to Wheeler a bit earlier.

After his usual checks, Blacky and breakfast, Scott was on his way again heading for Wheeler.

There was only one thing that bothered Scott why was Billy intent on going to Wheeler according to the dandy Billy made no secret about his destination so there had to be a reason for it, of course Billy thought Laura had died which means apart from the other members of the gang no one knows his destination is wheeler, as far as Billy is concerned there is no pursuit, the question still is why, what is so important about Wheeler.

1)   Is his family there.
2)   Does his girlfriend live there.
3)   Is it a safe haven for him.
4)   Maybe there is something there that belongs to him.

Billy is a young man with a load of money in his pocket who likes to gamble and thinks whether its cards or gun believes there is no one better than him but is all wrong this is why Billy gets into trouble.

The other problem is that being young and with people like the dandy and Bates who are a bad influence for him, and has taught him to think little about women, with his impetuous nature it would be impossible for him to keep away from booze and card games.

Since Scott could not understand Why Billy is determined to go to Wheeler, instead of going to town and asking question without known the situation, his best idea is to hang around the saloon, If Billy did want to drink and gamble that is where his place of interest would have to be.

Meanwhile the deputy with the dandy in tow, had arrived back in Jayton riding down Main Street, Laura had previously asked the doctor to put her in a chair by the open window so she could get air and watch the activity in the town as she was bored, she suddenly grabbed the doctor and with a crackling voice said.

"Look doc" she pointed in the street as the dandy rode past.

"Yes Laura" Doc spoke in a faint voice.

"Doc he is doing it; Scott has caught him" she croaked.

"Yes Laura" Doc said finding it hard to keep the tears from his eyes.

As the doc looked at Laura A smile came on her gaunt face, a crackling noise came from her throat as she attempted to laugh, then her body slumped in the chair, Laura died happy. Doc could not prevent the tears.

Scott walked into the Silver Dollar Saloon in Wheeler, strolled over to the bar, ordered a beer, turning drink in hand his back against the bar, he slowly made a survey of the room in particular each game played at each table keeping his eye out for Billy

Each night Scott carried out the same routine, each night Scott would take care and walk around the room checking every corner of the room his ears were tuned into the sounds around him, as a careless word may help him, after repeating this routine for three nights without picking up anything to help him and was thinking it is about time to ask questions.

Scott is still reluctant to ask questions as this was Billy's chosen destination and therefore may have friends here, if Scott asked question word might get to him, this could make him disappear or brazen as Billy is, Scott might get a bullet in the back, reflecting on the possible actions Billy could take, Scott decided to carry on with his search routine a little longer and rely on his instants to be able to apprehend Billy.

On the fifth night Scott stood at the bar thinking if there was another path it would be possible to explore, when a sound came to his ears, the sound was someone saying the name Watts, the name came from an unexpected source, his ears tuned in Scott turned slowly to look at the two saloon girls not far from him, the two girls did not realise Scott had tuned his ears into their muffled voice conversation about Billy Watts.

Looking at the two girls Nicky and Julia were a short distance away even though they were trying to keep it down, and what they thought was whispers between each other Scott could hear them.

"Why did that bastard Watts come back" Julia announced.

"I agree it would have been better if he had stayed away" Nicky agreed.

"It's bad for Sandra Mason and Clive Collins" Julia stated

"Yeh!" Nicky murmured.

"Sandra never wanted Billy in the first place, and I think she made that clear to him the last time he was here" Julia said to Nicky.

"If Billy gets his way, the sod will kill Clive" Nicky omitted.

"You know Nicky, I have never seen Clive wear a gun, I would bet that Clive knows little about guns" Julia summarised.

"If I was Sandra, I'd take a rifle to the scene and say loud and clear, if you kill Clive, I will kill you" Nicky declared.

"Excuse me Ladies is there a quiet place where we can talk" Scott asked.

"I think the office out back is empty, I don't think anyone will mind" Julia stated.

"Wrong the boss would" Nicky said.

"Yeh we are working girls" Julia admitted.

"As working girls, it is your job to entertain and get me to spend right" Scott said

"Yes, that is right" Julia agreed.

"Look miss would you go to the bar buy a bottle of champagne two glasses and a beer for me and let everyone see it, I don't think your boss will complain" Scott stated.

"Right" Julia said taking the money Scott handed her, then left.

Scott and Nicky sat and talked about the town and what it is like until Julia returned.

"OK mister what do you want of us" Julia asked

"Ladies drop the mister, my name is Scott, right girls I heard you talking while you were at the bar earlier and I am interested and want to know the full story" Scott asked them.

"Scott, I am Nicky, and this is Julia, you are not a friend of the sheriff" Nicky asked.

"I have never met him" Scott told them.

"Look you seem like a nice man and to us a stranger, everyone in town knows what is going on, but we have to know who's side you are on, it is dangerous to talk about Billy Watts" Julia explained.

"From the way, you too talked in the bar you are not a supporter of Billy and to what you have just said you know the sheriff is crooked, I am on your side, I think I can trust you not to talk, so I will tell you my secret can I trust you girl's" Scott asked.

"Yes, you can trust us" the girls chorused.

"My name is Scott Burrows, and I am a bounty hunter; my job is to capture or kill Billy Watts for robbery and murder" Scott told them

"Oh!" Nicky said putting her hand over her mouth.

"God!" Julia exclaimed.

"Now you know, I now need to know what is going on in this town, one, so I can carry out my job and two, I need to know who would be on Billy's side, and by the conversation you two know and can give me answers" Scott told them.

"Scott, we are willing to talk to you, but only if you promise not to tell anyone, if certain people in this town get to know about this Nicky and I will be dead, but we do like and trust you" Julia informed him.

"Billy Watts was born just outside town, his father is a well of land owner and it is needless to say his son was spoilt, if he got into any trouble his father would get him out of it, so mister Watts had influence and had word with the sheriff to keep Billy out of trouble, about four years ago, Billy started to swagger about the town, and acquired a holster and Gun, Billy at this time did not kill people but nothing in town was safe as you never knew what the boy would shoot at for practise, no women were safe either all women gave him a wide berth if possible." Nicky paused to sip her drink, so Julia carried on.

"Scott, no one would admit it, but Billy was getting out of control. Then the Masons came to town, mister Mason the Bank Manager, his wife and his beautiful daughter Sandra Mason, Billy fell in love with her, after a few days Sandra learnt enough about Billy to tell him she did not love him and told him she was not interested in him, grabbing her everyone believes Billy would have raped her but her father came to her rescue" Julia paused to drink and Scott realised the bottle was empty, Scott asked Nicky to get more drinks.

"Sure Scott".

Nicky returned with three beers. Nicky continued talking.

"Billy was not happy about Sandra turning him down, It was then when Billy became impossible molesting women all over town, the women of the town knew the sheriff was being paid by mister Watts senior, the women all congregated outside the sheriff's office, we believe the sheriff had a word with his father because Billy stopped molesting the women, but (and it is a big but) Scott, Billy began to gamble, the only women that would tolerate him was the girls in the cathouse, but that is when it all began, one night Billy sat in on a card game, after drinking heavily and losing heavily also it was probably an hour at the table when one of the men at the table called Billy a cheat, Billy stood up drew his gun and shot the man, the barman went for the sheriff, on his arrival took a quick look did not ask question, proclaimed it was self-defence and rushed Billy out of the saloon, the man Billy shot did wear a gun but it was in his holster the loop on the hammer" Nicky stopped to have a slurp of her beer Julia took over.

"Now there is no way to prove it but most people we know thinks the sheriff took Billy home and suggested to his father that for his health Billy should drift for a while.

Everything has been fine in town no shooting, (no shooting up the town, no abusing women of the town) we have all got down to living a peaceful life, two weeks ago Billy rides back into town, his pockets full of cash and for the first few days Billy returned to his old ways, now for the past week we have not heard him it's been quite speculation is that once more the sheriff saw Billy's father who ordered his son to pack it in, we have nothing to substantiate that claim but we all think that is what happened.

"Anyway, yesterday in front of everyone Billy stood in the street in front of Sandra and said loud enough for anyone to hear.

"You are mine"

"I am not I am getting married next week, and it is not to you" Sandra yelled back.

"Who are you marrying" Billy called loudly.

"To me" a voice from the left calmly told him.

Clive is a brave young man who does not believe in guns, I think Billy would have shot Clive there and then, but Billy saw Clive did not wear a gun.

"You get yourself a belt and gun and be on the street at noon tomorrow" Billy said.

"Tomorrow at noon Clive is going to meet Billy on the street, Clive is no coward but is not going to let Billy get away with it" Nicky cut in.

"Girls grab the tray, let's go to the bar and have a drink, and your secret is OK with me" Scott said. Watching the saloon owner coming to them.

"Barman a bottle of champagne and three glasses please" Scott said loud enough for the saloon owner to hear.

"Oh! Champagne eh!" the owner said.

"Yeh! You know your girls are great" Scott told him.

"What have you two been up to" the owner asked.

"Boss. You know better than to ask a girl that question" Nicky winked.

The manager smiled then moved away.

"Right girls I will leave the rest of the bottle to you; excuse me I have to see a pal" Scott walked to the livery stable.

Walking over to Blacky's stall Scott greeted him.

"Hi! you badding how are you" as the big horse muzzled his shirt and Scott patted the thick neck.

"Hello, nice horse you have there" a sweet female voice declared.

"Yes, this is my pal" Scott informed her.

"Your pal looks good I bet your horse has character "she said.

"Yes, you're right this monkey likes to play"

"I could tell" she said.

"Miss, it is getting dark, you should not be out by yourself at this hour" Scott said.

"I have a lot on my mind, I needed some fresh air to clear my mind I guess I lost time" she told him.

"Come on miss I will see you home, my name is Scott"

"I am Sandra Mason" she replied.

"Ah! You are the banker's daughter" Scott realised.

"Yes Scott"

Standing by the gate of the banker's house.

"Sandra, go in have an evening drink, go to bed have a good night's sleep forget your problem everything will be OK, trust me" Scott assured her.

(Oh! What a lovely girl) Scott summarised.

Scott headed straight back to his room, there was things that must be done before morning concentrating on his weapons getting them ready for tomorrow, the first item was his revolver, unlocking the barrel Scott slid it off and removed all the bullets which were placed in order on the bed picking the main part of the gun, with a thin bottle type brush the barrel was cleaned, pulling back the trigger Scott checked the action then put a couple of drops of light oil on the mechanism, satisfied with the main part of his gun, the next job is the barrel and bullets, picking up the barrel wiped it with a clean cloth, then using the thin brush cleaned out each hole in the barrel, then slid the barrel into place, after wiping each bullet he loaded the revolver, satisfied with the revolver and its action placed it on the bed, looking at his belt, making a good examination checking for any splits in the leather, removed each bullets wiped each one returning to the loops making sure all the loops have been filled, his final job Scott attended to was the holster itself with drops of oil inside the holster making it smooth so his revolver could slide easily in and out giving him a smoother draw, after a couple of practise draws, checking the time realised there was time for a beer before turning in for the night.

Ordering a beer his back to the bar Scott surveyed the room, it was a bit quiet at this time of night, the night being almost over, so relished the cool beer, half way through his drink, a friendly voice of a person that was known to him sounded from behind him.

"Hi! Scott buy me a beer" the words omitted from Nicky's mouth.

"Nicky, where is your shadow" Scott asked.

"If you mean Julia, she does not work at night, she is at home with her husband and little boy" Nicky explained.

"Barman, two beers and have a drink yourself" Scott ordered.

"Thank you, sir," came the reply.

"The name is Scott"

"Bert" the barman said.

"You're not married then Nicky" Scott enquired.

"No! no one has asked me, and as yet I have not met anyone I want" Nicky answered.

"I know you and it's just a matter of time before you do" Scott assured her.

"Scott, I feel lonely tonight, the bed in your room is it big enough for two" Nicky asked.

"Yes, it is, and I'd love to share it with you if you want to" Scott said.

"Thanks Scott I need a cuddle" Nicky said.

When they completed drinking their drinks, Scott put his arm around her, she followed suit putting her arm around his waist as they climbed the stairs. Once they stepped into the room and shut the door Scott took Nicky into his arms and kissed her long and tenderly after the kiss her eyes still closed, she murmured.

"Oh! Scott" opened her eyes and started undressing.

After they had both undressed, they climbed into bed, as the two bodies came together their arms around each other a contented sigh came from Nicky's lips as they cuddled the two naked bodies clung to each other, the tender kissing and words of love whispered in her ear soon changed into passionate kissing, the night went well they made love a few times, between bouts of love making they talked finding out about each other in the end both of them enjoyed it there was no pressure just two relaxed people having a pleasant time together.

After a while Scott said to Nicky.

"I must get some sleep; I have a gunfight tomorrow"

This statement puzzled Nicky, (What does he mean) she thought, she and everyone else knew Clive and Billy was facing each other tomorrow what does it mean, (Have a gunfight) she looked at him, Scott kissed her then turned over and slept, Nicky followed, Nicky woke up feeling aroused by the hand between her leg which opened and she whispered "Oh! Yes Scott" and made love again.

"Thank you, Nicky I have had a wonderful time, and a wonderful night and you were fantastic," Scott kissed her "you are beautiful now I must get up I have things to do but you if you are still tired, you and that beautiful body can rest as long as you wish" Scott smiled. Nicky was happy because of the compliments Scott gave her.

"Yes, we have had a lovely night, thank you, I am not lonely anymore" she replied.

Scott now dressed, leaned over and kissed her, then left the room locked it and Nicky saw the key being slipped under the door.

At the livery stable, Blacky seeing his master gave out a neigh, Scott smiled walked over to him and greeted him by patting his neck and talked to him, topping the trough up with water then giving him a nosebag, Scott waited until the big horse had his breakfast, last of all Scott released Blacky into the corral to roam a while.

Even though Scott had said that Blacky had his breakfast it was really a very late breakfast due to his early morning activities, a smile came to his face because of his thoughts, walking a couple of hundred yards down main street, stopping outside the café the smell of food seemed to draw him in, by this time it was eleven am, finding a table by the window, Scott ordered an all-day breakfast, with coffee to follow, just before midday Scott called for and paid his Bill.

Looking up the street Scott saw the young man Clive wearing a gun belt and gun the holster too high for a fast draw, slowly walking down the middle of the street at least the young man is no coward needing to avenge his girl Sandra, lower down the street

Billy stepped from the saloon then starting his walk up towards Clive, who was coming the other way, the street was clear doors shut as people sneaked a peek at the scene in the street, when the two men stood about ten paces apart, Clive stood right opposite the café door.

Meanwhile Nicky in Scott's room had woken, climbed out of bed still naked splashed water into the bowl and with a wet towel washed her body then dried of then dressed, she felt great so went to the window to get some air and saw the two young men in the street facing each other, she stayed at the window to watch to her amazement Scott came out of the café walked over to the shocked young man Clive, and punched him in the jaw rending him unconscious, quickly turning Scott faced Billy his hand hanging by his side the loop already of the hammer of the gun.

"Billy Watts you are under arrest for robbery and murder" Scott announced loudly.

"What robbery" Billy asked.

"The Wells Fargo office Jaydon nearly three weeks ago" Scott told him.

"I don't know what you are talking about" Billy said.

"That's not what the witness said" Scott informed him.

"What witness" Billy asked.

"Billy Laura sent me" Scott told him

"Laura" a look of understanding came to his face

"Yes! Laura, you remember Laura, don't you Billy" Scott nudged Billy.

"I don't remember a Laura" Billy said

"In a cave, not far from Jaydon you left an almost naked girl with two bullets in her back, she survived and with her bare hands dug her way out" Scott told him

"Who are you" Billy asked.

"Scott Burrows"

For a second a strange silence fell on them, everything seemed to stop as Billy's hand went for his gun hoping to take Scott by surprise, Scott watching Billy's eyes the normally dull grey eyes flickered, Scott drew and fired twice, Billy did manage to get his gun out of the holster but before aligning it two bullets hit him in the chest, the pale blue shirt turned a sticky wet looking red colour as his blood soaked into the shirt, his face had an amazed look on his face, his slight body fell backwards to lay out stretched on the dusty street, for a second air escaped from Billy's lips then his head rolled to the left lying still eyes wide open.

The sheriff ran to the scene.

"What's going on here" the sheriff demanded.

"You know what goes on here, but you have ignored it, if you had done your job there is at least six or seven people would be alive today, you will have in your office a dodger on this man. Who should have faced the law, but you allowed him to go free and protected him for money from his father letting him kill" Scott proclaimed loudly?

"And who are you to accuse me" the sheriff demanded.

"Scott Burrows bounty hunter" came the reply.

"Bounty hunter"

"Yes, you know murder was to be committed on this street today, and you made no move to stop it, go to the counsel offices and return the badge you are not fit to wear it be out of town in an hour, you're finished in this town" Scott ordered.

"You take this stinking badge to the town council" the man threw the badge at Scott.

The sheriff grabbed his horse and rode out of town, Scott picked up the badge with a little help wrapped Billy's body in a tarp and laid the body at the livery stable ready to load on his horse before leaving, proceeding to the courthouse Scott asked for the mayor, a man standing a couple of paces from Scott spoke up.

"I am the mayor, this is Mr Mason, and this is Mr James the gunsmith we are members of the town council, you did an excellent job out there" the Mayor said.

"Mayor you are going to need a new sheriff here is his badge" Scott handed over the badge.

"Thank you, Mister,"

"The name is Scott, Scott Burrows, I'm a bounty hunter and I will be taking Billy's body with me" Scott informed him.

"OK Scott, you can have him thank you" James replied.

"Mr Mason, you are the banker" Scott asked.

"Yes, I am"

"I will be along to the bank to see you shortly" Scott told him.

Scott returned to the saloon went up to his room, packed his bags went downstairs ordered a beer, as the beer was cool it felt great the sound of a female voice spoke out.

"Gunfight, I see what you mean" she stepped in front of him put her arms around his neck and kissed him.

Scott loaded his belongings onto a horse at the hitch rail, (Billy's horse) and walked to the livery stable, stripping the horse, Scott put water in the trough gave each horse a nosebag of oats, now he had tended to the horses a few things needed to be done before leaving the town, the café for a meal, the general store for supplies needed for his trip on leaving town, then his last place of call the bank entering the bank and asked for the manager two people had followed Scott into the bank.

"Scott, Scott, I think you have met my daughter and son in law," Mr Mason indicated the young couple behind him,

"Thank you, sir, but that was my fight" Clive the young man greeted Scott.

"Scott thank you for helping my future son in law" Mr Mason said.

"I guess I must thank you for rending me unconscious Clive said rubbing his jaw.

"Scott, I see what you meant last night, I must thank you for saving my fiancé" Sandra Mason said.

"Scott, you came here on business please come into the office" Mr Mason ushered Scott through the gate to his office,

"Thanks" was his reply.

"Mr Mason Billy Watts did not have a money belt, so I assume his money is in the bank is that right" Scott asked.

"Your right Scott Billy Watts does have an account" Mr Mason told him

"What is the balance left" Mr Mason called for Billy's account.

"According to this there is $12.700 dollars in his account" Mr Mason informed him.

"The money in Billy's account is part of $100.000 dollars stolen from Wells Fargo office in Jayton where they shot three men when stealing it, I am going to send a wire informing the sheriff in Jayton, I would like you to send the money to the bank in Jayton" Scott requested.

"I will do as you request Scot and thanks again for saving my family" Mr Mason said.

"No Dad I must thank Scott the most, when walking me home to keep me safe last night I did not understand, when telling me (not to worry everything will be OK) I do understand now. Thank you for saving Clive" Sandra said in a faint voice.

Half an hour later Scott rode out of town, riding down Main Street, the people of the town waved to him, Nicky standing outside the saloon threw him a kiss, some of the town folk actually came from their homes to wave.

As Scott had removed the sheriff, his destination was Wellington, where the sheriff and the people of Wellington applauded him.

CHAPTER SIX

BEN I LOVE SCOTT

After getting rid of Billy, Scott now had a problem according to the dandy Wes Arnold rode east and Bates and Dutchy rode north, finding the first two men of the gang was easy because of the fact of knowing their destination but the next three men were different knowing roughly where they were heading for the one thing that might help is there new occupations.

Scott came to a decision, go back to Turkey as that was the last place all five men were together, looking at the map of Texas it came to him it would be easier going east from Turkey, that made him think of going after Wes Arnold first, going by the map east had a lot less towns to cover than going north, travelling to Turkey took two days arriving in Turkey at dusk on the second day.

Riding straight to the livery stable, after making Blacky comfortable Scott headed straight to the café as the café would knowing it would be shutting soon, (great it's open) talking to himself as approaching the café sitting at the table against the wall Scott called the waitress over.

"Howdy miss I'm glad I caught you open"

"Only just," she looked at the door as it was being closed.

"What do you still have on miss" Scott asked.

"Steak pie, cold chicken or eggs with beans and fries"

"Steak pie sounds good to me" Scott declared.

Scott had his meal and made his next destination the saloon, because of riding most of the day, his pangs of hunger has been satisfied and now looked forward to a cool beer then it's a night in a bed for him.

The next morning. Scott decided to check for chatter, as there was little chance of sign because of his being here before but if while away someone like the sheriff, a barman, a barber has heard anything about the three criminals. His first call must be the sheriff's office.

"Hi! Sheriff "Scott greeted.

"Scott helloes it's nice to see you, I heard you have been busy" the sheriff replied.

"Yeh! I have done the easiest bit, now the work begins" Scott answered.

"How do you mean" the sheriff asked.

"The first two proved easy to find, the next three seem to have more brains and harder to find, not to worry I have had to search in the past it will make the job take longer, with a lot of perseverance and a lot of questions to ask, I will get them for Laura's sake." Scott ended.

"Who is Laura" the sheriff enquired.

"Laura is the remarkable young lady who started me of on this job" Scott said.

After a questioning look from the sheriff, Scott told the sheriff about Laura her part in the robbery, and how she escaped from the cave just to tell someone about the five men, so they could be caught and brought to justice my next job is to find Wes Arnold." Scott told him

"I maybe a little help to you" the sheriff said

"How do you mean that sheriff" Scott asked.

"You know how word gets around; it is surprising how something carried out miles from town gets about" the sheriff said.

"So, sheriff what's the word" Scott asked.

Three days ago, I decided to stop at the saloon to have a beer, a stranger passing through town also called into the saloon, I heard him telling a crowd of drinkers about a gunfight in the town called Tula, this man told the crowd that the man who won the gunfight was called Wes Arnold." the sheriff told Scott.

"Thanks sheriff, shut the door let's go for a beer, you have saved me a lot of work and given me a place to start" Scott acknowledged. They walked over to the saloon

"Two beers barman please" Scott called out. The barman came over with the beers.

"No need to pay mister, I heard you caught up with Billy boy, these drinks are on me thank you"

"Hi! don't you say hello to your friends" a female voice came from behind him.

"Tammy what a pleasant surprise, barman a drink for the lady please." Scott said.

"Nice to see you Scott, she gave him a hug and a kiss"

"When did you start working in the saloon" Scott asked

"When Mandy quit" Tammy explained.

"You know I met Mandy and Jake last week they are getting married" Scott told them.

"Good" was all Tammy said.

"That's good news, I am glad she is putting the ordeal she went through behind her everyone in this town liked her" the sheriff said.

"How are they Scott" Tammy asked.

"They are both happy and love each other, they are riding far away from this town and treating it as an adventure"

Scott had a long drink, with Tammy and the sheriff, then walked around town, looked in on Blacky then spent the night in town before going to bed Scott spent some time studying the map of Texas, just after dawn Scott rode out of town travelling in an easterly direction.

Obviously Scott took it easy, there was no urgent need to hurry finding himself riding through a beautiful valley, the countryside was a beautiful green valley a winding stream ran through the middle with an abundance of trees and brush, Scott sighed as the job left his mind for this brief moment, marvelling at the site of mother nature, there was fish in the stream, birds flue about singing there songs and small animals scurried about, Scott brought Blacky to a halt hooked his leg over the saddle horn pulled out the makings and rolled a cigarette.

"Ah! This is wonderful, mother nature is fantastic" Scott omitted.

This period may not be relevant to most people but when you are constantly alert like a bounty hunter normally is, because of the intensity of the job, it is a privilege to come across such a beautiful place with warm sunshine filtering through the trees and a beautiful pool of water to have a swim.

The sheriff had told Scott about the gunfight, but that had happened a week before which meant no haste was necessary apart from taking the kinks out of Blacky Scott kept moving at a steady pace mainly walking, leaving the lovely fertile valley behind they moved across the country, at the end of the first day Scott started climbing some hills, after completing the climb there was a place that was just right to make camp for the night as sunset rapidly approached. His camp area was just outside the mouth of a cave making camp has been done by him many times so it became automatic, using the mouth of the cave as a windbreak, in a ring of stones a fire was lit taking water from the canteen, put it over the fire to boil the water for coffee, now the camp is made up while waiting for the water to boil and it was still light, taking the map from his saddle bags sitting on his bed roll starting to studied the map.

As darkness came over the land, Scott put fuel on the fire, with his pistol under the saddle his head was on and fell asleep.

Suddenly Scott's eyes opened, his hand went straight to his pistol, he lay still his ears worked overtime listening to the night sounds, climbing silently to his feet creeping silently to the edge of the cave, peering out in the distance, gun flashes could be seen in the darkness of the night the noises of the firing guns had woken him up, the flashes were too far away to bother him, making a mental note of there positions, Scott found no reason for him to worry about, going back to his bedroll and slept the night away.

At dawn, the light filtered into the cave, Scott's eyes opened but lying still his ears working hard all that could be heard was Blacky crunching away at some grass at the mouth of the cave, climbing to his feet raising his arms Scott stretched and yawned.

"Morning boy I see you have breakfast, are you ready to ride" Scott said talking to the big horse as is his normal habit.

Scott went through his normal actions at the start of each day washing, shaving, cooking and eating breakfast, as usual clearing up the camp area making sure it was left as near as possible to when arriving having a final look around to make sure nothing had been forgotten, mounting up Scott rode out to continue his journey.

There was nothing that could be done about the shooting last night but Scott was more alert because his estimation was that his destination would mean going past or very near the area where the shooting took place, riding for a few miles without incident but his senses were on full alert, keeping his eyes open Scott turned a bend, immediately spotting the top of a wagon riding nearer Scott was about to call out a greeting which is the normal thing to do when approaching a camp area.

When about to open his mouth when Blacky stopped sniffing, pointing to the wagon Blacky had been taught to tell Scott when everything was not right, the big horse had heard an unusual noise which Scott had not heard, slipping from the saddle, unsheathing his rifle then starting to creep forward until getting to an angle where it was possible to view the camp, It looked like his arrival had happened at an appropriate moment, three bodies lay on the ground, a young lady stood facing three men with guns one of the men had started stripping her, as she now stood in her underwear as one of the men completed disrobing the girl who now stood naked, Scott found a good position raised his rifle lined it on the one who looked to be the leader.

"Raise your hands I have you covered" Scott's voice rang out in the clear air.

The young lady dropped to the ground as the three men went for their guns, the unfortunate leader disappeared from the scene as the bullet from Scott's rifle hit him so hard at this distance causing his body the fly for a second before dropping to the dusty ground, the other two men ran and leapt behind a cluster of rocks about twenty yards away, Scott fired a few bullets to help them on the way, It looked like one of the two men were nicked in the arm. In the end, the accuracy of Scott's shots told the two men who had tried to shoot it out with him, but because of his shooting the two ambushers ran for their horses and managed to escape with Scott's bullets came near to killing them the barrage of fire was too much for them.

Scott still alert slowly crept into the camp, the first thing was to check the man that had been shot was dead, there was no mistaking the man was dead the rifle bullet at close range had put a large hole in his chest and a larger one as it exited from his back blood covered the ground the man lay on.

Turning around Scott's mouth fell open his eyes almost came out of his head never had there been anything more beautiful in his life, walking over Scott held his hand out to her which she took and climbed to her feet.

"Err! Err! Miss Emm !! get yourself dressed" Scott said stumbling over his words.

"Thank you" she said and smiled at his discomfort.

"What's your name" Scott asked.

"Danny" she replied.

"Danny"

"Yes, Danny short for Daniella" she told him.

"Do you prefer Danny" Scott asked

"I have been called Danny all my life, I 'm going to splash my face to freshen up a bit" she replied.

"OK Danny"

Scott started to look at the bodies of Danny's Mom and Dad, carrying the man's body behind the wagon where the body was straightened out clothes arranged, going back to the woman, checking the lady was dead, the same routine was carried out on her body Scott going to the third body a young man a little older than Danny who must be her brother, bending to check the man Scott felt a faint pulse.

"Danny quick the canteen"

"Ben, Ben" Danny called as she picked up the canteen and ran to them.

Scott put a couple of drops of water on his lips, then started to look for wounds and found two wounds one in the shoulder and a grazed head and by the looks of it, the young man had lost a lot of blood and Danny was upset.

"Danny calm down, take a couple of deep breathes, find some bandages" Scott ordered her.

"I'm good" Danny said.

"Good, Danny we need a bowl or Bliley and a clean cloth, we will wash his wounds before putting on the bandages" Scott told her.

"OK" Danny replied. After cleaning and dressing the wounds, they lifted him into the wagon and made him comfortable.

"Danny keep him warm, nurse him until your brother comes to, we will take him to the doctors in the nearest town" Scott instructed her.

"I'll look after him" Danny said.

"Danny, would you like me to bury your folk out here, or would you like to take their bodies elsewhere" Scott asked.

"My Mom and Dad loved the outdoors, so it would be nice to pick a good spot and bury them out here in the countryside" Danny explained.

"OK Danny look after your brother I will let you know, when I am done" Scott said.

"Thank you, mister," Danny said.

"Danny my name is Scott"

"Thank you, Scott," she replied.

Before digging Scott checked the dead ambusher the leader of the men who killed these folk and were about to rape Danny the thought of Danny made him pause as his thoughts of her standing in front of him naked, (God she is beautiful) then came back to the job at hand, the man turned out to be, 'Jerry the bear Simpson' wanted for murder Dead or Alive bounty $300.00 three hundred dollars wrapping the body in his tarp and lashing it, placing it in the shade.

About ten yards from the camp Scott found a small knoll, a grassy patch with brush and trees all around, it was there the graves were dug and where Danny's folk were to be buried, in a small beautiful shady area.

"Danny, do you want to see your mother and father" Scott asked.

"No Scott I want to remember them as they were, please bury them, let me know when you have" Danny told him.

When the graves were dug each of the bodies were wrapped in blankets, double wrapped them in their tarps (waterproof coats) lowered the bodies into the graves, after filling in the graves Scott made two crosses which were put at the head of each grave.

"Danny come here please" Scott called for her.

"Yes Scott" Danny left her brother and stood beside Scott.

"Danny, I hope it is OK for you" Scott asked her.

"Oh! Scott, it is a beautiful place, and you have done a wonderful job thank you, I know if my Mom and Dad were looking at this spot they would be happy" Danny said then she omitted a prayer, as tears welled up in her eyes, Scott put his arm around her, pulled her close and held her until the tears stopped.

"Come Danny we will have a meal, break camp then starts moving slowly towards town, we will have to sleep out tonight and will reach town sometime tomorrow, we must make a move" Scott informed her.

"You are right and thank you" Danny

Going back to the camp area they did exactly what Scott suggested they had a large sandwich each, a last cup of coffee pouring the remainder on to the fire, clearing up the camp did not take long, Tying Blacky and the horse with the dead man onboard to the back of the wagon, Danny climbed inside to nurse her brother, Scott climbed on the box started moving the wagon slowly.

"Scott drive slowly" Danny instructed.

"I will" Scott replied.

An hour before sundown, Scott found the ideal place to camp for the night, pulling up a short distance from the stream, both Danny and he set up the camp securing the wagon and tethering the horses.

"Danny, you told me you felt dirty, I am going to look after your brother Ben, I want you to take some clean clothes with you, the pool of water is inviting, go and bathe in the water, by the time you have done so the coffee will be ready" Scott told her.

"Oh! Thank you, Scott," she replied.

Danny did exactly what Scott had told her, picking up her clean clothes she also took a bar of soap with her, Scott had already seen her in the nude so without embarrassment Danny who went to the water's edge and stripped of her clothes, It would be impossible for any man not to look at such a wonderful sight, Danny is eighteen years old and her naked form looked fantastic, (by god I have never seen anything so beautiful) Scott said to himself. Danny did not stay long in the water just long enough to bathe, as Danny walked out of the water Scott saw her, (Phew I could watch her all day) once more admitting to himself.

"I'll take over now Scott I feel great" she told him.

"Danny, you look great" Scott returned, Danny blushed.

"Thank you"

"Anytime Danny you are beautiful"

"Thank you" she repeated then climbed into the wagon a smile on her face.

Scott made a round of the camp site, checking the chocks on the wagon wheels seeing that Blacky and the other horses were calm for the night, the next thing on Scott's mind was food before going to bed, coffee had already been made putting the skillet on the fire, and began to cut slices of bacon, the sizzling sound and the smell was fantastic which did not go unnoticed by Danny.

"Oh! Scott that smells great, I am starving" Danny omitted.

"Could you get the bread out for me please"

"Yes of course" she answered.

Danny and Scott sat down to a plate of Bacon, beans and potatoes with a slice of bread each this gave them a little time to talk.

"What are we going to do next" Danny asked.

"In the morning after spending the night camped here, we will move out going to the nearest town which is 'Tula' taking it easy no rush we should reach town just after noon, we will go straight to the doctors, we will look after your brother together, don't worry Danny Ben will get better" Scott assured her.

"And what happens in town" she asked.

"Once you and Ben are settled into the doctors, I will take our friend to the sheriff's office, take the wagon and horses to the livery stable. I then have a little business to take care of in town, then I will arrange for rooms for us at the hotel" Scott explained.

"OK Scott, thanks for your help" she said in soft tones.

"Danny since the first moment a saw you and heard your voice I could not help the feelings I have had for you in the short time we have known each other, you don't know me so as soon as we can after arriving in town I want to talk to you but not now out here, I like you and admit I would like to see more of you "Scott said she smiled.

"See more of me, don't you think you have seen enough of me"

"I could never stop looking at you, I have seen you naked and you are beautiful, but you are also beautiful dressed you are witty, and I love the sound of your voice and I know I can never get enough of you" Scott said tenderly a smile on his face, leaning over, Scott kissed her tenderly.

"Danny"

"Thank you Scott, I also like you, I am already curious to what you want to tell me, but at this time I must look after Ben" Danny said in a low husky voice.

Danny climbed into the wagon.

"Scott" the loud urgent call came from the wagon, Scott was there in seconds.

"What's wrong Danny" Scott asked.

"Ben is burning up" she cried.

Climbing into the wagon Scott had a look at Ben and new Ben had a fever, picking up the canteen poured water on a cloth and applied it onto Ben's forehead.

"Danny Ben has a fever it happens to most people after they have been shot, we have to keep him cool by putting wet towels to his forehead and put drops of water on his lips, when the fever breaks, Ben will then be on the mend" Scott informed her.

"Scott, I am glad you are here" Danny replied.

"Danny don't worry we will get through this together" Scott said.

"Thank you again"

"Look Danny you have been looking after your brother all day, I'll take over you get some sleep, you can take over again later" Scott told her.

"Scott wakes me in two hours" Danny ordered.

"Sure" Scott assured her.

Danny was very tired, and Scott was determent to make sure she had a good rest so just let her sleep, staying with Ben all night. At around four thirty in the morning Bens fever broke, making sure Ben was wrapped up and sleeping peacefully Scott climbed out of the wagon and made a pot of coffee, settling down to have a smoke.

At seven o'clock Danny woke up, Scott smiled at her, she went to Scott anger on her face and was about to yell at him about to explode when Scott put his finger on her lips.

"Shhh! Ben's fever broke during the night and is sleeping so be quiet" Scott said.

"Oh! You I'll" she got no further as a pair of lips met Her's, the kiss was full and tender, she showed she liked it by her response after kissing for a few moments.

"Now you go and freshen up then look on to Ben, I will start breakfast"

"All right but when I get a chance, I am going to have a few things to say to you and you know what I mean" she said with a stern face, she could not stop the smile that came to her face.

"Danny, I am about to break camp, you know it is nearly a day since I met you, I have never been so attracted or happy to be with a woman before" Scott told her.

Danny smiled, deep in thought she climbed into the wagon.

There was lots of things to do so they continued getting ready to move off, Danny tidied up the back of the wagon making sure everything was stowed so nothing could fall on Ben as they moved, also checked Ben was secure and wrapped up, Scott on the other hand washed and stowed everything away, put out the fire, cleaned up the camp a area, saddled and loaded Blacky, saddled up the ambushers horse putting the man' body over it, and tied both horses to the back of the wagon, attaching the team to the wagon everything was ready to move.

Danny with Scott by her side went to the two graves and said her last farewell to her Mom and Dad, as Scott turned away Danny slipped her arm through his. Danny climbed into the back of the wagon Scott climbed on the box (driving seat) took up the reins and rode out travelling slowly.

Between one and two in the afternoon they rode down the main street of 'Tula' going straight to the house with the doctor's shingle outside the door, as per usual there was always some willing hands to help, getting Ben into the Doctors proved easy. The doctor went straight to work, cutting the bandages cleaning the wounds, tending to them and rebandaging them, turning to Danny and Scott doc told them.

"You did, an excellent job and being a strong healthy young man, he will be up and about in a couple of days"

"Is it alright to stay with him doctor" Danny asked.

"Yes miss"

"Danny, I will leave you for a while, I will be back soon" Scott said.

Needless to say, his first stop is the sheriff's office.

"Howdy sheriff I have a present outside for you, this fellow taking a dodger that was pinned to the wall down, I'll relieve you of $300.00 three hundred dollars while I am here" Scott told the sheriff.

"OK mister you've earned it" going to the safe in the corner of the room.

"Scott, Scott Burrows sheriff".

"Scott Burrows, I have heard of you, you're a long way from your normal stomping range aren't you" the sheriff admitted.

"Yes, I am sheriff, I understand you are in a position to help me, I'd like to ask you a few questions" Scott told him.

"Shoot! Scott how can I help you" the sheriff asked.

"Three weeks ago, five men robbed the Wells Fargo office in Jayton and killed three men and got away with $100.000 One hundred thousand dollars, I have been on there tail for a while, I have heard that one of these men came through your town, I wonder what you can tell me about him" Scott asked

"Who you are asking about" the sheriff asked.

"Wes Arnold".

"The gunfighter".

"Yes".

"His reputation says Arnold is fast".

"Maybe that bit I will worry about when I face him" Scott replied.

"OK it's your neck"

"I heard about him being in your town a week ago, and you might know what his destination is when leaving here" Scott asked.

"I don't know for sure, I have heard on the grapevine that his destination could be the town of 'Muleshoe' east of here, as there is a woman there known to him it's been a week I doubt if Arnold would be there now" the sheriff explained.

"Thanks sheriff at least it is a place to start, it seems Wes has not settled down and does a lot of moving around".

"What now Scott"

"My next move is personal, I'm interested in a young lady, I don't know how she will react to the fact that I am a bounty hunter after a gun slinger".

"Good luck Scott" the sheriff smiled.

"Oh! By the way, Wes Arnold shot it out with someone in your town could you tell me who and why they fought." Scott asked.

"The man Arnold killed was called Chance Morgan, I think it was over a card game and called him a cheat". the sheriff said.

"Was Wes cheating".

"I wasn't there Scott and no one else was willing to say so" the sheriff replied.

"Thanks sheriff".

Because of what the sheriff said Scott made his next destination the saloon. Scott stood at the bar; the bartender approached him.

"What's your poison friend"

"Howdy I'm Scott and I'd like a beer, and some information" Scott asked.

Being a stranger in town and asking for information certain persons around the bar tensed and stopped drinking and listened intently ears straining to hear what information the stranger wanted.

"There is no problem about the beer friend that's what I am here for, but information is something different, of course it depends on the question" the Barman asked.

"A week ago, in this saloon I understand the supposed gunfighter challenged one of your citizens to a shootout, I want to know if you know anything about it, if not could you point out anyone who was there that night" Scott asked.

"I was on duty that night, the thing is it was a very busy night, the whole staff were rushed of their feet, I did not realise what was taking place until there was a loud voice yelling and the crowd in the bar subsided and there was a deadly hush as Arnold made his challenge" the barman told him.

"Understood "

"Wait, Johnny over here" the barman called out to a man who had just entered the saloon

"Hi! Ken how can I help you" the new man asked.

"John, I know you were in the game last week when Wes Arnold challenged Chance to a shootout in the street, Scott here wants to ask you a couple of questions" the barman ended.

"Thanks, Ken, for volunteering me, how can I help you mister" the man asked.

"My name is Scott and It's simple all I want to know is what happened at that table that night and what happened to get Wes Arnold's back up" Scott informed him.

"Scott it was a normal evening in the saloon, having a couple of beers and a game of cards, the night was like any other night everything normal except for the fact that Wes Arnold seemed to be winning every large pot, Chance then called Arnold a cheat, needless to say Arnold jumped to his feet drawing his gun, then a strange thing happened, Arnold did not shoot Chance instead gave out a challenge to Chance, (If you think I am a cheat meet me out in the street at noon tomorrow or retract your statement and get out of town)" Arnold said to him.

"Could you tell me if Arnold was cheating, Chance believed that Arnold was cheating so much, facing a gunman in the street proved it" Scott said.

"I am uncertain about this, Arnold did win all the larger pots and I thought it was possible because of it that cheating could be taking place, but I could not see how, even though I kept my eyes on him, Look I have known Chance for a long time if Chance saw him cheat, that means the man cheated" Johnny told Scott.

"Thanks Johnny"

"Ken, thank you, give Johnny a drink on me" Scott left the saloon.

Scott smiled and did not admit it but found the interview fascinating and had to reflect on what could be done to capture or kill Wes Arnold, with this in mind Scott proceeded to the doctors.

"Hi! Doc how is Danny and the invalid" Scott asked.

"Come in Scott"

"Scott this is Ben" she said excitedly

"Howdy Ben I'm happy to see you are awake and obviously getting better".

"I hear from Sis, that you had a lot to do with my recovery" Ben said.

For the next hour, Scott, Danny, Ben and the doctor sat and talked for quite some time, until Scott broke it up by asking Danny to dinner.

"I'd love to Scott; will you be alright Ben"

"Sure, you go and enjoy yourself, Doc will stand in for you" Ben laughed.

"Oh! I see, you are getting better" Danny said.

Scott turned towards the door Danny stepped alongside him slipping her arm into his they made their way to the hotel, where Scott had already booked a table in the restaurant.

Taking a table in the corner where directed, Scott pulled the seat out for Danny to sit, there dinner was good which consisted of, Roast Turkey, potatoes, vegetables gravy and sauce, a glass of wine to wash it down with fruit pie and ice cream as sweet followed by a cup of coffee, after the meal Scott and Danny sat together gathering her hand in his, looking into her eyes.

"Danny, we have only known each other for a couple of days, but I know how I feel about you, I won't hide the fact I have had a couple of girlfriends, but I have never felt for any other woman the way I feel for you, I don't know if it is love, I do know how I feel for you. Because of the way I feel for you I want to talk to you about me, I have to tell you about what I want to do in the future then what I am doing at this moment it is important to me" Scott said to Danny.

"OK if you deem it important" Danny agreed.

"As I have said I love you and if you agree I would like for us to build up a ranch in south Texas where there is miles of grass and long summers we could have a good life together", Scott paused," At this present time I am a bounty hunter, I am half way through a very special job and must complete it", Scott explained to Danny about the job and the reason why it was important to finish what was started, Danny I must keep my promise to Laura, before meeting you I was quite happy to carry on doing the job I am doing. Now I have met you and if you would agree, after I complete this job, I would like to marry you and start ranching." Scott explained.

"I have put myself on the table to you, hoping you will think about it, Danny I love you, if you want to, I would like us to settle down together" Scott ended.

"Thank you Scott, I did not know you were a bounty hunter, why are you" she asked

"As a boy, I lived with my mother and father who ran a small store in a small town, it was a very small store and the money it made was just enough to get by on, one day two men entered the store, they pulled their pistols and told my father to hand over the money, my father said we don't have any money opened the cash drawer and gave him the ten dollars in the drawer, the two men were angry they shot my Dad and raped and killed my Mom, I that day made a vow to bring every killer and rapist to justice and I have been successful I have a reputation of catching these people" Scott told her.

"I see" Danny said.

"Danny tomorrow morning I have to leave town to continue the job I am on, please think of what I have said, I do think your wonderful, I'm also certain I love you; I have told you everything it is now up to you" Scott told Danny.

"Thanks for telling me, I will give it some thought." Danny said.

The evening went over well, they enjoyed each other's company, after dinner over a drink the two of them talked therefore having a pleasurable night together when leaving the hotel arm in arm the two of them strolled back to the doctor's office Scott, Danny, Ben and the doctor chatted for a while, until eventually Scott made his excuses, leaving the doc's Scott walked in the direction of the livery stable.

Blacky was happy to see his master as Scott walked over to the big horse patting his neck and slipping him a cube of sugar, started mucking out the stall making sure there was fresh straw down, topping up the water trough and giving him a bag of oats all the time talking to the big horse as the chaws (Job) are completed, as usual Blacky enjoyed the brushing down, when brushing the mane it shone and Scott talked all of the time as was his habit.

"You know Blacky I cannot get Danny out of my mind; she is beautiful and great to be with, boy I'm certain I love her".

Talking to himself, on his completion of looking after his pal. Scott decided before going to his room to prepare for leaving tomorrow, a beer would be lovely, the beer was cool and slid down his throat sighing as it quenched his thirst, going to his room his first task was to clean and check his weapons.

Meanwhile Danny was a little disturbed and worried on finding Scott is a bounty hunter, her father called them bounty killers and told her these men kill for money she likes Scott but could not marry a man who's living is to murder people (Oh! What can I do, who can I talk to.) she thought about confiding in Ben her brother but new his opinion as their father would be the same as Her's, the only other person she has come in contact with her was the doctor, then it came to her, (The Sheriff if anyone could tell her about Scott, it would be him.) the sheriff's office was only two doors down from the doctors, picking up her purse two moments later she walked into the sheriff's office.

"Howdy Marm how can I help you" the sheriff asked.

"What can you tell me about Scott Burrows" she came straight to the point.

"Ahh! You're the lady, Scott told me about and is interested in I don't blame him" the sheriff acknowledged. Danny blushed.

"Thank you, now about Scott" she asked.

"Miss" she cut in.

"The name is Danny sheriff"

"OK Danny, a rare breed, Scott is the best of the few men who are like him a rare breed. I have heard of him, but the man does not normally work this far north of Texas, like most sheriff's I am glad of his presence, when we (I mean sheriff's) cannot capture criminals we get help from men like Scott and we are happy to have him around" the sheriff paused.

"How do you mean" Danny asked.

"The man has skill's very few people have, people say Scott can track a fish through water, because there is only a few men who can track like him, the job is dangerous the people that commit crimes killing, murders, robbers and rapists, when they realise or find it difficult to escape most of them try to take him out, none have succeeded" the sheriff explained.

"Isn't Scott a killer" she blurted out.

"Who told you that"

"Scott is a bounty hunter, they kill people, my father called them bounty killers" Danny said.

The sheriff burst out into laughter

"Miss Danny, there is some disreputable men who call themselves bounty hunters who kill, but most of the men who do this job are good men like Scott who try to bring the men in to face justice, but to save his own life may be forced to kill to protect themselves" the sheriff explained

"Mmmmm! I want to believe" Danny stated.

"Danny, did Scott tell you anything about his present job" the sheriff asked

"Yes, the job is to catch five men who robbed the Wells Fargo and shot three men and Scott said the job was being done for someone called Laura" Danny said

"Let me tell you about the job Scott is doing" The sheriff said.

The sheriff spent the next hour explaining about the job Scott was doing and also about Laura, and how Scott always completes a job that has been given to him.

"Look Danny did Scott tell you about capturing the first man"

"No"

"The thing about the west is the grapevine works well and it is just coming through about Scott's catching the first man of the five did Scott tell you about it" the sheriff asked.

"No" Danny said.

The sheriff then told Danny about the job in the red-light house.

"The red-light house" Danny was in hysterics and could not stop laughing.

"Danny the next morning no one could find the girl, Scott left tied up on the bed and as the Dandy's horse had gone, they broke into the locked room, when the gag was removed, the girl was so excited they could not shut her up, the story flowed from her mouth everybody laughed but as I said this story has just reached us, as you can tell Scott did not kill the man who is at this time facing justice" the sheriff explained.

"Ha Ha Ha" Danny laughed her heart out.

"Danny, you can see by our conversation that Scott tries to bring the men back to face justice and does not kill for no reason at all, plus try's to take them alive, which is going to be hard to do with the next man on his list" the sheriff told her.

"What do you mean" Danny asked.

"His next target is a man called Wes Arnold, Arnold is a man known to be good with a gun (a gunfighter) this man will not come easy and Scott may have to kill him" the sheriff explained.

"Oh! No" Danny already knew she loved Scott but being told by the sheriff that there is the chance that the man she loves could be killed worried her.

"Are you all right miss" the sheriff asked.

"Yes, thank you sheriff I must go" Danny replied.

Danny left the sheriff's office and went straight to the doctor's house.

"Well sis how did the dinner with Scott" Ben asked.

"Ben, it was great we get on well together and I love him, now I have something to tell you, I need to tell you" Danny announced.

"OK what's your problem" Ben asked.

"I have told you I love Scott" Danny stated

"Yes, you have told me that, what's wrong" Ben asked.

"Ben Scott is a bounty hunter" Danny blurted out.

"WHAT! Danny, you cannot marry a killer" Ben said in a raised voice.

The raised voice brought the doctor to then.

"He is not a killer let me tell you what the sheriff told me" Danny said to them.

Ben and the doctor went silent and became interested and astounded as the story unfolded, Danny told them about the job Scott was doing and why, she told them about Laura, and both the men ended up in screams of laughter as she explained how Scott had taken a man alive from a cathouse.

"Ben, Scott is not a killer like you think "Danny told him

"What now sis"

"I must see Scott, I will see you in the morning" was Danny's answer as she left the room,

CHAPTER SEVEN

FIFTEEN HE IS ONLY A BOY

Sitting on his bed having a smoke, the room was claustrophobic so opened the window and removed his shirt, started to clean his weapons. Being in the job of bounty hunter one of the main things to take care of his weapons coming to the end of his routine cleaning, there was a tap on the door, gun in hand he unlocked the door.

"Danny" the word coming loudly from his surprise lips. Danny pushed the door open and walked straight passed him.

"Hi! Scott" she greeted.

"Are you OK"

"Yes" she said.

"I dropped you of at the doctors as it is not safe for a young woman on the street"

"I had to come and see you" she told him,

"Why"

"You are riding out in the morning, I needed to see you, and I am sorry" Danny said.

"Sorry why" Scott asked. Danny was quiet for a moment.

"Scott Ben and I were told by our dad that bounty hunters were bounty killers a man who goes out to kill people for money, they warned us not to have any time with this sort of person, I had a lovely evening with you tonight, and when you told me you are a bounty hunter I could not believe you were a killer and I was troubled," Danny paused.

"Danny, I" Danny cut him of

"Scott, I sat talking to Ben and the doctor, but I could not get you out of my mind, what can I do I thought, after thinking for a while I decided to go see the sheriff, who told me about you and the job you are doing, and about Laura" Scott looked up, "Yes the sheriff told me about Laura" she ended

"Look Danny I have heard of men who kill people for the money, I always try to take them alive, yes I will not lie to you I have had to kill people who try to kill me ", Scott assured her.

"The sheriff has told me you are going after a gunfighter; this man is a killer and likes doing it" Danny asked.

Scott sat beside her, put his arm around her.

"I have been doing this job for some time now, during that time I have had to face men who are gunfighters, all you have to do is find their weaknesses everyone has one" Scott explained.

"I do love you Scott" she said. Drawing her close they kissed.

"Oh! Danny that is wonderful, I hoped tonight to make an impression on you, and you would at least think about me" Scott spoke softly.

"Scott, I do love you, but I could never marry a man who is away from home months on end chasing criminals who could kill him" Danny explained.

"Danny, before I met you, I could just carry on doing the job I am doing but from the moment I met you I wanted to be with you always" Scott told her.

"Oh! Scott that sounds good"

"Look I am in the middle of a job I promised to do, and I will complete the job I always do, but I will make this promise to you, and if you do know me I keep my promises, Danny darling I promise you, if you agree to marry me that I will give up doing the job I am doing, will set up a ranch where we can live together, now the question is, will you marry me" Scott asked her.

"I will marry you but only when this job you are doing is complete" Danny said.

"Oh! Danny thank you" Scott drew her to him and kisses her tenderly.

"Darling, I love you" Scott whispered in her ears.

"Thank you" Danny blushed but loving every tender word spoken.

Kissing her, caressing her, his hands made pattern on her back, shoulders and spine as the tender kissing changed to passionate kissing more wanting, her thoughts were (Oh! That is wonderful).

Kissing her lips, then her neck and throat and nibbled her ears, her temperature started to rise, her eyes closed and had a wonderful feeling, putting his hand where the gingham dress covered her beautiful soft firmed tits, (Ohhh, Ohhh) she omitted in a low voice in her head she heard herself say (Ahhh, nice don't stop Ahhhh,) the way his hand smoothly stroked her breasts, then it would stop squeeze the tit as his thumb flicked the nipples, his nimble fingers undid the top five buttons on the gingham dress she did not stop him.

Brushing the top of the dress aside the lips still kissed her lips, neck, throat, and ears but now added the shoulders to his slow moving routine of arousal, her body twitched as she felt the hand cup her beautiful round smooth breasts, Ohhhh yes, Ohhh more, a low husky sound came from her lips, pushing back the top part of her dress, then unclipped her bra, which dropped to reveal the perfect pair of breasts which made him have a catch in his throat, his mouth covered the nipple of her left breast as his hand covered the right breast, Ahhh, Ohhhh, as the flicking tongue caused the nipple to vibrate, her breasts swelled the nipples protruded making the breasts more sensitive giving her the next stage of arousal, but the continues sounds of pleasure omitted from her mouth sounded fantastic to Scott's ears, Ohhhhh! More Ohh yes, Ohhh yes.

Scott pulled her gently to her feet pushed the dress of her shoulders and let it drop to the flour as she threw her arms around him, her lips searching for his, sliding his hands down the side of her remaining underclothes gently pushing her to fall backwards onto the bed relieving her of her clothes leaving a beautiful naked body in front of him on the bed Scott's remaining clothes disappeared in seconds, Danny's eyes opened wide as she saw the released erection, Ohhhh! Will that fit Ohh, lying beside her there lips came together his hand once more invading the tingling sensitive breasts, Danny's body arched pushing her breasts up asking for more.

"Oh! Danny my beautiful baby, Oh! Danny, Oh Danny" Scott whispered.

"Scott, Scott, "she whispered.

Danny tensed as she felt the teasing hand travel from her breasts down her body to pause slightly at her belly button, moving over the beautiful smooth skin of her tummy, as the fingers moved through the pubic hair hiding the private entrance to her body, gently rubbing the lips caused the legs to open slightly, Ar, Ar ,Arhh, the look on her face, her lips pursed, eyes closed and head back, Murmuring, Danny gasped as the finger invaded her inner body, Scott's finger probed and swirled around inside her body driving her wild with pleasure, as the finger caught her clitoris it drove her wild Ahhh, Arr, Ohhh, she was in ecstasy, as the finger probed and swirled more and more her legs opened wider and the juices of love started to wet the lips of her crotch, Danny was out of this world as she grabbed at his erected penis, Arrrr Danny, yes, Scott, Scott they both called out

"Ohh Arrrr Ahrrr.Scott, Scott,"

"Oh! Baby" Scott said as Danny gasped loudly as Scott's erection entered between the lips of the private entrance, (Oh it's in me were her thoughts as the erection slid into her magnificent body, the erection probed deeply as his body moved in and out the moving erection as it moved in and out smoothly it sent her to a new level of erotic pleasure, starting slowly and building up the speed and thrust, Ohh! Yes, Yes Ohhh! Scott, she called as she experiences the new sensation, Danny's head went back as Scott's body jerked, as his seed past into Danny's body. (Ohh! Scott fill me, fill me.) she cried, the sensation was so great she felt as if her body had been taken apart and lovingly put back together again, Scott new that Danny had experienced a climax.

A sigh came from her lips as Scott withdrew and the two sweat covered bodies lay together fighting to get their breath back.

"D, Darling that was fantastic, I love you", Scott whispered in a deep voice.

"Thank you, Scott," her voice was husky she was elated at Scott's compliment, they held each other and cuddled the two sweat covered bodies enjoyed holding each other, Scott kissed her tenderly.

"You are beautiful my darling" then kissed her, as Scott caressed the beautiful smooth skinned naked body lying in his arms, after lying for a while the feeling in his penis caused him to put his hand between her legs a finger brushing the private entrance her sex organ.

"Yes "Danny whispered.

Scott and Danny made the best of the time they had together which is only one night as Scott had a job to complete, they made love a few times during the night, in-between talking of love and plan for the future, before finally falling asleep cuddled together, as dawn arrived as usual Scott's eyes opened and a smile came to his face as the first thing visible was the beautiful sleeping face of Danny, putting his face nearer to her Scott kissed her tenderly which changed to passionately as Danny woke put her arms around him and kissed him. Getting his breath back.

"I love you Danny" Scott said. This started them of making love again.

"Scott, I know you must go and complete the job you started, could you please assure me this will be the last job, and we can settle down, get married and have a family" Danny asked.

"Danny I can honestly say I want us to get married and settle down, I would definitely prefer to have a wonderful night like we have just had rather than sitting around a campfire in the middle of nowhere "Scott assured her.

"As you may know I was a virgin tonight, because I love you, I decided before I came to your room, I wanted you to make love to me, it has been wonderful and I want you to do it again, only you, but I cannot do it if every time you go out the door you may not return. Scott get the job done I love you and will wait for you to complete the job." Danny explained.

"Danny there is three men left to get, then I am no longer a bounty hunter if you will have me, the job will be complete when I get back to JAYTON, when Ben is fit enough to travel, go to Jayton and wait for me." Scott informed her.

As they lay side by side in bed Danny reached over and put her lips on his they kissed, then in a husky voice she said.

"In two hours, you ride out, that gives you time to make love to me again, and time to see Ben before you go" as she rolled his penis in her hand their lips coming together,

"Darling you are fantastic "Scott said, kissing her passionately and placing his hand between her legs, they made love again, an hour later hand in hand they walked into the doctor's house.

Watching his sister walking arm in arm with Scott, made Ben smile and was happy for her, she is his little sister only eighteen, but she now looked happy, and more sure of herself, Ben felt happy for her.

"Hi! Ben" Danny greeted him jovially.

"Hello Ben" Scott said.

"Howdy you two I see you did more than talk last night, and I am happy you two have come to visit me" Ben commented.

"Ben, I hoped you would be alright to the fact I love Danny; we have talked about marriage and I hope you have no objections" Scott asked.

"Ben, I love Scott" Danny butted in as Scott put his arm around her.

"Sis has told me you are a bounty hunter" Ben queried.

"That is true at the moment, I have a job to do but I have made a promise to Danny I will give that line of work up" Scott told him.

"I'm glad you sorted it out between you I knew Danny loved you and also knew she would not marry a bounty hunter, as long as you are true to your word and you are both happy, I am happy for you," Ben told them.

Danny threw her arms around him, hugged him and kissed him, now her mother and father is dead Ben is the only family she has left to confide in.

"Thank you, Ben," Danny said.

"Now Ben I have to get on with the job, so when you are fit to travel, I would like to ask you, if you could take Danny to the town of Jayton as that is where the job I have to do will be complete, there is no hurry I expect the job to take two to three weeks, It's up to you but I did tell Danny, you could use the wagon, you could sell the wagon and buy a buggy, but both these ways give you no security, my advice would be for you to travel by the stagecoach with Wells Fargo, they have guards on them who will give you added protection, these guards carry rifles, now I don't want any arguments Scott said to Ben, take this two hundred dollars, with the money of the sale of the wagon plus what I have just given you will be more than enough for you to live on and purchase your stage fares" Scott informed them.

"We cannot take your money" Ben said.

"Our money, this came from the sheriff for the body of the man who shot you, so the money is mine, Danny and yours. So, use it" Scott said.

"We will darling" Danny said.

Scott grabbed her arm, put his arm around her waist pulled her close and kissed her long and tender.

"I will see you in Jayton darling" Scott told her. Then walked out of the door.

Standing as still as a statue with her mouth open due to the surprise of it all, her face was red as she saw Ben and the doctor looking at her a smile on their faces, she was flustered for a moment then got the bravado back and spoke.

"That was lovely I liked that" smiling back at them.

Picking up Blacky, loading up making sure there was food and his canteen was full, riding along Main Street heading north, passing the doctors Danny was at the door waving to him, Scott threw her a kiss, as he rode out of town.

Now the problem facing him is the word passed to him about Arnold being in Muleshoe seeing a girl was a week old, after studying the map it would take three days to get there, the puzzling thing is if Arnold had a permanent place in Muleshoe why does the man continue to move around the territory. After a bit of thought coming to the decision was to carry on towards his destination, but to call into to the four small places on route called Canyon, Hereford, Dimmill and Farwell.

Riding north out of town Scott started off at a fast pace for two reasons, one to take the kinks out of Blacky after his lazy night, and two his destination was known therefore it was not necessary to look for sign, coming across an area which was his ideal place to camp checking the sky and his surroundings came to the conclusions it was not far of sunset and decided to make camp, reflecting on his progress and carrying on at the same pace it's possible they would arrive in Canyon at sunset tomorrow.

As normal Scott went into his normal routine of setting up camp, first getting a fire started "Ah Blacky I'm looking forward to a cup of coffee" Putting a pan of water on the fire, "Well boy a stall for you tomorrow night we should be in Canyon" while talking to the big horse Scott rolled out his bedroll placing the saddle for his head once satisfied the making camp is complete, taking from his saddlebags a package of sandwiches that had been bought back in Tula, contentedly sitting on his bedroll with a mug of coffee.

When dawn arrived and the ribbon of light showed on the horizon, the eyes of the sleeping man opened, his body remained still, his ears straining for sound after a moment hearing only the dawn chorus Scott relaxed climbed to his feet picking up his pistol at the same time.

Kicking the fire back to life, Scott put a pan of water on the fire to boil to make coffee, "Morning boy" Scott called out and received a 'neigh' back, as normal after shaving, washing and breakfast the next move was to break camp.

Riding out there was no need to hurry, apart from giving Blacky his head to take out the kinks the speed was kept to a brisk walk, satisfied with his progress and enjoying the scenery around him it was a pleasant warm sunny day after riding for about three hours turning a bend in the trail out in front of him was a large type valley which has a carpet of high thick grass spreading as far as the eyes could see, it was beautiful at the end of this expanse of green there is standing a range of hills which started with a shear rock face.

Bringing Blacky to a halt about a hundred yards from the face Scott hooked his leg over the saddle horn and reached for the makings, rolling a fag (cigarettes), while smoking he surveyed the rock structure in front of him, Scott's luck is with him today when bending forward to pat the big horses neck, Scott heard the two shots ring out in the clear air, but also heard the whine of the bullets whistle past where his body was a moment ago, yelling 'Yah.' and a sharp nudge of his heels sent Blacky from a standstill to a gallop in less than a second causing him to run forward to get under the cover of a large part of the rock formation, with the rock over hanging the way it does meant they were in a safe position for the moment.

Most men would have turned their horses and rode of putting some distance away from the rocks, not Scott who saw the benefit at being under the rocks, on hearing the sound of two rifles it is therefore logical that there are at least two bush whackers who happened to be stationed directly above him, pulling his rifle from the scabbard. after a bit of thought he decided to move to his left dismounting slowly began to creep along the rocky base.

Finding a break in the face with enough space to climb the rocks, as he was about to climb looking up he saw a man with a rifle who was intent on something giving Scott the time to be able to flatten himself against a part of the cliff face, retracing his steps to the position where blacky stood, he started to move in the opposite direction, but unfortunately the same occurred on finding an opening a man had stationed himself above with a rifle in his hands once more going back to where Blacky stood, he was left him with only one option, examining the rock face there was quite a few hand holes visible so realise it could be possible to climb the face putting moccasins on and taking his rope, Scott looked at the face sighed before gingerly starting to climb.

When starting the climb, Scott was lucky to find it a little easier to climb because of the numerous hand holds available to him, the two ambushers has obviously decided to wait for Scott to show himself, hopefully they will not expect him to climb the face, It has been a few years since any job had required some serious climbing, but it had to be done, but you don't forget things like that in fact it came back to him quite quickly.

Slowly and painstakingly Scott climbed the face, it took over an hour to get to the top and pull himself over the edge to lie behind a large rock, having a quick look to the right a man stood a few yards away from him with his back to him looking down, the cliff, a quick peep to the left gave him the same picture, except the man looked in the opposite direction.

Scott knew that as soon as they see him both men will turn and fire, the best solution would be to distract one of the men or better still disarm one of them, after a bit of thought Scott looked at each man to see who it would be best to shoot, the man to the left stood up therefore presenting a large target, the man on the right was partly hidden by the large rock beside him or the man was sitting presenting him with a smaller target, taking careful aim at the man on the left, aiming for his right shoulder, taking a deep breath, he squeezed of a shot, quickly switched his aim to the other man who had jumped to his feet.

"Hold it right there, touch that gun and I will blast you" Scott ordered.

The man surrendered then moved as ordered to be with the other man, Scott had shot the other man in the right shoulder because of the fact of him being right handed, that meant a) the man could not draw his revolver, 2) the rifle but could not go on his right shoulder, 3) it would be impossible to pull the trigger of the rifle, with him being incapacitated it meant there was only one man to concentrate on.

"Right you two start climbing down, you mister can help your buddy" Scott ordered.

"I can't climb down I am wounded" the shot man complained.

"Mister you can climb down with your mate's help, so do it" Scott told him.

"I can't" the wounded man still complained

"Look mister I am a stranger to you, but you bushwhacked me, now you are going to either climb down or I will push you over the overhang, there is something else I can do and that is shoot you, move now" Scott ordered them again, motioning them with the movement of the rifle barrel.

It took some time getting to the valley floor, but it was achieved.

"Where are your horses" Scott asked.

"Around the other side of the hill" the man not wounded replied.

"Ok start walking" with groans and grunts they started walking, the two men had admiration in their eyes when Scott whistled, and the big horse followed them.

Arriving at the position of the two horses with Scott's assistance the two men were tied and mounted taking the reins they set out heading for town, arriving just before sundown. Halting outside the sheriff's office, physically Scott pushed the tied men from the saddle and marched them through the office into a cell.

"Howdy sheriff I have a couple of customers for you" Scott informed him.

"Thanks, but what did they do" the sheriff enquired.

"Attempted assassination" Scott informed him.

"How do you mean" the sheriff asked.

"Wait sheriff, You two in the cell, what is my name" Scott asked.

"We don't know your name" they said.

"Then why did you bushwhack me" Scott asked.

The two men shrugged their shoulders but stayed silent.

"Sheriff, I was on my way to this town, riding over a plain with long grass, at the end was a range of hills just south of here" the sheriff broke in.

"Yeh! I know that place so what about it" the sheriff asked.

"I rode within rifle range of the hills when two shots rang out, which just missed me" Scott explained.

"So"

"You two, I want to know, were you trying to kill me, 1) Were you sent to kill me if so, who sent you, 2) It was robbery, which talk." Scott enfersized the last two words.

"So, you did try to kill this man why, you do not kill a man without a reason I can only assume it was for robbery, you are now arrested on attempt of murder" the sheriff told them, then sent for the doctor.

"Sheriff, do you know Wes Arnold" Scott asked.

"Sure, I know him his wife owns the golden nugget saloon in town" came the reply.

"I didn't know about him being married"

"Oh! Yes, Jacky is a good person mister"

"The name is Scott does Arnold come here often" Scott asked.

"Yeh! About once a week"

"That's interesting, when are you expecting him next"

"You just missed him, left town yesterday morning" the sheriff told him.

"If you want me sheriff, I'll be at the hotel, I will also be riding in the morning" Scott informed the sheriff.

True to his word, at dawn Scott and Blacky rode east of town heading in the direction of Hereford his next destination, one thing for certain Scott wanted to know why Arnold did not remain in one place, with a wife in town the question was answered, it is two days ride to Hereford and Scott saw no need to hurry, so keeping Blacky to a walk it is a lovely warm sunny day, to go faster would tire Blacky when it was not necessary.

Bringing Blacky to a halt, dropping from the saddle and rolled a cigarette, Blacky snorted then munched some grass as Scott sat on a rock drew on his fag and thought of Danny

"Oh! My beautiful darling, I wish I was with you now" talking to himself.

Crushing the fag end out with his boot Scott mounted up and carried on with his journey until sunset finding a place to camp stopped there overnight, but as usual woke at dawn and continued his ride in a westerly direction, just over an hour they passed a boundary marker informing them they were crossing the lazy T ranch, after crossing the markers, half an hour later they saw a short distance, three mounted men driving a dozen steers, but as they were a little distance away Scott rode on.

What goes on at the ranch was really no interest to him therefore carried on his way at a normal pace, so just drifted carrying on for another hour it was close to ten am when the smell of smoke and then he smelt the coffee, going over the brow of a hill in front of him was a camp with chow wagon and a dozen hands, pulling Blacky to a halt Scott called out.

"Hello the camp"

"Come ahead stranger" a voice called out.

"Howdy, I smelt your coffee" Scott said.

"Sit, help yourself"

"Thanks"

"You come far friend"

"Canyon"

"I see"

"It's quite busy on this ranch" Scott said,

"How do you mean busy"

"Oh! About an hour ago I saw three of your hands driving a dozen head travelling north, I don't think they saw me I was too far off" Scott told them.

"Pete, Sonny stay with the herd the rest of you mount up, mister could you take us to where you saw this herd" the foreman asked.

"Sure trouble"

"Mister there should be no movement of cattle in that area" the man said.

"The name is Scott, you mean rustlers"

"Yeh! Possible rustlers let ride"

Scott and the party of men kept their horses at a canter, which ate up the miles meaning it did not take long to get back to where Scott saw the men moving the cattle, the cattle left a lot of flattened grass, making it easy to follow the sign, driving cattle is a time-consuming job, this slowed the riders down, in about an hour later they saw the rustlers ahead of them.

Riding over the Brough of a hill, about a quarter of a mile ahead they spotted the herd, as they started moving towards them, one of the three men with the herd saw them yelled, the three men rode off to the left of the herd.

"Scott, Frank, Jack, turn the herd and start back, the rest of you follow me" the foreman ordered.

The remainder of the crew, went after the rustlers, Scott decided to help with the herd there was no need to hurry, but Scott knew by the time they get the herd back, it would mean that another night out, meaning it would not be possible to get to Hereford in the morning as planed it would have to be the next morning.

Everyone heard the shooting, like all rustlers when the others caught up with them they knew it would either be a shootout or the rope, rustling is a federal offence meaning a hanging offence, needless to say they decided to shoot it out, by the time it took to return the cattle to the herd the remainder of the hands rode into camp.

"Scott, thanks for your help, look cookies got grub ready will you eat with us" the foreman asked.

"Sure, I'll take you up on that offer, saves me from my own cooking" Scott replied.

"OK Scott you are welcome, I am Jack and your welcome"

"Thanks, I will eat, then I must get underway I have lost a little time, which is not important, but I make my own timetable and try my best to stick to it." Scott informed them.

Being a man of his word, after completing his meal Scott washed his plate, said good bye to the hands mounted up and rode out of the camp, because of his extended stay it was only possible for him to get a few miles before sunset but as usual Scott squeezed every minute out of the day because of the meal earlier it was not necessary to eat but after making camp, made sure there was a pot of coffee handy, drinking a cup Scott turned in for the night.

Once again as his usual routine, at the first sign of dawn, Scott's eyes opened, a few moments later Scott rose, an hour later mounting up they rode on, pulling out the map checking his route, due to the activity of the last twenty-four hours, it means another night camping out,

Ten am the following morning Scott rode down the High Street in Hereford. The first stop was the livery stable, apart from looking after Blacky it is one of the most important places to get information, Scott's intension was to stay overnight, as both of them were a little weary so a good night's sleep will be good for both of them making sure the big horse had been fed watered and had a clean stall, worst luck the holster was not available so the decision was to leave the questions until later.

Booking a room at the hotel, Scott was able to precure a room at the front of the hotel where it was possible to look down over the high street, his room was no different from any other room, just inside the door on the right stood a bureau with a large bowl and jug filled with water, enabling Scott to freshen up before proceeding to the local café for his lunch, the Snack Box is the name of the local café, was a small but clean the place it only had six tables and looked like a popular place, Scott was lucky to get the one remaining place left, of course it was lunch time, Scott ordered the days special delivered by a smiling waitress. A young man came around the café selling the local rag The Hereford Post, seeing the headline of one of the articles on the page Scott bought one.

SHOOTOUT IN HEREFORD.

Yesterday the well-known gunfighter Wes Arnold faced Richard Hall, This was MURDER and Arnold hid behind the self-defence rule, many People saw this so-called gunfight and saw this murder take place, so far It has been impossible to find the reason for this incident, but most of the People of this town knows that Hall was no gunfighter.

This article gave Scott the first lead a positive bit of information needed to enable him to start investigation and know knew that the editor of this paper was no friend of Wes Arnold, leaving the café Scott made his way to the local newspaper office, finding the place by the board that proclaimed. HEREFORD POST editor Wayne Collins.

"Mister Collins" Scott asked the man in the shop

"Yes, I'm Wayne Collins" this surprised Scott as the man was young most newspaper men Scott had met were middle aged.

"I'd like a word with you please" Scott proclaimed.

"Sure, how can I help you" Collins asked,

"I have just read your article about the gunfight; I'd like to ask you about it"

"What would you like to know" Collins said.

"You said Hall was no gunfighter"

"Yes"

"How do you know"

"I knew Dicky, yes he wore a gun like most men, but I have never seen him shoot, in fact in all the time I have known him I have never seen him draw a gun, look mister even I know to be good with a gun you must practise, Dick has not had any training, I know" Collins explained.

"You say you knew this man, how do you know this friend did not practise in secret" Scott asked.

"One I have known dick for a long time, plus there was little time for him to do anything, courting my sister kept him busy" Collins explained.

"I see OK thank you" Scott told him.

"Why all the questions" Collins asked.

"I needed to gather information about Wes Arnold"

"Why"

"I have my reasons, for wanting to know about him" Scott said

"The best person to ask about Arnold is his wife, Lucy she works in the general store" Collins informed him.

Scott was surprised but did not show it.

Scott had once more found out what was required, leaving the office with not much left to do, Scott spent the rest of the day strolling around town browsing, his thoughts of Danny came to him when seeing a wedding dress in the millinery store window at the end of the main street a little further on was a bit of open country the town folk called the park it is a nice pleasant day so a stroll through the area seemed a good idea, strolling down a make shift path brought the thoughts of Danny to his mind, (My beautiful Danny I wish you were here my darling) it would have been wonderful, this brought the job back in his mind, "let's get this job finished" the sooner the better.

Now we know why Arnold moves around it looks like there is a wife in each town.

Going back to the hotel Scott prepared for the next morning by checking his weapons, to the general store for bacon and beans then to the livery stable to attend to Blacky, when satisfied after a substantial supper in the hotel restaurant, he drank a couple of beers then of to bed at last to retire for the night.

Once again it is time to ride another dawn had arrived, due to all the preparing the night before, Scott only needed breakfast, it would be ready to ride, looking at the map the night before Scott worked out it would be three days to his next destination the town of FARWELL.

"Hi! Boy you ready to ride" Scott greeted the big horse, Blacky neighed and nodded his head as if the horse understood, believe it or not Scott was once again happy to be on the trail again, on his mind was the picture of a smiling Danny with thoughts of getting the job done as soon as it was possible.

Scott believes that what he has uncovered about Wes Arnold it is possible for him to be able to take him, which makes him want to continue after him so made his plans to follow him with the chance of taking him down, in the meantime the more information that can be gathered, going to Farwell then on to Muleshoe gives him time to accumulate more about Arnold it will do no harm to do so, time does not count.

Riding for three days Scott rode down the Main street in Farwell without coming across any incident for a change, the street was silent, and people stood around watching the funeral procession coming towards him, Scott stopped Blacky and removed his Stetson as the procession went passed, the crying woman in black who followed looked at him briefly and nodded her head.

Moving to the sheriff's office, dismounting then spotting the sheriff standing on the boardwalk also watching the funeral procession passing.

"Hi! Sheriff" Scott greeted,

"Yer! How can I help you" came the solemn return?

"Did you know the deceased" Scott asked.

"Yer! We all knew him" the sheriff said.

"Who" the sheriff cut in.

"James Hunt fifteen years old" the sheriff said shortly.

"Fifteen"

"Yes, fifteen only a boy"

"How did the boy die" Scott asked.

"Wes Arnold".

"The gunfighter"

"That's him, it was pure murder, Arnold knew that the boy was not good with a gun when goading him into a shootout" the sheriff explained.

"I would say you are right, if Arnold killed that young man, it was murder"

"Yes, but Arnold hid behind the (He drew first rule) and the boy did go for his gun first, so Arnold gets away with it pleading self-defence" the sheriff told Scott

"How did it all start" Scott asked.

"I'm afraid you will have to ask his mother"

"I see, I came to town thinking I will have to spend a lot of time searching for clues and information, I arrive in town to find things laid out in front of me" Scott said.

"Mister you ask a lot of questions, who are you" the sheriff demanded.

"Scott Burrows".

"The bounty hunter"

"Yes"

"I've heard of you, what's your interest in Wes Arnold".

"Sheriff, can we go to your office or somewhere it is safe to talk" Scott requested.

The pair of them retired to the sheriff's office, the sheriff topped up two mugs of coffee.

"Now mister suppose you fill me in" the sheriff asked.

"The name is Scott sheriff"

"OK Scott, now why are you interested in Wes Arnold"

Sitting in the office Scott took a slurp of his coffee and as it warmed his belly, Scott told the sheriff about the robbery and murder in Jayton and of all the incidents that had occurred since and what information picked up about Wes Arnold.

"The person that could tell you the most about Arnold would be his fiancée, June Armstrong, she works in the café as a waitress" the sheriff told him.

"Right, that leaves me with two people to interview June Armstrong and missus hunt the boy's mother" Scott informed him.

"Where's Arnold now"

"I don't know Scott, nobody saw him leave but Arnold took of fast straight after the shooting" the sheriff informed him.

"Well, I guess I should go to the café and have a late breakfast" Scott said.

Being true to his word Scott did exactly that, and made his way straight to the café to partake a late breakfast, due to the time normal breakfast was over but like most café's in the west they do normally have all day breakfasts on the menu, on entering there was a vacant table in the back right hand corner of the room, at this time of the day the café is not busy, mainly had a few people drinking coffee and there was a few empty tables but Scott preferred his back to the wall, the waitress came to him.

"Could I take your order sir" the waitress asked.

"Sure, do you do all day breakfasts please miss" Scott enquired.

"Yes sir"

"Thanks, the name is Scott not sir, OK"

"OK Scott I won't be long".

Scott did not wait long after a few moments the waitress returned with his order.

"Excuse me miss are you June Armstrong".

"Who are you".

"My name is Scott burrows, I am looking for Wes Arnold I hear you are the person to ask".

"Who told you that" the waitress asked

"The sheriff told me you are engaged to Arnold".

"Was,"

"Was, you mean you are not his fiancée" Scott asked.

"I am not"

"Would you be willing to tell me why".

"We had a disagreement that's all".

"I see".

"No, you don't see, Wes told me about the gunfight between him and young James Hunt, I told him Jimmy was only a boy and begged him not to do it"

"No" Wes said.

"To cut the story short, we had a fallout when I told him that Jimmy was just a boy, laughing at me callously said"

"That so-called boy you talk about wears a gun"

"The way Wes said it made me mad, I took of the ring gave it to him and told him we are finished and for him to get out, the next time I saw him was when the boy was killed, I have not seen him since" she told Scott.

"I see did Wes tell you about the disagreement between him and James".

"Not really but I understood it to be about a girl"

"Thank you miss June, you did the right thing breaking up with Arnold, as far as I know Arnold has three wives already" Scott told her.

"Thank you, mister," the lady said.

Scott had been so busy, there had been no time to look after Blacky, going to the hitch rail outside the sheriff's office, climbing into the saddle they went to the livery stable, finding a stall that was clean and had recently mucked out, Scott unsaddled Blacky gave him a bag of oats and made sure the big horse had clean water.

"Can I help you sir" hearing the voice behind him, turning the holster stood in front of him.

"Maybe, how well did you know James Hunt"

"James was a good friend".

"Do you know why they fought".

"No but James was young and proud and at the age, that made him frightened of nothing" the holster explained.

"Thank you, the name is Scott,".

"No problem, I'll look after your horse mister"

"No, you can take the nose bag of him when Blacky stop's eating but do not pat him try to put reins on him or try to ride him, my pal is a one-man horse, touch him and you will regret it" Scott informed him.

"Thanks Scott my name is Billy"

"Billy, where does James and his mother live" Scott asked.

"Misses Hunt and family live in a cabin north end of high street behind the gunsmiths" Billy informed him.

"Thanks" Scot said and walked in the direction to go to the cabin.

Reaching the cabin Billy had told him about, there was quite a few people around the place dressed mainly in black as it is James wake, Scott knocked on the door which was answered by a young girl of approximately fourteen to fifteen years old.

"Hello, I am sorry to bother you all at this time, but it is important I talk to Misses Hunt, could you ask her if that would be OK, please" Scott asked, the girl left then returned.

"She said yes please come with me" Scott followed her.

"Hello Misses Hunt, I am sorry about your son, and I hope you can forgive this intrusion, I'm afraid I must ride out in the morning, and would like to know as much as I can about this incident" Scott asked.

"What do you want to know" Misses Hunt asked.

"How did it happen, your son was a young man of fifteen years old, how did the boy get into a gunfight with a man like Wes Arnold" Scott enquired.

"It was my fault" the young girl blurted out.

"Becky darling how is it your fault" Mrs Hunt asked.

"Miss, it will maybe help me, to catch this man if I know what happened" Scott said

"Mister"

"Scott not mister"

"Scott this is my daughter Becky"

"Hello Becky, this man Arnold is a bad man, and I have the job to bring him to justice, as I have said it would help me if I have as much information as I can get about this man so could you please tell me your story" Scott explained.

"OK Scott, I was outside the house just watching some people further down the street when this man called Arnold came to me and started asking question about the town so I answered his questions, he told me I was beautiful and gave me a kiss on the cheek, Arnold continued talking kissed me on the lips, I was not thinking and liked his kisses, after moving me to the side of the house, I was pushed against the side of the house, kissing me again only this time I felt his hand up my dress between my legs, I pushed him away and called out (No Stop) putting his hand over my mouth I was pushed violently against the house wall and once more he put his hand up my dress, James must have heard me call out because I heard him call out.

"Mister you leave my sister alone" James repeated this twice more, Arnold let me go.

"Mom James came to my rescue"

Arnold hit James which knocked him to the ground, James jumped up anger on his face that man Arnold pulled a gun. Holding James at gunpoint the man told James.

"If you want to defend your whore of a sister, get a gun and meet me on the street" the girl started crying.

"It was my fault; James was defending me". her mother put an arm around her.

"Miss Becky, it was not your fault, any man who sees a woman being abused or attacked would defend her, your young brother might be fifteen, but James was a man, and miss thank you for the information" Scott said.

"Are you going to get this man" Mrs Hunt asked. As she looked at the man in front of her, she saw the man's face go taught, his eyes turned like steel glinted in the light his jaw went tort, solid and omitted.

"Yes"

"Good" Mrs Hunt replied.

"Scott now knew that Wes Arnold would have raped Becky if James had not arrived when he did, Scott made the decision, to remain in town overnight.

At the crack of dawn, Scott was on his feet an hour later after breakfast intended to ride out of town, Scott had made up his mind the night before, that it was now time to take Wes Arnold down, so his intension was to ride to Muleshoe it only takes a day to get there meaning it will be possible to get to his destination by dawn tomorrow, once there his idea is just to wait until Arnold arrives.

After saddling up Blacky Scott rode to the café and tied him to the hitch rail, the café had just opened on his arrival, where after a substantial breakfast, Scott asked for a large pack of sandwiches and to fill up his canteen with fresh water, June the waitress came over to him.

"Hello Scott, your horse is outside I take it you are leaving us" she said.

"Yes, June I am"

"You asked about Wes, Why? Who are you what do you do" June asked?

"June, I am a bounty hunter, I am often hired by lawmen to do jobs they are unable to do, like at the moment, I most of the time do normal work catching small time criminals but this job is different it is a special job" Scott informed her.

"And Wes was part of it" June asked.

"Yes June, Arnold is a murderer and rapist, you are well shot of him, June did you know that the shootout with that young boy Jimmy was because the boy stopped Arnold from raping his young sister" Scott told her.

"No, I did not know about Wes. In fact, there is a lot of things I did not know about him, thank you" June said.

"June, my job is to go after him and take him Dead or Alive, preferably Alive and take him in to face the law but this man it could be impossible because the man believes in the gun, but we will see, thanks for the sandwich's now I must get going" Scott told her.

"Good luck Scott" June said.

Riding down Main Street on his way out of town, a hundred yards the sheriff waved and said "Good luck Scott" then continued doing his rounds, once clear of the town Scott nudged the big horse into a gallop, when completing a mile the kinks taking out of Blacky they slowed down to a walk to cool him walking another hundred yards Scott brought Blacky to a halt to let him blow, taking the makings from his shirt pocket rolled a cigarette , taking a long drag then letting the smoke leave his lips Scott extracted the map from his saddle bags it looked like a straight forward walk but from past experience it was not like that due to hills a forest area's that had to be negotiate but you just plod on.

As it happened his trip to Muleshoe was uneventful Scott had to camp out overnight but it was warm so there was little problems, the next morning after cleaning the camp sight saddling up, rode on, at nine o'clock in the morning, entering town they moved down the main street of Muleshoe, riding down the street Scott kept his eyes open surveying the town checking where everything was situated, most of the building were the same as most other towns, In Muleshoe the building that stood out the most was the Golden Palace Saloon, the saloon in most towns was the biggest building in the town but in Muleshoe the saloon was exceptionally gourdy lots of gold paint and covered with coloured lights.

In Muleshoe the livery stable was at the far end of town so needless to say that was Scott's destination, on his arrival at the livery stable, the holster was nowhere to be seen so Scott found an empty stall which had recently been mucked out, proceeding with the normal routine of removing the saddle and other pieces of equipment, Blacky was in a playful mood, talking to the big horse, and playing games together made Scott laugh while feeding and watering, unknown to him a few people had heard them and were attracted to the scene, the first indication that there was spectators was when a voice behind him, (female laughter) greeted him.

"Hello" Scott greeted.

"You have a good horse" the young lady said.

"Yes, this is Blacky my pal and has saved my life a few times, we have travelled a lot together and is a one-man horse" Scott informed her.

"I'm happy to meet you, and to see such a magnificent animal"

"Thank you, I'm Scott burrows"

"Call me Jo, Jo Taylor I 'm the holster here at the stables, don't worry about your horse I 'll look after him" Jo told him.

"I'm not worried about him, but I pity anyone who tries to touch or take him as I have said Blacky is a one-man horse and does not like strangers, Jo you can give him water, you can feed him, but do not touch him, I will be in frequently to see to him" Scott instructed her.

"OK Scott"

"I have to admit you are the first lady holster I have met" Scott said.

"I wanted a job, and I am good with horses when the position became vacant, I asked Mister Rodgers for the Job, and as I am known by him to like horses his answer was yes" Jo explained.

"I'm going to breakfast would you like to join me" Scott invited her.

"I don't normally go to breakfast with a stranger but why not "she shrugged her shoulders.

"Well, I promise you, it is just breakfast, I'm not coming on to you or anything else" Scott assured her.

"Why not am I ugly" Jo demanded.

"I'll tell you a secret, I am engaged to be married, after this job I am going to marry Danny my fiancée"

"Then I will be happy to have breakfast with you". Jo said.

"Jo and Scott walked side by side down main street to the café, finding a table Scott ordered two breakfasts which they ate, over coffee" Jo asked.

"I have never had breakfast with a stranger before, since I have not seen you before you are obviously a stranger" Jo looked at him enquiringly.

"Yeh! I only rode into town an hour ago" Scott stated.

"What do you do" Jo asked.

"You ask to many questions" Scott said.

Scott looked at Jo, she had gone quiet and looked down at the floor an embarrassed look on her face, she knew it was not a thing you would ask a stranger, as she is getting to personal, even though they had only met thirty minutes ago Scott had taken a liking to this feisty girl so decided to be honest with her.

"Jo at this moment I am a bounty hunter" Scott said.

"A bounty hunter" she exclaimed.

"Yes"

"You said at the moment" she asked in a faint voice.

"Yes, the job I am doing is the last job, then I'm going to marry Danny and settle down" Scott told her.

"Since this job is important to you, can you tell me about it" Jo asked.

"Jo, you are a nice young lady, and I like you, but the brief time we have been talking I have found you are quite talkative, I want to keep the job a secret"

"Scott, it is up to you if you don't trust me, but I will make you a promise I will not tell anybody what you say" Jo said. Scott studied her for a moment.

"OK Jo, I will tell you, I must warn you I will find some way to punish you if you do tell anyone, do you understand" Scott told her.

"Yes, Scott I understand".

"Jo Five men robbed the wells Fargo office in a town south of here, they took a payroll and murdered three men, I did not take the job to retrieve the money I took it to bring the five men to justice, but worse was to follow when escaping from the town the five men took a young couple hostage, the nineteen year old boy who was unarmed tried to protect his seventeen year old girlfriend they shot him in cold blood then the five men raped the seventeen year old virgin to death" Scott paused as a gasp and a look of horror came from Jo.

"So I am determined to bring these men to justice dead or alive, if I can but if I have to kill them I will because they are animals, the first man I took back alive to face the law, the second young man decided to shoot it out with me , I won, in a day or two I hope to have the third man, this man is bad a robber, murderer and rapist and I am here to take him" Scott told her.

"What's his name" Jo asked.

"Wes Arnold".

"You're here I assume you are waiting for him, how do you know Arnold is coming here" Jo asked.

"I have spent a lot of time gathering information about this man and I know a lot about him, one thing I do know is after the rape of the young girl Arnold told his confederates about having the biggest and best saloon in this area, and there it is down the street you can see where the stolen money went" Scott told her.

"Are you sure, the saloon is ran by a woman" Jo pointed out.

"That must be the third or fourth wife".

"Third wife".

"Yes, as I told you I have investigated this man, there is a Mrs Jackie Arnold in Canyon then there is a Mrs. Susie Arnold in Hereford, there may be more but I definitely know about those two so far" Scott explained.

"Does the lady in the saloon know" Jo asked.

"I don't know about that, Jo because you like horses the way you do, and because I love horses also, I like anyone who likes horses for that reason mainly I have told you what I have about this job, I trust you not to pass it on OK" Scott said.

"I won't I promise"

"Jo do you know Wes Arnold"

"Well yes everyone knows him".

"Question"

"What"

"Is Arnold liked in the town, or does he have any friends" Scott asked.

"I don't know for certain" Jo paused "Scott you know I am the holster in the livery stable and I hear gossip, from what I understand not many people like him but his reputation as a gunfighter stops people from talking, no one wants to go against him" Jo explained.

"Thank you, Jo," Scott replied, then paid for the meals.

Talking to Jo made him happy, it helped with his investigation it helped him with his ideas, Jo is a nice girl and well known in the town also liked and well thought of but she is a woman and talkative, she promised not to pass the word around but she will tell someone, during the conversation Scott had gathered little bits of information that will come in handy and will help him.

Strolling around the town, Scott kept his eyes and ears open, looking into every space in particular places like the general store, café and saloon, these are places where people congregate therefore is the places Arnold can be walking a little further along the street arriving outside the sheriff's office.

CHAPTER EIGHT

ARNOLD LAURA SENT ME.

"Hi!, Sheriff" Scott greeted.

"Howdy stranger, how can I help you"

"I'm Scott sheriff"

"OK Scott how can I assist you"

"Would you know Wes Arnold"

"Everyone around this town knows Wes Arnold"

"Do you know when Arnold is going to be back in town"

"No, but like a bad penny, Arnold will eventually turn up as usual".

"I take it by your manner sheriff, you don't love this man".

"Look, the man is trouble, I don't like him swaggering around town trying to gourd people to draw, but as word has circulated that Arnold is a gunfighter, nobody wants to take him on" the sheriff explained.

"Thanks sheriff, that is exactly what I wanted to know, Arnold is not liked, and no one will miss him" Scott said.

"Why".

"I am a bounty hunter, I want Wes Arnold by asking around as discreetly as I can access what opposition I might have, you are the second person that has told me that no one will go against him because of his expertise with a gun" Scott told him.

"If I am not being to forward or it is not a secret who was the other person"

"A young lady by the name of Jo Taylor, I met her at breakfast this morning"

"Jo Taylor Mmmmm"

"When someone says Jo Taylor the way you do, I feel I am missing something and I get curious sheriff"

"Two months ago John Taylor her father was on his way into town, I knew John a good decent man, well someone ambushed him the assassin using a rifle shot John who was found later, look Scott I cannot prove it, but all the sign I could pick up indicated that Wes Arnold had carried out the assassination, I could not prove it as all I found was circumstantial" the sheriff told him.

"Oh! I see"

"Sheriff I have more than enough proof, I can use against Arnold, what I would like to know, do you know of anyone who would side Arnold and will try to stop me"

"If you can prove you can take Arnold out, I don't think you will have anyone challenging you" the sheriff said.

"Thanks sheriff".

Scott left the office and continued his stroll along the main street, his next place of call is the bank, after entering the bank, spotting the managers secretary behind the barrier

"Hello miss, could you ask the bank manager if I could have a word with him please"

"I will find out if it is possible to fit you sir" the young lady disappeared.

After a few moments she emerged from the manager's office opening the gate.

"Please come this way sir, that's the manager's office please go in" the young lady pointed out.

"Thank you miss".

"Hello Mr. Stuart, could I have a word"

"Of course, Mister"

"Scott"

"Yes Mr. Scott" the manager replied.

"Not Mr. Scott, Mr. Stuart just Scott"

"Mr. Stuart, I have a letter here from the governor of Texas, this letter is instructions from Wells Fargo"

"OK what's this all about" the manager asked.

"About a month ago the Wells Fargo office in Jayton, was robbed of $100,000 one hundred thousand dollars and three men were killed, five men carried out this crime one of the was Wes Arnold" Scott informed him.

"Wes Arnold"

"Yes, Wes Arnold, you know why I am here, I want you to freeze Arnolds Asset's if necessary, tell him you had message from the governor"

"OK prevent him from being able to draw money"

"Thank you, Mr Stuart, you have seen my authority, I will be back to see you soon" Scott held out his hand.

Time was getting on before Scott new it half the day had gone and found himself just outside the café so entered to have lunch, arriving at that time was very convenient because the café was quiet just before the midday rush. After eating Scott went straight to the livery stable, Blacky was happy to see him.

"Hi! You rascal lets go for a ride".

"Hello, can I come also" Jo's voice said behind him.

"I can't see any reason why not" Scott replied.

Saddling their horses Jo talked all of the time excitedly, a few people took notice of the two of them as they walked their horses' side by side out of town, riding north for a couple of miles Scott surprised Jo when yelling loudly.

"Yeh!"

Kicking Blacky into life, Blacky went from a slow walk to a gallop in seconds leaving the surprised Jo standing still her mouth open as she gasped leaving her dumb founded, a mile further up the trail Scott pulled Blacky to a stop.

When Jo caught up to him, Scott had dismounted and sat on a rock rolling a cigarette.

"Wow that horse is fast" Jo commented.

"Yes, every day we come out for a ride, we do a fast mile to take the kinks out of him, you being good with horses should know that"

"I see you are right" she said as she looked around nervously.

"Are you alright Jo" Scott asked.

"We have stopped at the spot my father died, someone ambushed him" Jo explained

"Oh! I am sorry Jo come on we will go back" Scott said

"No! Scott, you do not have to be sorry, it is something I will have to get used to as I have to ride by here every day" Jo told him.

"Jo, you said your father died on this very spot"

"Yes" Jo said in a faint voice.

Scott stood on the spot made a circle looking all around him.

"If I planned an ambush, I would shoot from either those rocks to the left or that small bunch of trees to the right. I'll check the rocks first," Scott told her

"Blacky stay" talking to the big horse, Scott wanted Blacky to stay on the spot, (the big horse stood still, if the reins were just dropped Blacky would wander but when ordered would stay in one place) so it was possible to give him a view of where Mr Taylor had been.

Moving slowly studying the ground, climbing slowly each time there was a place a man could conceal himself Scott stopped and looked back at Blacky, it did not take long for Scott to realise that the shooter did not ambush Mr Taylor from the rocks.

Going back down to the trail, Scott crossed the trail into the brush, then walking for approximately twenty yards entered a small crowd of trees, the first thing that was noticeable the ground was wet and his feet sank into the ground but most of all there was a set of boot prints not his, checking the prints, Scott moved forward knowing that this time there has been someone here.

Studying the tree's Scott picked a position that looked like the best place to see the trail where Mr Taylor would be on the horse, the man who took the shot had found a sapling with a small branch giving the perfect vee in which a rifle could be aligned, the man wore expensive tailored boots, which Scott would recognise if seen again, this man stands about five foot eight inches tall, his horse stood tall was brown in colour and the left rear shoe is broken, all this Scott told Jo who was impressed by the information but said.

"All you have said fits quite a few men".

"How about Wes Arnold".

"Yeh! Even him will fit that description worst luck there quite a few men who will fit that description" Jo said.

Scott and Jo rode at a canter back to the livery stable.

"Jo don't talk to anyone about what we have learnt today"

"I won't" Jo replied,

"Also, I notice whenever Arnold's name is mentioned, you grimace I take it you don't like him, do you want to tell me about it"

"I have a good reason to detest this man, Scott we have got along quite well and I trust you, I have not told anyone even my mother the reason I hate this man, the day after my father died Wes Arnold caught me alone in the livery stable, and tried to kiss me, I stopped him and yelled NO hoping someone would be nearby, I turned to walk away from him, an arm came around my waist and a hand grabbed my breast, we both heard someone coming I was about to yell, taking his hand from my breast, clamped it over my mouth, through me into a stall there was a pitch fork in the stall I picked it up and Arnold disappeared, if we had not heard someone nearby Arnold would have raped me, I hate him and stay well clear of him" Jo explained.

"Yeh! That is his MO (Method off) doing things and has done this before I'm afraid" Scott told her. Jo kissed Scott on the cheek.

"Scott thank you it was wonderful to be able to ride and confide in someone".

"You need anyone to talk to I'm available, so long for now" Scott after attending to Blacky walked of.

Scott decided to have a little time to himself, making his way to his room locking the door, removing his Stetson and gun belt, putting a chair by the open window putting his heels on the window sill taking out the makings rolled a cigarette looking at the street below Scott analysed all the recent information gathered.

As the shadows of the building lengthened across the street, looking at the clock it told him it was time for dinner, making his way to the café it was early evening and still light, the sun from the day kept the evening air warm, sitting at a table at the rear of the room, lying on the table was a new edition of the local paper, the headline caught his eyes.

ATTACK ON WAGONS CONTINUED.

Yesterday once again a wagon carrying families east has been attacked, this is the sixth wagon so far in the last two months, the wagon was found by a lazy T cowhand two people dead wagon ransacked, no idea of the identity of the killers.

His dinner arrived and it filled the large plate Scott being hungry dug into it, the meal was good, but the large mug of strong coffee was fantastic, relishing the brew made him sit contentedly for a while on completion Scott went to the saloon had a beer, retired for the night.

When the ribbon of light spread across the horizon of the morning sky, Scott woke to the call of a crowing cock, in the morning air the noise sounded extra loud , with a sigh Scott climbed to his feet, first retrieving his pistol from under his pillow, placing the pistol on the bureau as water was poured into the bowl, after the completion of his ablutions picking up his gunbelt slung it around his waist, buckling the belt dropped his gun into the holster tied the thong around his leg, drawing the gun Scott checked the load swung the gun on his finger dropped it into the holster.

Scott's day started in its usual way by making his way to the stable to look after Blacky, it was normal for Scott to look after the big horse first before himself, Blacky as was part of his morning routine greeted Scott with a neigh, snuffled his shirt, patting the big horses neck, putting the feed bag with oats in it plus putting fresh water into the trough, as Blacky ate, picking up the two brushes, he started brushing the sleek black coat (It shone as the light reflected from it), by the time the job of brushing the big horse was complete the big black horse had finished eating, leading him to the corral behind the stable Scott slipped the reins and set him free to run around, then returning to the stall began to muck out.

"Morning Scott" Jo's pleasant tones rang out.

"Morning Jo"

"Everything OK".

"Sure, I have just looked after Blacky, I told you I would be in each day to see to him" Scott told her.

"Yes, you did, you carry on with what you have to do, I will muck out it is my job you know" Jo told him.

"OK Jo thanks" Scott left.

Now that the big horse was happy for a while Scott felt his belly rumble and thought of breakfast so made his way to the café, 'Sandie's Place' the local café was a clean place that sold good food, eating a substantial breakfast followed by a good cup of coffee made Scott feel good and ready for the day ahead, pausing outside the café after rolling and lighting a cigarette, at a leisurely pace Scott in a contented mood strolled along the street.

Proceeding along the street, stopping outside the sheriff's office and with time on his hands Scott decided to visit the sheriff.

"Morning sheriff" Scott greeted.

"Morning Scott, you're here early can I help you" the sheriff said.

"I'd like to scan your wanted dodgers"

"Sure, Scott go ahead they are pinned to the board over there go check them out" the sheriff pointed to the far wall.

Sitting at the desk opposite the sheriff, Scott thumbed slowly studied the bunch of dodgers in his hand, picking out two dodgers which were low paid only $100 OO dollars each, his reason for pulling these dodgers was because the two faces were familiar after studying them Scott shrugged his shoulders, carried on looking through the rest of them, not certain what or who it was possible to find but it did give him knowledge of the local criminals which will come in handy and it helped him to pass the time, almost at the end of his search Scott came across a printed sheet among the wanted dodgers the sheet was a warning notice which mentioned a big man called DUTCHY. This fact alone made his trip to the sheriff's office worthwhile, It gave him a start on his next part of the job, Scott memorised the message before returning it to the pack. The sheriff did not need to know so the clip with the dodgers were hooked back on the wall.

"Well, there is not a lot here that I would be interested in" Scott said.

"What are you really doing here Scott" the sheriff asked.

"I already told you why I am here, I am waiting for Wes Arnold to get back in town"

"How do you intend to take Arnold".

"Oh! That is easy, I intend to challenge him to a duel"

"There is not a man in this town who would go up against Wes Arnold mainly due to his reputation, what makes you think you can take him"

"Sheriff, can you tell me one man with a reputation that Arnold has gone against"

"Everyone I have talked to told me Arnold took Frank Williams gunfighter"

"Yes! Frank Williams did have a reputation but when Arnold faced him, the man was old, had not shot in anger for a sometime, giving his age was the man still fast or had Williams slowed down" Scott asked.

"Well Williams did have the reputation" the sheriff pointed out.

"Let me tell you something very few people know about, the last gunfight Williams had was against the twins 'the Albert brothers. As you know Williams took them both this gave him a reputation but what no one knew is that Williams took a bullet in the arm, climbing into the saddle rode out and kept riding until feeling safe and well away from town, found a doctor to look at the arm, the result was not good, the doctor told him his arm will never be the same it will be stiffer so will impede his draw, the years after that Williams lived of his reputation, no one wanted to take him on" Scott explained.

"Well, I will be damned" the sheriff burst out.

"It's true"

"Scott remembers Wes Arnold has shot it out with a few people since then"

"Sheriff name me one of those men you mention who had a reputation."

"Mmmm, I see what you mean".

"Sheriff, I have spent the last two weeks, looking into Wes Arnold and I know Arnold has goaded young boys and men who are not good with a gun into a gunfight sheriff this is murder".

"I agree about it being murder, but when Arnold says it was in self-defence there is not a lot I can do".

"My main problem is I do not know who I can trust, who will back up Arnold when I challenge him meaning who will stick a gun in my back to prevent me, that is the type of knowledge I am trying to gather" Scott said

"As far as I know, Arnold has not got many friends in this town, it must be possible for him to have a supporter, if there is, I don't know who that will be"

"I'll leave things as they are and take my chances when the time comes" Scott told the sheriff.

Leaving the sheriff's office, Scott realised the conversation with the sheriff had taken so long, they had forgotten time, and they had talked all morning, tipping his Stetson forward to shade his eyes a bit more from the noon day sun, Scott walked to the café as lunch was in his mind. The only table left available was by the wall just past the window.

"Afternoon miss could I have a steak well done with fries and peas please, and one of your lovely cups of coffee" Scott ordered from the waitress.

"Yes sir" came the smiling reply.

A few moments later the waitress dropped of a cup of coffee, then Scott watched the approaching Jo.

"Could I have another cup of coffee please" the waitress looked at Jo. Smiled and then nodded.

"Hi Jo. Pull up a chair, do you want something to eat" Scott asked. The waitress came to the table put a cup of coffee in front of Jo. Then put the plate of food in front of Scott.

"Pearl, could I have a bacon sandwich" Jo ordered.

"Put it on my bill miss" Scott said.

"OK" she replied.

"I'd like to talk to you and hope you will help me" Jo said.

"OK Jo what's your problem".

"I have a sixteen-year-old brother, 'Johnny' named after my dad and at this time is playing with a gun and holster, I have watched him practise, Johnny thinks a lot of himself, but I don't think so, could you help maybe persuade him otherwise, I cannot get him to listen to me" Jo explained.

"Jo that's a hard problem, boys from thirteen to seventeen are at a rebellious age, when you try to tell them anything, they most times ignore and don't believe you, it often does not work and can make the problem worse" Scott explained.

"Oh! I do understand, when I tried to talk to him, I was told to shut up and get lost please, please Scott" Jo informed him.

"Arnold is not here and Blacky needs a run, OK I'll come along with you and see what I can do but Jo no promises" Scott assured her.

"Thank you, Scott,"

Even though John Taylor was dead the family as far as they knew still owned the family homestead just outside town, Jo and Scott went to the livery stable and saddled up, it was a pleasant ride out to the homestead Jo and Scott gets along well together and have in a short while become good friends.

Riding into the yard of the homestead, Jo saw her brother by the barn wearing a gunbelt in a cross-draw position practising drawing a gun. Directing her horse to go across to him, Scott followed.

"Hello Johnny" Jo greeted.

"Hi! Sis who is your new friend".

"Johnny meet Scott"

"Howdy Scott"

"Hi Johnny" Scott replied and stuck his hand out.

"Johnny what are you doing" Jo asked.

"Sis I'm practising drawing and shooting".

"I see you favour the cross draw" Scott said

"Yes, I think it is best and faster" Johnny said.

"Johnny, I have tried all the ways to draw, and I find the straight draw to be the best" Scott informed him.

"Well, I don't think so" Johnny said in an angry voice.

"Would you believe me if I proved it to you".

"Well, yes of course I will" Johnny sneered.

"Give me your gun"

Johnny handed Scott his gun reluctantly, Scott unloaded the pistol then pointed the gun in the air and pulled the trigger twice handed his gun back to him.

"Right Johnny put these in your pocket" handing him the bullets.

Jo and Johnny watched with interest as Scott lifted his revolver from his holster and once more took the bullets out of his own gun, pointing it to the sky pulled the trigger twice.

"Johnny holster your gun then stand and face me" Scott said putting his own pistol into his holster and faced Johnny.

"Now Johnny let your hand hover over your gun, Jo count to ten silently then call draw OK" Scott told them.

"OK Scott" Jo replied. After a few seconds Jo called.

"Draw".

Surprising Johnny's draw was not bad, succeeding to clear the holster but before aligning the gun a loud double click could be heard, looking down there was Scott's pistol cocked pointing at his stomach Johnny was amazed.

"Johnny, you can reload your gun now" Scott told him.

"Right Scott"

"I am not telling you what draw you should use, but I have tried all the methods of drawing a gun and as far as I am concerned the straight draw is the best for me, I am also not trying to stop you wearing a gun almost every man in the west does, and you also must learn to use a gun properly, but Johnny do not try to be better than other men because there will always be someone better" Scott told Johnny.

"All methods, how many ways are there to draw a gun" Jo asked.

"There are quite a few ways to handle a gun but there is only five ways that are mainly used" Scott said.

"And what are they" Jo enquired.

"The straight draw, the Cavalry twist, the Cross draw, the swivel holster, and the spring-loaded holster." Scott informed her.

"Well," Jo said.

"Well, what" Scott asked.

"How do they work"

"What"

"Tell me about the different ways to draw" Jo said

"The most common draw is the way I draw the straight draw, the belt crosses the body from the left hip to the top of the right leg, where the holster hangs on the upper right leg, the belt is adjusted so the gun is levelled with a hanging hand, this means you only have to grip the butt, cock as you draw level the pistol then squeeze the trigger". Scott explained.

As Johnny asked Scott a few questions, Jo left them for a few minutes, returning with a tray with three glasses of beer.

"Thanks Jo that looks good" Scott said as a gulp flowed down his dry throat.

"I agree with Scott thanks sis" Johnny commented.

"Well, what about the second method" Jo looking at Scott

"The Cavalry twist, means exactly what it means it does not matter whether you were in the confederate or union soldier your belt was high with a holster that had a pistol but forward you had to twist your arm to grip and draw the gun, after the war on leaving the army many men had modified holster made, the belt and holster fitted exactly the same as the straight draw only the holster was fitted so that the gun was butt forward, that means you twist your arm to grab the butt lift and twist the gun into the firing position the problem with this draw is if you are too eager you could shoot yourself". Scott paused to take a slurp of his beer.

"Get on with it, what is next" Jo demanded

"Is she always this bossy" Scott asked.

"Sometimes worse" Johnny smiled.

"The cross draw, I don't have to explain to much about this draw, as I have already demonstrated this draw, I think a split second is lost as you reach across your body." once more taking a drink from the glass.

"Scott what about the swivel holster you mentioned" Johnny asked.

"Yes, I am curious about that" Jo said.

"For this type of draw the holster was fitted to a belt high up, it has no thong to tie down as the holster could not swivel, it has to be high to be able to control it, now the holster is attached to the belt with a large metal stud, to fire you grab the butt of the gun swivel the holster and pull the trigger, the downside is you lose a fraction of a second reaching to draw plus because of how it is situated on the body it has a limited range if you move to his blind side the man has to move" Scott explained.

"What about the spring holster you told us about" Jo and Johnny said at the same time.

"This way of trying to speed up the draw is the newest method, you have a spring in the bottom of the holster, when you push the gun down it clicks into a notch, then with the movement of the leg you release the spring which propels the gun up into his hand, the only other point about the draw is you must have a special type of gun, a flat gun like a Webley, this gun carries eight bullets in a magazine, in the handle of the gun" Scott concluded.

"You definitely know about guns" Jo said.

"I need to know about weapons in my present job" Scott told them.

"What is your job" Johnny asked.

"I am a bounty hunter at the moment" Scott told them.

"Bounty hunter" Johnny exclaimed loudly.

"Yes, Johnny a bounty hunter, but after the job I am doing I am going to marry Danny my fiancée we are going to settle down, Johnny don't get any ideas I am a bounty hunter for a special reason and to be a bounty hunter it takes a lot of learning and dedication otherwise you will be dead, there is lots of men who have decided to be a bounty hunter and are in boot hill, my advice to anyone is don't do it unless you have something to drive you to do so, now I have found Danny I am looking forward to settling down and having a family" Scott told Johnny.

"Now you two have a good day I must get back to town, it has been a nice change for me to be able to visit you out here it has been a pleasant distraction, but I must get back see you" Scott whistled and Blacky ran to him, mounting they headed for town.

"See you Scott and thank you" Jo said.

Scott had to admit the time spent with Jo and Johnny had been so enjoyable that time had sped past, so it was early evening by the time Scott arrived back in town, after checking Blacky into a stall for the night, going to the café for his evening meal, a couple of beers it was time to turn in for the night.

At dawn as, usual Scott woke up in his usual way, his body was tuned into waking him up at a certain time, because of the many times this had been done over the years constantly waking up at a certain time each morning his body clock automatically takes over.

"Well it's another day" Scott said talking to himself.

After rising, the normal routine of his ablutions were carried out, Scott headed for the stable to tend to Blacky, Scott had just started by giving Blacky his morning nosebag when a familiar voice came from behind him.

"Blacky knows me now Scott you go to breakfast" Jo announced.

"Thanks Jo"

Scott had his breakfast which was substantial as usual, but did not hurry, sitting with a cup of coffee, and admitted to the world.

"Ah! Breakfast the best meal of the day" sighing then paid the waitress.

Making his way back to the stable Scott picked up Blacky and took a ride, during which the kinks were taken out of the big horse, finding a quiet place they stopped to let Blacky blow, also giving him time to roll and smoke a cigarette, this gave Scott a pleasant morning, he was not in any hurry knowing Wes Arnold will show up eventually, there was nothing that could be done before the man arrives. The last couple of days have been calm waiting for Arnold to get back in town.

Getting back to town going to the livery stable, stripping Blacky of the saddle and other equipment, then put him in the corral to run free, being it near to lunch time, walked to the café, the only table free was at the window, as the waitress served him she looked through the window she exclaimed.

"Oh! No"

"What is wrong miss" Scott asked she pointed through the window.

"He's back, Wes Arnold is back" she omitted.

"I'll have todays special miss" Scott ordered.

"Yes sir" came the reply.

Scott studied the man riding down the street, the piebald horse was big like Blacky looked like it has a lot of stamina, the man on the horse wore all black except his shirt starting with his boots, they were black made to measure patterned soles, trousers are black, the trouser belt and the gunbelt was also made of black leather, his low crowned Stetson with a silver band on it that shone in the sun last of all Arnold wore a long three quarter length black coat and looked more like a gambler than a cowman or the look of a normal western men.

The waitress arrived with his food and Scott as usual found the food to be good and tucked into his food with relish as the food was so good Scott took his time following his dinner with a large slab of apple pie and cream but most of all, relaxing over a large cup of coffee.

Stopping on the boardwalk outside the café Scott rolled and lit a cigarette, adjusted his gunbelt and tied the thong around his leg, taking the revolver from the holster checked the gun twirled the gun on his finger lowered the weapon into his holster but left the thong of the hammer, now everything is checked, Scott threw the cigarette end away started walking towards the saloon.

Scott stepped into the saloon, stood for a moment to get his eyes used to the light of the room and scanned the room to see if there will be any visible chance of opposition then looked at Wes Arnold standing at the end of the bar talking to the barman, Scott walked to the middle of the bar lifted his pistol.

"Wes Arnold, you are under arrest" Scott called out loudly.

"Mister drop your gun" a voice came from behind him.

Most of the people in the saloon all jumped as the loud noise in the confinement of the room of the sound of a rifle being fired the bullet ploughed a hole in the bar right in front of the man challenging Scott.

"Tubby put your gun away or I will shoot you" Standing at the top of the stairs stood the lady saloon owner with a rifle in her hands.

"All of you in these premises keep out of this, carry on mister" she backed up her words by levering a shell into the chamber.

"Wes Arnold, you are under arrest for robbery and murder" Scott once more called out loudly in a firm voice.

"You are not a lawman" Arnold returned.

"I am making a citizen arrest." Scot informed him.

"You can get stuffed" Arnold told Scott.

"Arnold the dodger in my pocket says dead or alive, I only have to let the hammer drop and believe me I will if I have to" Scott told him. The saloon lady broke in.

"Mister I don't want any unnecessary shooting in my place, I would be happier if you could take your business outside"

"I agree Arnold you seem to have some misguided support plus I know you are a murderer but these people do not want to get killed, and because of what I know about you I agree, so I am offering you a chance you can walk to the jailhouse or meet me on the street in a shootout, and that is all the offer you will get, well make up your mind" Scott challenged him.

"I agree to your challenge" Arnold agreed.

Scott with his pistol trained on Wes Arnold's spine marched him into the centre of the street, when standing fifteen feet apart faced each other.

"Arnold remove the loop from the trigger move your hand away from your gun" Scott told him.

Arnold carried out the instructions given to him, lifting his hand away from his side calmly a smirk on his face, the two men faced each other, along the street people peered through curtains the drinking had stopped in the saloon and a face showed from almost every spot, the same with the café people looked from windows and doors, the two men studied each other's faces, Scott saw the difference in his eyes and knew Arnold was about to draw, Scott spoke

"Laura sent me"

As the two men s hands were going for their guns, when hearing the word Laura Arnold very briefly paused, Arnold's shot flew an inch from Scott's head, the white shirt Arnold wore became a sticky red as the two bullets ploughed into his body the bullets caused Arnold's body to go over backwards to lay sprawled in the street, keeping his pistol pointing at the body, advanced to the body checked Arnold was dead stood up and holstered his colt.

The first person at the scene was the sheriff

"Well Scott you did give him a chance"

"Yeh! I have to admit Arnold was faster than I thought, because of the soft targets Arnold had been doing lately I became complacent I expected him to be slower" Scott explained.

"I'll get the body to the undertakers for you" the sheriff said

"No sheriff I want him wrapped in his tarp, when I ride out, I wish to take him with me" Scott told him.

"Where to Scott"

"I know a town not far from here who will be very happy to know Arnold is dead".

"OK considerate it done" the sheriff replied.

Before leaving town, Scott had three important things that must be done, Saloon, Bank, and telegraph office.

On his way to the saloon Scott met the lady from the saloon who handled a rifle so well, Scott was still puzzled by her actions, as she was married Scott thought the lady would support Wes Arnold rather than him. Scott stopped removed his Stetson.

"Howdy Marm I was on my way to see you" Scott greeted.

"Mister I am on my way to the café, to have lunch with my son and daughter, why don't you join us" she invited him.

"Begging your pardon Marm you do not seem to be upset about me killing your husband" Scott stated.

"I have my reasons for that, two days ago I would have shot you where you stood but because of information I have since acquired I say good riddance to him" she said.

"Looks like my lucky day"

"You could say that, also I must thank you" she replied.

"Now you do have me intrigued why!"

The lady went quiet and remained that way until arriving at the café, on their arrival Scott opened the door to allow the lady through, on entering the lady made her way to a table at the far-right corner and Scott had his answers, sitting at the table was Jo and Johnny Taylor.

"Mum, Scott" Jo omitted in surprise.

"Ma what are you doing with Scott" Johnny.

"Afternoon you two I believe you know this gentleman" the lady said. Jo smiled.

"Mister Burrows"

"Marm the name is Scott"

"And my name is Barbie".

"Scott, it is needless to say, because of you my son and daughter came to see me, and told me quite a few things about Wes, things like wives, like the attempt to rape and a few other things I did not know of" Barbie said. Scott sat quietly for a few seconds, and they all heard him sigh loudly.

"Look Barbie, I have a lot of things I would like to talk to you about, first why did you marry Wes Arnold" Scott asked.

"Wes asked me to".

"Did the man ask you to marry him and leave your husband before your husband was ambushed" Scott asked.

"Why yes, but I told him no I am happy and have a family" Barbie said

"Then after your husband died, once more Arnold proposed again"

"Yes, wait a minute why do you ask"

"Mmmm! I wish I had something stronger to drink, two days ago I saddled Blacky to go for a ride, Jo asked me if I was leaving and I told her I was only going for a ride asked if she could ride with me, we had a pleasant time just talking until we came to a junction in the trail, this is when she told me about her father, and the fact of him being ambushed at that spot, I asked Jo to wait while I investigated, I found the killer rode a brown horse, was about six foot eight inches tall, there was some black threads there but the most distinctive sign was the pattern of some fancy made to measure boots, after beating him in the shootout I checked to see if I had succeeded in killing him and could not help noticing his boots, Barbie Wes Arnold killed your husband John Taylor" Scott paused, Barbie had tears in her eyes Scott continued.

"Barbie I think Wes Arnold asked you to marry him, you said no to him, I also believe that no woman had said no to him, so

Wes ambushed John, and showed sympathy to you, asked if you were OK and said how sorry about you husband's death after a while waiting a bit of time, Wes once more asked you to marry him, and you excepted" Scott told her.

Barbie made a choking noise put her face in her hands Jo put her arms around her mother and consoled her.

"Thank you, Scott," Jo said in a faint voice

"No! It is I who must thank you" Barbie broke in.

"Barbie take your time to compose yourself, but I have a few things I must talk to you about, they concern the saloon and any finances Wes Arnold may have, in a town called Jayton five men robbed the Wells Fargo office of $100,000 one hundred thousand dollars and killed three men, one of those robbers was Wes Arnold, I have been employed to capture or kill these five men and retrieve what money I can, you being Arnolds wife, the saloon was his property and will I suppose go to you, it is important that we talk" Scott explained.

"I take it by the way you are talking the saloon will have to be sold to recuperate the money" Barbie replied.

"Yes, I have to get as much of the stolen money back, maybe I can get more money that is required, there may be some left, I don't know yet, if there is some over, It will most likely be split between you and Jackie and Susy Arnold his other two wives" Scott stated.

"I'm not worried about the saloon, the only reason I lived there is because that is where my husband lived, I still have my son and daughter, plus we still have the homestead, we will grow vegetables out back, maybe get a couple of chickens, if we have the money we can have a couple of cows for milk, we can live of the land hunt for food, what do you two think" looking at Jo and Johnny.

"Oh! Mum it's good to have you back" Jo told her.

"Scott, you can do what has to be done, if there is nothing I don't mind, of course I will take what furniture and other items that belong to me at home, otherwise it is up to you what happens just let me know" Barbie told him.

"OK Barbie I will see you before I leave, now I must make a move I have a lot of things to do, before I track the next one" Scott told them.

"Next one" Barbie omitted.

"Yes, I told you there was Five murderers, Wes Arnold is number three there is still two more of them to go" Scott reminded them.

Leaving the Taylor family, Scott directed his feet in the direction of the bank as it is now time to find what assets Arnold held to enable him to recuperate as much money as possible to return to Wells Fargo.

"I'd like to see Mr, Stuart please" Scott asked the secretary.

"Yes, I will tell him you are here sir"

A moment later the young lady returned and ushered Scott into the office.

"Hello Mister Stuart"

"Yes, Mister Burrows, how can I be of assistance"

"I take it you have heard of the demise of Wes Arnold"

"Yes, I have"

"Mr. Stuart I would like to hire you to collect all of Wes Arnold's asset's together organise the sale of the saloon, could you calculate their worth and let me know what will be left after you have taken your fee" Scott instructed him.

"I might not like Wes Arnold, but the man was very astute when it comes to business, because of that the assets could be substantial, I'm afraid it will take at least two to three hours to get an idea how much Arnold was worth" the manager told him.

"In that case I will be back to see you in the morning, this means delaying my departure, but it is only time" Scott said.

It was now getting a bit late so Scott decided to leave the telegraph messages until the morning, it means there will be an unwanted delay for another day, of course unbeknown to him the western grapevine was passing the word of Wes Arnold the gunfighter being dead, in a duel in Muleshoe.

Leaving the bank, as time was getting on, Scott's next call has to be the café to have a meal a drink before turning in for the night, Scott did find out that the people of Muleshoe did not like Wes Arnold, because of his reputation people were afraid to show there feeling but know they congratulated Scott patting him on the shoulders, as usual the meal was fantastic but when asking for the bill they told him there was no charge, looking in on Blacky, having a drink at the saloon, not feeling like celebrating Scott turned in for the night.

The next morning Scott woke up in his usual way and therefore did his normal duties washing, shaving, going out to the livery tending Blacky then having breakfast all in all Scott agreed it was a good start to the day.

"Well, I guess I had better get started the sooner I get the job done the sooner I Ride" Scott said to himself.

Walking down to the telegraph office, Scott sent the news to Jayton that Wes Arnold is dead and will inform them of any further development. When Scott arrived at the bank mister Stuart must have informed his secretary about their meeting as she ushered him straight through to his office.

"Hello Mister Stuart, have you had time to access what Wes Arnold was worth" Scott enquired.

"Look Scott as you know Wes Arnold married Mrs. Taylor by the law the Taylor homestead is his, so it depends on whether that property is included" the bank manager stated.

"No take the homestead back out and recalculate, Mister Stuart I want you to do something for me, do you have the deeds for the Taylor homestead" Scott asked.

"Yes, they are in the safe" the manager told him.

"Right, I want the homestead signed over to Mrs. Barbara Arnold for life I will witness it" Scott informed him, this was illegal, but Mr. Stuart agreed.

"OK Scott I understand ".

"The Taylor family are not going to lose their home because of that monster that family has gone through enough this is between me and you OK" Scott ordered.

"I agree"

"Make the deed unbreakable, making sure no claim can be made against it"

"I will sort it"

"I will be back later Mister Stuart" Scott informed him.

Danny and Ben had just arrived in JAYTON, as they had been travelling for quite a time on the stage, and admitted being very tired as their Suite had two bedrooms and a lounge.

"Ben, I am going to lie down for a while, I'll see you in a couple of hours" Danny said.

"OK I agree with you it's a great idea" Ben agreed.

After a period of rest, both Danny and Ben after a wash to take the sleep out of their eyes, which made them both feel much more relaxed, walking out of the hotel together their destination being the café as it had been a while since they last ate, during the meal it gave them time to talk, taking a piece of paper from her pocket wallet, read the name Scott had told her to contact.

"Ben after lunch we had better go to the Wells Fargo office and see if we can make contact with this Alex Morrison, we can introduce ourselves and ask if there is any news about Scott "Danny said.

"Danny, I think you have mentioned Scott every day since you have met him" Ben stated and smiled.

"Oh! I am sorry I miss him" Danny said softly.

"You only knew him a few days" Ben pointed out.

"Ben, I know how I feel" Danny said.

"Oh! Yeh! Love at first sight" Ben said a little sarcastically.

"Ben, I don't think I can make you understand because it is a feeling inside me it is a beautiful feeling something I have never felt before. Oh! Ben one day you will get those feelings. I love Scott" Danny explained.

"OK Danny lets go" Ben put his hand out as she rose from the chair left the café.

"Right Ben", Danny said as she slipped her arm through his.

Arm in arm Danny and Ben walked down Jayton main street looking for the Wells Fargo office, Danny being a woman found and stopped outside a few shops, stopping Ben to look at the goods on display, In the Milliners, the furniture shop, and the Cafe arriving at the office Ben and Danny approached the counter.

"Could I please see Mister Alex Morrison" Danny asked.

"Alex" the man yelled.

"Hello, how can I help you" Alex asked the beautiful young lady in front of him.

"My name is Danny Knowles, this is my brother Ben and I have a letter of introduction from Scott Burrows my fiancée, Mister Morrison do you have any news about Scott" Danny asked.

"Miss, Scott is a good man, so I bet before proposing to you, his job would have come up in the conversation" Alex stated.

Danny nodded her head.

"I was told by Scott about a job that had to be done before we can marry, but gave me no details, could you tell me what it is all about please "Danny asked.

"Miss Danny, Ben please come into the office" Alex invited them.

"Charlie three coffee's please" Alex yelled.

"OK Boss" came the reply.

"Please sit the story I have to tell you is quite long" Alex informed them.

For the next hour Alex explained starting with what had happened in this office they were sitting in, Alex left nothing out and explained in detail about the robbery, about the agents killed, about the rape of the young girl, Alex told them about the part that Laura had to do with the attack her escape, every detail that Alex knew came out, that is what happened Alex ended.

"Mmmm I see" Danny murmured,

"Look! Miss Danny, Miss Laura who I have told you about in the story was so incensed by the deceit and there leaving her for dead, with her dying breath asked Scott to get these men as they were animals, then moments before she died she saw the first man brought to justice, she died with a smile on her face" Alex explained.

"Why Scott" Danny asked.

"Miss Danny when Scott was boy his mother and father was brutally murdered and even then as a boy, made a promise to bring every killer to Justice, of course as he was only a boy no one believed him, but as soon as a job became available Scott went to work and with his wages bought a gun the holster and practiced for hours on end, he accumulating everything a man would need to do ride, hunt and track, put this knowledge to use by tracking everything animal or human, after a couple of years Scott started his promise by becoming a bounty hunter, over the years slowly his reputation grew and became known as the best, yes Scott carried on bringing criminals to justice but when the law had difficulty in catching people who rob and kill, a job like we have, we would seek to employ him, you asked Why, there is no one better at doing the job" Alex informed Danny.

"I see, Scott when proposing to me said when we marry his intension is to give up bounty hunting, so we can settle down together and this is his last job" Danny said.

"Then I will wish you and Scott good luck, over the last few years, Scott has done a great service to the law of this land, therefore has earned his new life, we will be sorry to lose him, but good luck to him anyway" Alex told her

"Alex thank you for telling me Scott's story it has only made me love him more than I did before." Danny murmured.

"Alex thanks, come on sis I don't know about you, but I could do with a cup of coffee" Ben said,

"I agree let's go" she replied.

Back in Muleshoe Scott after having his lunch once more walked back towards the bank for his meeting with Mister Stuart.

"Mister Stuart I want to get the financial part of this job over, so I hope you have a figure for me" Scott asked.

"OK Scott I have spent a lot of time sorting out Wes Arnolds expenses, I even had to spend a bit of time on this case last night because you needed it done as quickly and as soon as possible, anyway this is what I have turned up, after taking of Arnolds depts., the standard bank fees, and omitting the Taylor homestead, it appears the remainder of his estate comes to around $26.000 "twenty six thousand dollars," mister Stuart concluded.

"Arnold's share of the robbery came to $20.000 twenty thousand so please send that amount to the bank in Jayton made payable to Wells Fargo, what money is left is to be divided between the three wives, now Mister Stuart do you have the deed for the Taylor homestead" Scott asked.

"Sure Scott" then handed it to him.

Scott compared the signature to a copy of Wes Arnold's signature they were identical,

"Good who knows about this" Scott asked.

"Just me and you," the bank manager said.

This statement meant the bank manager (Mister Stuart) had forged Arnolds signature himself.

"Mister Stuart when I complete the job, I am doing I am going to get married to get away from my reputation I am travelling so I'm sure we forget the deed" Scot said.

"OK Scott thanks"

"As I leave town, I will drop the deed of to Mrs. Arnold" Scott told him.

"I will see the three widows get their share of the money thanks" the bank manager stated his hand out which Scott shook.

Walking to the livery stable, Scott saddled Blackie and Wes Arnolds horse, then rode to the sheriff's office to pick up Arnold's body.

"Hi! Sheriff" Scott greeted walking into the office.

"Hello, Scott, here for Arnold"

"Yeh! Give me a hand" between them they loaded Arnold across his horse.

"Well sheriff, thanks for your help, got to get going" Scott stuck his hand out they shook hands.

"Good luck Scott" the sheriff said.

Riding at a steady pace it did not take long to come across a smaller road going off to the right of the Main trail Scott followed the track until coming across the homestead

"Hello, the house" Scott called out,

"Come ahead Scott" came the reply

"Howdy Jo" Scott said as Jo went straight to Blacky and patted his neck.

"You're the only other person I know who can do that" Scott said.

"All of the time we were in the stable together we became friends" Jo told him.

"Nice to see you Scott" Barbie omitted as she walked towards him.

"Hi! Barbie, I need a word with you" "OK let's have coffee" Barbie returned.

Scott, Barbie, Jo and Johnny sat around the table on the veranda it being late afternoon the sun still up but in the shade of the porch it felt just right.

"I must get going soon, Barbie I stopped off to give you this" handed her the deed.

"Thank you, Scott," Barbie replied she looked at the signature and smiled.

"The bank had it among Arnold's papers" Scott said

"How did they get there" Barbie asked.

"Barbie when you married Wes Arnold you may not have realised it, but Arnold did know that by the law anything you owned became his not just you but all you owned" Scott informed her.

"You mean I could have lost the homestead" Barbie said astonished

"Well we found it in Arnold his papers as we recuperated the stolen money, now it is yours keep it safe it's your proof of ownership "Scott told her.

"Thank you" she kissed him.

"Johnny look after these two, I must get underway now bye folk" Scott said mounted up and rode back to the trail, they waved, and he waved back.

CHAPTER NINE

I GOT THE MEN WHO KILLED YOUR PARENTS.

Leaving Muleshoe on the main trail, Scott rode for a few miles then stopped to have a smoke sitting in the saddle his leg hooked over the saddle horn reached back and extracted the map then checked it.

When checking the map Scott picked what was thought to be the best route back to the town of Farwell and then possibly the best place to camp as Scott knew it would be the next morning before getting to town. The next morning at around ten am Scott rode into Farwell, as per usual when Scott rode into anywhere with a body over a horse there was interest.

"Hi! Sheriff" Scott greeted pulling up in front of his office.

"Scott it's great to see you" the sheriff exploded.

"I want to know if you will take a body of my hands".

"Whose body are you talking about Scott".

"Wes Arnolds"

"By god Scott, thank you, it will mean a lot to this town".

"Yes, I know".

"Thanks again".

"Well, I must get going there is still two to catch" Scott said climbed in the saddle.

"Good luck Scott" the sheriff said.

About five miles out of town Scott pulled Blacky to a halt to let him blow for a short while, during the time Scott hooked his leg over the saddle horn took out the makings and rolled a cigarette. Picking up the map and began checking the route and distance to his next destination, the town of VEGA.

When riding most of the days Scott came across a river, going through the water to the other bank, Scott turned north riding along the riverbank looking for the ideal place to camp for the night.

"Let's have a early night Blacky" Scott said, then dismounted.

The big horse snorted stopped at a rich grassy part then started to eat, to the horses pleasure, Scott started to relieve the big horse of its Burdon, consisting of the bedroll, rifle and scabbard, saddlebags the saddle and blanket, then slipping of the reins letting him roam, after setting up camp Scott came to the main reason for setting up camp early, laying his change of clothes, taking of his gunbelt, stetson and boots, emptying his pockets, then threw himself into the water, on taking of each item of clothes and washed them, the swim was refreshing, dressing in his spare set of clothing, hanging up the wet clothes to dry, with the coffee ready, and beans in the pot on the fire, plus bacon on the skillet, Scott had a quiet evening for a change putting the job out of his mind for a short moment.

As the first sign of light heralding the coming dawn which also meant it was time for Scott to get back to work, going back to his morning routine, pocked the fire back to life, putting a pot of water on to boil for coffee. Scott washed and shaved had his breakfast, it was back to work.

There is a few sheriff's that after a big disturbance in their town instead of sending a wanted notice out they sometime send a warning notice out to the surrounding towns, Scott while in the sheriff's office in Muleshoe took time to look through the wanted notices, in doing so found a warning notice from a town that has had a problem with a big Dutchman, Scott new that it might not be Dutchy but the man the sheriff reported has done just what Dutchy would be expected to do, it is at least a place to start.

Saddling up and breaking camp Scott took out the map check the direction of travel taking out the makings rolled and lit a cigarette, mounted up and rode out, keeping Blacky at a brisk pace, because of Scott's early night the day before it would take about two and a half days to get to Vega. The first part of the day up to midday proved to be a leisurely ride it being a pleasant day, they rode along the sun making it a good day to ride as they enjoyed the near perfect day.

Getting near to midday Scott was on the verge of stopping for a break when the sound of gunfire came to his ears, Scott nudged Blacky into a faster speed, a brisk walk, remaining alert ready to pull up at any time, by the increased loudness of the gunfire his estimation was the shooters were near, Scott slipped from the saddle pulling the Winchester rifle from its scabbard as hitting the ground on a run to get to a large rock.

Creeping around the large rock formation looking into a clearing where a wagon stood, it looked like there was a man, a woman and three children in the wagon, looking along the barrel of the rifle pointing in the direction of the two shooters, as one of the gunmen had managed to get quite close into a shooting position this man was on the verge of pulling the trigger, Scott adjusted his aim took a breath held his breath squeezed the trigger, the bullet hit the man in the chest this caused the man to jump up revealing his face for the first time before going over to lie flat on the ground, when the man jumped up Scott recognised him as one of the men who had attacked and killed Danny's parents, the second man on witnessing his buddy go down, jumped on his horse and rode like hell, aiming after the running man Scott fired but missed the man who laid low over the horses neck making the target small. Sheathing his rifle back in the scabbard Scott rode to the edge of the clearing stopping short of the wagon then called the greeting to the wagon.

"Hello the wagon"

"Come ahead stranger"

"Howdy folks" dismounting, Scott walked over to the body and checked the assassin was dead.

"Thanks for your help mister"

"The pleasure is mine; the name is Scott".

"Scott, I am Charles this is my wife Greta and these two are the trouble makers".

"I'm happy to meet you all".

"Would you like a coffee Scott" Greta asked.

"Thanks, I will, I was about to have a break, when I heard the shooting".

"In that case why not stay and eat, you are welcome" Charles invited him.

"Why does these men attack us" Greta asked.

"These two men have been attacking and robbing wagons for a while, they pick people who are vulnerable and sometime defenceless".

"This is the second time I have intervened when these men attacked another wagon the last time, they killed my father and mother in laws my fiancée and her brother survived thank god."

"What do you intend to do next Scott" Greta asked.

"This man here I am taking with me, and now I have recognised them as the men who killed my father and mother in-law, I am going to take them to the sheriff in Vega" Scott explained.

"Scott is it far to Farwell" Charles asked.

"It is about a day's ride from here to Farwell, if you start out soon about half way to town you will come across a river, it is a mild river about two feet deep if you turn right as soon as you cross ride about three or four hundred yards you will come across a good place to camp then carry on in the morning, you should get to Farwell around midday tomorrow" Scott explained

"Thanks Scott"

"What do you do Scott" Greta asked.

"Greta" Charles omitted.

"It's alright Charles, I'm a bounty hunter Greta"

"Bounty hunter" she exclaimed.

"Sure"

"Bounty hunters kill people" Greta said.

"You have it wrong Greta, I go after criminals to bring them to the law alive if possible, I always do my best to take them alive, I do have to admit, if the criminals decide to try to shoot me I have to shoot back"

"You killed that man" she pointed to where the body was lying.

"That man was a fraction of a second from killing your husband"

"You still killed him".

"Yes, I did, to save your husband".

"You could have called him to stop".

"Greta, Charles would have been killed, I did not have time to call him".

"You still killed him".

"Greta, I have seen these men kill before they show no mercy, Charles was the only one that had a rifle, these men would have killed him then your two boys, then you would have wished they had killed you before they did" Scott explained.

Scott could see the tension in Greta's jaw, he knew Greta did not like the idea of Scott being around the children and she was determined not to give in, Scott stood up and drank the coffee.

"Greta, it was nice coffee, thank you, I am sorry I have upset you".

Walking over to the horses, taking the reins of the dead man's horse, Scott loaded the dead man onto his horse.

"Charles when you get to Farwell could you go to the sheriff's office and report this matter, I know the sheriff" Scott explained

"Sure, Scott and thanks for saving my life"

"By folks" Scott said climbed into the saddle and rode off.

Getting a little distance from the family Scott lashed the body properly, started looking for sign to get after the man who had ran away. It did not take long to pick up the sign as the man had been in a hurry to get away. It was easy to find out that the man rode a piebald whose rear left shoe was cracked and because of the fact the man was in a hurry so did not attempt to hide his tracks.

One of the easiest reasons he could follow him is the fact that the man did not slow down, kept the horse at a gallop this means the horses hoofs were closer together and deeper, keeping Blacky at a fast walk means they could travel all day but the other man's horse will soon tire, the longer the man keeps his horse at a gallop the sooner the man will have to stop. Scott just carried on following the sign and came across a wooded area where his quarry was forced to slow down, this meant Scott had closed the gap, because the man used the wooded area to hide and rest the horse and could not go on for a while it enabled him to watch the trail behind him that was how the man was able to find out about the man hunting him seeing Scott the man thought of jumping on his horse and running looking at the horse with his head down knew there was no way the horse could make it across the wide open stretch of land in front of him without being seen.

Knowing there was no way possible to avoid the man hunting him, the decision was made up for him meaning the only thing left for him to do was to take Scott out, his next action will have to find a place where it will be possible to ambush the man following him, hunting around the man being hunted found a clear space with flat rock to rest his rifle on facing the trail and approaching man

Riding across the small open area between two tree covered sights Scott spotted the tree covered area ahead and the same idea came to his head that had entered the mind of the hunted man, Scott knew if Blacky needed a rest its certain the big horse would get one and the wood ahead looked just like the place to stop.

Bringing Blacky to a halt hooking his leg over the saddle horn Scott reached into his pocket and extracted the making to roll a cigarette lit it and took a deep draw scanning the tree's it front of him, as the smoke came out slowly through his lips, his thoughts were (What would be the best thing to do) putting himself into the hunted man's mind, (If I was in the position of the hunted man I would find a place where I could shoot the man approaching his position) Scott had stopped just outside rifle range and Knew the man concerned was at that time looking along the barrel of a rifle, when getting to the wooded area it will be a game of cat and mouse but the job is getting there.

Looking at the distance to the tree's Scott realised the distance was not great, keeping low and moving fast it is possible to get to cover without getting shot, finishing the smoke extinguishing the cigarette butt he tethered the dead man's horse then,, Yelling 'Yah!' loudly Blacky went from a standstill to fifty miles an hour in seconds Scott lay low along the neck of the big horse, the sound of two shots being fired could be heard but with the speed of the big horse nothing came near them, often long distance shooting was very hard and is even harder when the target is moving and because Blacky is exceptionally fast the chance of the ambusher hitting the target was small.

Getting to the tree covered area leaving the saddle fast, drawing his rifle at the same time, before advancing into the tree's, now the real game begins, knowing the man that shot at him was on the side of the tree's facing the trail, it was time to think will the man stay there or after shooting did the man decide to move to another position, Scott paused stood still listening to see if it was possible to hear any sounds that would maybe tell him the man moved and in what direction, it was very quiet the birds had stopped singing, small animals had either stopped or hid as the humans intruding into their territory all animal activity ceased.

Hearing a slight noise of to his left Scott now knew the man had moved therefore creeping slowly in the direction of the sound being careful taking one step at a time making almost no noise at all, hearing a small noise to his right this made Scott adjust his direction after a few yards, stopping once again to listen but hearing no noise, he decided to play the oldest trick in the book picking up a stone throwing it in the direction of where his quarry was thought to be, this should maybe make the man move but alas no sound was heard, lowering his body to the ground it was possible to look under the bushes after looking all around there was no visible signs, remaining on the ground his mind was working overtime trying to think what the man could do, putting his ear to the ground, no sound was detected. (If there is no sound and there is nothing on the ground the only way is up).

Looking up Scott saw a slight movement in a nearby tree, letting the rifle go grabbing his revolver he rolled over shooting three shots into the tree as a rifle bullet hit the ground where his body was before moving, a loud scream came from the tree as a rifle dropped followed by a body, getting quickly to his feet Scott rushed over to the prone body pistol in hand quickly relieving the dazed man of his revolver and picking up the rifle.

"Stay still or I will shoot you" Scott ordered

"You shot me" the man screamed as his hand held his shattered knee

Scott did not on purpose shoot the man's knee but the luck of it was in his favour it means the man can give him less trouble. Dragging the man onto a clear patch ignoring his screams the man omitted as the leg scraped along the ground on the left of the clearing stood a stout tree, putting his arms around it the tied them together, retrieving the man's horse bringing it into the clearing also giving out a whistle, mounting up, ignoring the man's screams Scott retrieved the dead man and his horse they returned to the clearing , building a fire Scott made camp putting water on for coffee, taking the bedroll of the assassins horse taking out his spare shirt and ripping it into strips of cloth with apiece of the cloth and the canteen approached the wounded man.

"Right I'm going to attend to your leg" Scott informed the man,

Taking the knife from the sheath in his boot, the man's trouser leg was cut to just above the knee who yelled when Scott straightened the leg with water from the canteen and the cloth, the wound was cleaned making a pad from the damp cloth and using another strip of cloth wrapped the leg, hunting around the clearing two large sticks were found which were also lashed to the leg.

While continuing to sort out the camp the wounded man fell asleep, taking his time first having a cup of coffee then a smoke getting the skillet out started making bacon sandwich's, the wounded man must have smelt the bacon because just at that time the man woke up, untying one hand to allow him to eat the sandwich and drink the coffee Scott settled down with his also.

"Mister we are going to Vega which is a day and a half from here" Scott told him.

"So" the man said shortly.

"So, we are going to take it easy, I want no trouble, or I will have to shoot you"

"I'm not likely to give you any trouble with this leg am I"

"Mister I was not born yesterday" Scott said

"What do you mean by that"

"You know, and I know that you and your two friends, murdered quite a few people therefore you will hang and I know desperate men will do desperate things and leg or no leg if you get the chance you will try to escape" Scott explained.

"So, you think I will try something"

"If you could yes".

"I see"

"In a moment, we start riding by Sundown we should be over those hills up ahead where we will camp then into Vega tomorrow afternoon" Scott informed him.

As soon as they completed eating, Scott cleared the camp, helped the wounded man on his horse then tied him to the horse, they rode on towards the hills, through his experience at being a bounty hunter Scott remained alert,

The next morning at the break of dawn Scott woke up as normal, washed and shaved, woke the prisoner, had breakfast, broke camp, loaded the horses then once again hit the trail as the cavalcade moved out, Scott being a bounty hunter for so long was alert, even though the three men that attacked the wagon and killed Danny's parents were now accounted for it is possible they could have worked with other men so that is the reason for staying alert.

As predicted they cleared the hills by sundown, travelling a mile they found the perfect place to set up camp for the night, now the job of making camp becomes more difficult because there was not only the wounded man to take care of but also his dead partner of course this meant everything takes longer, first task was to see to the wounded man by helping him from the horse, then tying him hands and foot to make sure the man is in no position to cause him trouble while preoccupied making camp the second task was to relieve the horse of the dead body, laying it out just outside the camp area, the third task was to relieve the three horses of there burdens, each horse had on them, Bedrolls, Saddlebags, rifles and scabbard, saddles and reins, the two horses belonging to the prisoners had to be tethered on long ropes, Blacky was left to roam as the big horse will come when Scott whistled.

The heavy work done Scott made camp, coffee and sandwich's, untied the man to allow him to eat then retied him again, at dawn Scott had to do things all over in reverse before the cavalcade could ride on, and with luck they will reach Vega before nightfall. They kept moving all day stopping a couple of times to let the horses blow, Scott and the wounded man had jerky meat and water, stopping a few moments longer each time for Scott to have a smoke, before carrying on, late afternoon Scott leading the other horses rode through the centre of Vega stopping outside the sheriff's office, after tying the horses to the hitch rail, dragging the wounded man from the saddle forcing him to hobble into the sheriff's office.

"Howdy Sheriff I have a couple of presents for you" Scott said as the man was marched into an empty cell, walking to the wall beside the desk, taking down the wanted dodgers thumbed through them and removed the dodgers for the two men.

"Looks like you owe me $800.00 dollars sheriff".

"Who are you" the sheriff demanded.

"Scott Burrows bounty hunter".

"Scott Burrows I've heard of you, in fact I received this wire from Farwell for you".

"Thanks"

From, Sheriff's office, Farwell.   Stop

To, Scott Burrows, sheriff's office, Vega.   Stop.

Greta says she is sorry, now understands, stop.

Charles says, thank you, stop

Good luck Scott, stop

"Scott, you do not normally work this far north" the sheriff said.

"Yes I do come from south of here, but the job I am on has brought me north and that is what I am going to tell you about later, the important thing is that I deal with the job in hand, sheriff these two men were (there was three of them a few weeks ago) and they attacked and killed a man and woman who would have been my future in-laws, now two days ago these two men attacked a wagon travelling to Farwell with a man, woman and two children, also the fact that you have two dodgers for these men proves the point" Scott pointed out.

"OK Scott"

"According to the dodgers you owe me $800.00 dollars".

"Your right Scott" the sheriff said and turned to the safe.

"I was in Farwell a few days ago when looking through the dodgers I came across a warning notice about information of a large Dutchman" Scott enquired.

"Yes, I did".

"Sheriff it is now getting late, so I will see you in the morning, I need to ask you about this man, and I will tell you about the job I am doing" Scott informed him.

"OK Scott here is your money I will see you in the morning".

Leaving the sheriff's office Scott made his way with Blacky to the livery stable at this time of day it was busy so they were lucky to find one empty stall, giving Blacky a nose bag fresh water and checked the stall had clean straw the next stop was the local café, as his target all day was to get to Vega apart from jerky meat had not eaten all day, needless to say Scott was looking forward to a delicious meal.

"The local café was called THE HOLE which is probably because of the sense of humour of the owner, as it was anything but a hole on entry it was a bright, clean and looked good and well taken care of and a lovely place to eat, with tablecloths on each table, Scott enjoyed his meal in the pleasant atmosphere.

After enjoying the wonderful well-cooked meal his thoughts came to partake a lovely long cool drink as the saloon came into sight, standing at the bar after a well-earned beer, and with money burning a hole in his pocket he found a place in. a game at one of the tables.

"Howdy boys I'm Scott" introducing himself.

"This is Jack, that's Billy, he is Alf and I am Mike, and this man is Drummond another stranger to the table," Mike introduced everyone.

"The game is five cards, a dollar to play, a dollar to draw and a dollar to see" Drummond explained.

The game was jolly, everyone seemed to get along with each other, jovial jokes and remarks as they played, an hour into the game, Scott laid his pistol on the table the barrel pointing at Drummond.

"Mister I don't like cheats" Scott challenged the man.

"Who are you calling a cheat" Drummond said loudly.

"I'm calling you a cheat" Scott accused him.

Alf disappeared from the table straight through the batwing doors.

"I can see you want to use that gun, I must advise you not to do it, as you can see my finger is on the trigger of my gun, if you make a move for it you will be dead I promise you" Scott told him.

"What gun" Drummond asked.

"Drummond, you have a derringer up your right sleeve, the slightest move of that arm you will die" Scott warned him.

At that moment Alf returned into the saloon with the sheriff walking straight to their table.

"Hi! Scott what's going on" the sheriff enquired.

"First this gentleman has a derringer up his right sleeve" Scott pointed out.

"Has he now" the sheriff replied.

"Sheriff check his left sleeve, you will see he has cards in a holdout" Scott said as he raised the pistol, pointed it at Drummond and pulled back the hammer.

The sheriff checked Drummond as Scott suggested, and produced a couple of cards.

"Drummond take your coat of now" Scott ordered.

Drummond looked at Scott, but really had no choice with Scott's colt pointing at him with the hammer held back, so removed his coat, the sheriff relieved Drummond of the derringer.

"Mike could you separate the aces and kings from the pack, sheriff can you look at Drummonds fore finger on his left hand you will find it slightly discoloured" Scott said.

"Your right Scott" the sheriff replied.

"Now look at his belt you should see a small pot" Scott advised.

"Yes, it is there why?" the sheriff asked.

"Mike put the aces and kings face down on the table" Scott said.

"Sheriff draw your colt and keep our friend covered." Scott asked.

Scott lowered the hammer on his gun and holstered it, moving his attention to the cards on the table.

"Sheriff if you look at these cards, you will find the aces are slightly different to the other cards, look at the corners they are discoloured the aces one side the kings the other side, you will hardly see them unless you know what to look for" Scott explained.

"By god your right" the sheriff exclaimed.

"You have to have sharp eyes and know what you are looking for, our cheat here has been using a new technique called dubbing, he dips his finger in the pot and flicks the corner of the cards to mark the cards he requires" Scott explained.

"Right mister how did you come to town" the sheriff asked.

"On the stage" Drummond sullenly mumbled.

"You will spend the night in a cell and will be marched to the stage in the morning" the sheriff informed him.

"I'll see you in the morning sheriff" Scott said.

"OK Scott" the sheriff replied, escorted Drummond to the jail house.

"Barman a beer please" Scott ordered.

The barman poured the beer but refused to take Scott's money.

Scott drank the beer, after having a busy day he felt tired so decided to turn in for the night.

As dawn was breaking, Scott's eyes opened after a brief moment he rose carried out his normal morning routine, stood up, stretched, washed, shaved and dressed once satisfied left the hotel made his way to the livery stable to check on his pal, Blacky, who spotted his master and looked happy, the big horse wanted to play Scott played for a while before giving Blacky a nose bag filled the trough with fresh water, at that time the holster arrived.

"Billy after Blacky has finished his breakfast could you let him roam in the corral and muck out the stall for me" Scott requested.

"Sure, will do Scott" came the reply.

Scott proceeded to 'The Hole' to partake in the most important meal of the day breakfast and being able to relish in peace the first mug of coffee, one thing Scott loved was his morning mug of coffee.

From his seat in the café his attention rested on the telegraph office as the agent opened the office, (good) he said to himself as his intention is next to send a wire, completing his breakfast his legs carried him there. Where he sent of a wire to Jayton.

To; – Alex Morrison, Wells Fargo office, Jayton. Stop
From; – Scott Burrows.   Stop

Alex, when my fiancée 'Danny' arrives.   Stop
Could you inform her I have taken the men who killed her Mum and Dad?   Stop
Tell her I love and miss her.   Stop

See you all Scott, stop.

Next stop for Scott is the sheriff's office, arriving just in time to help by escorting the prisoner to the morning stage, returning to the sheriff's office as the stagecoach departed, Scott got straight down to business.

"Sheriff my reason for being here in VEGA is to see you, while in Farwell I took time to look through the wanted dodgers (notices) among them I spotted a warning notice about a Dutchman from you, I have in my pocket a wanted dodger for a man called Dutchy, could you tell me if it is the same man. After examining the wanted dodger, the sheriff exploded.

"Yes, that's the man, the sod"

"Good, now tell me what you know about this man?" Scott asked.

"This man 'Dutchy' did not come into town alone, there was three men with him, but you could see Dutchy was the leader of the group, even though they had just entered town they started causing trouble, I can understand men getting drunk, getting angry and causing a problem, but these four men had just rode into town and were sober, It is obvious this quartet came in to harrow the town, and were determined to do what they wanted, the trouble started straight away at the livery stable, when the four arrived at the livery stable the holster a young man fifteen years old told the four men that the stable was all full up, 'Dutch' and his friends opened up all the stalls and drove all the horses out into the street, the young holster tried to stop them. And he was badly beaten, the boy was in the doctors for four days getting better.

Leaving their horses at the stable this group of trouble makers walked through the town harassing every man, woman or child that was in there way, their next stop was the café, first the waitresses were pushed around, next they stood picking food of other customers plates and threw it around the room, all customers left, the café owner shut what they could down then told the staff to leave by the back door, when the four saw there was no one to serve them they went mad and wrecked the place."

"Because of a bout of rustling taking place at the triple ex ranch (xxx) I was out of town I did not know about these incidents at the time." The sheriff explained.

"To carry on the four must have been hungry because the four men's next stop was the hotel dining room where they did eat, that was before smashing up the place, one of them did attack a female customer but was stopped before hurting her, that was when they decided to go for a drink, retiring to the saloon, there was a brief pause as the group partakes a couple of drinks, after which the four really caused a riot, by first killing two men who tried to stop them, they grabbed a bottle of whisky each then proceeded to shoot up the place and they really went wild shooting at everything including mirrors and decorations, they left the saloon in a mess as the gang paraded through the street braking all premises windows and shooting at anything that moved, just causing havoc, they left town travelling north."

"I arrived back in town, three hours later, I did try following them as best I could, but I have to admit my tracking skills are terrible, after two hours it was getting dark I had no choice but to give up, I felt I had to do something, I sent a warning notice to all town's in the vicinity" the sheriff ended.

"How about rape" Scott asked.

"That is one of the most surprising part of it all, these four men were bent on destruction, killed two men, attacked a few people including some women, but I have not heard of anyone being raped, I think that is unusual under the circumstance" the sheriff told him.

"It is unusual, but in a way, it is good news" Scott said.

"Your right it is good news" the sheriff replied.

"Looking at the map of north Texas, the four men would have to pass through either, Amarilla or Channing, do me a favour sheriff, send a wire to each of these towns for me find out if this gang passed through their town's it will let me know which way to go" Scott asked

"OK Scott, what are you going to do" the sheriff asked.

"Well, it's about time I checked Blacky has food and drink and is ready to ride, I'm going to the café for lunch, next I will wait until you get the answers to your messages, if there is enough time left in the day I will ride" Scott informed him.

Meanwhile in Jayton, Alex Morrison has just received Scott's wire, grabbing his Stetson he rushed towards the hotel, and rapped hard on Danny's room door, Danny answered.

"Hello Danny, I have a wire for you" Alex handed it over.

"Oh! it's from Scott, he is still alive" Danny smiled.

"Yes" Alex said as Danny read the wire

"Ben! Ben," Danny called out.

"What Sis" Ben asked, as he walked through to her

"Scott has caught the two men who killed Mam and Dad and shot you" she said.

"That is great news Danny" Ben replied.

"Alex thank you for bringing me this news, if you get any more please let me know" Danny asked him.

"Don't worry I will" Alex assured her.

"Thank you" she replied as she kissed the wire.

Just before Danny shut the door, the sheriff came rushing towards them.

"Alex" he called out loudly.

"What" Alex demanded.

"He's, done it, He's done it" he called out excitedly

"He and who has done what?" Alex asked.

"Wes Arnold is dead, Scott beat him in a shootout" the sheriff stated loudly.

"I'll be damned!!, Wes Arnold was known as a gunfighter, with the reputation of having a fast draw" Alex exclaimed.

"How" Alex asked.

"It seems, Scott waited until the last minute when he could tell Arnold was about to draw, then broke his concentration as he reached for his gun, Scott was heard to say, (Arnold Laura sent me) this made Arnold hesitate and Scott beat him to the draw" the sheriff explained.

"Weakness" Danny said, "Is Scott all right" she asked.

"Yes! Why? Who are you" the sheriff asked abruptly?

"I am Scott's fiancée" Danny replied in a stern voice.

The sheriff looked at Alex who nodded his head.

"You said weakness, what do you mean" Alex asked.

"Scott told me, everyone has a weakness you just have to find it, to me the weakness for this man Arnold was the mention of Laura" Danny explained.

"Well, I'll be damned" the sheriff omitted.

"I am engaged to marry Scott, I ask again how is Scott" Danny asked.

"He is OK! And I think he will be well on the way to find number four on the list I have just heard this news, and it is a week old" the sheriff explained.

"Oh! Good" Danny sighed with relief.

Scott did exactly what was said earlier in the sheriff's office and waited for the answer of the return messages, the first message to return was from Amarilla, that only informed the sheriff that the men mentioned have not been seen, the message from Channing said that the men described passed through town quickly and quietly after having a meal they rode on.

"Why" the sheriff exclaimed.

"They have either committed a crime and are running wanting to make some distance, or they are being hunted" Scott suggested,

"At least you know which way 'Dutchy' and his gang went" the sheriff told him.

"That is true, thanks for your help sheriff" Scott shook hands.

Going to the café he purchased a bag of food, topped up his canteens, checked his ammunition, all guns loaded and loops in his belt filled, satisfied with his checks, at livery stable, saddled up and an hour after talking to the sheriff he rode north out of town.

Scott estimated by sticking to a steady pace, Channing would be only two days away, so after checking the compass he adjusted his direction, the weather is good and at a steady pace no need to hurry, with frequent stops to allow Blacky to blow, have a rest and smoke. At sunset on the first day Scott arrived on the south side of the Canadian river, finding a good spot by the river Scott dismounted and started to set up camp, there was no need to hunt or cook as he has a bag of food that had been bought in town before leaving.

The next morning after breaking camp, they rode along the river bank until finding a ford, the river is wide but only about two foot deep at the deepest part making it easy to wade across, pausing to roll a cigarette on the other side Scott and Blacky ambled along, about five miles further up the trail the big horse stopped and Scott thought he heard a child crying, Blacky swung his head to the right pointing out where the sound came from so Scott directed the big horse in that way passing through a row of bushes following the noise as it became louder, moving about two hundred yards Scott spotted a young girl about ten years old, keeping his voice low he started talking to the girl.

"Hello" she did not answer and carried on crying.

"Where is your Mam and Dad" Scott asked.

She still did not talk but pointed through the trees.

"Would you like a ride on my horse" Scott asked.

"The girl nodded her head, Scott bent down put his hands under her arms and lifted her up to sit across his knee, with a nudge from Scott the big horse moved forward slowly.

"This horse is Blacky my pal" Scott told the girl.

The girl remained silent and huddled into Scott as they rode through a light wooded area it was beautiful, they travelled for about a mile until coming out into a clearing in front of him was a beautiful setting, a sort of place you dream of a picturesque view of a log cabin and a place you dream of.

Scott suddenly stiffened all was not right in the doorway of the cabin lay a man's body, bringing Blacky to a halt Scott climbed from the saddle then lifted the girl down walking slowly to the white picket fence, from that distance he could see the red blotch of dried blood on the head of the body.

"Stay here" he told the girl.

Moving forward slowly, treading carefully advancing to the cabin door, one brief look told him the man had been dead a few days, stepping around the unfortunate man his pistol in his hand as he crept slowly a step at a time into the cabin, the living room of the cabin was clear except for upturned furniture, but a peek into the master bedroom told a different story the first thing you noticed was the nude body of a woman sprawled across the bed, the lady had obviously been raped but the evidence of torture was plain to see, she apart from being black and blue all over she had belt marks and cigarette burns on her body the thing that put the woman out of her misery was the large knife pushed through her left breast into her heart, Scott shook his head in disbelieve, in this job, a job he had been doing for a while he had seen death many times, but cannot understand why certain people had to torture and make innocent people suffer in pain this way.

Scott straightened the woman's body then placed a sheet over her, going back to the girl outside putting a hand on her shoulder spoke gently to her.

"What is your name" he asked.

"Paula" came the reply.

"Well Paula, I'm afraid your mother and father has gone away" Scott did not know what to say to this young girl.

"I know they are dead, I hoped for the first day that they might be alright but knew as time went by that they were dead, that is why I was near the trail hoping to find someone to help me, and I have" Paula explained.

"OK Paula, I am Scott, let's go to your room" Scott asked, Paula showed Scott her room after looking at her room he told her.

"I see you have jeans and shirts in your cupboard, take that dress of and put the jeans and shirt on, while I prepare your mother and father for burial" Scott said.

"Yes Scott" she said.

"Oh! Paula, after you have changed get a bag and put in it what you need, I will call you after I have buried your parents" Scott told her.

"OK Scott" she replied.

There was a lot to do before they could move on, Scott found a nice, secluded place to put these poor people to rest, where he dug the two graves, getting two sheets from the house, wrapping the bodies then lowered them gently into the prepared graves, taking some pieces of wood from the white painted picket fence he made two crosses.

"Paula come here please" Scott called; she came to him he put his arm around her shoulder as they stood by the graves.

"Scott my mother always told me when you die you go to heaven" Paula remarked.

"Your mother is right Paula; all good people go to heaven and your mam and dad are good people they have gone to a wonderful place" Scott told her softly.

"Where are we going Scott" Paula asked.

"Paula about a day's ride from here there is a town called Channing, where I am certain there will be someone to look after you" Scott informed her.

"Why can't I stay with you" Paula asked.

"Paula, I have a big and dangerous job to do, so it is impossible for you to come with me, now let's saddle up can you ride" Scott said.

"Yes, that is my pony in the corral over there" she pointed.

"Let's ride the sooner we get going the better and the sooner we will get to Channing" Scott told Paula.

As it was, because of the time spent looking after Paula's unfortunate parents it was too late, they camped overnight.

CHAPTER TEN

STRATFORD

At dawn the following morning, when waking up Scott found Paula was still asleep, so he left (let her sleep) while freshening up, shaved, relit the fire, putting water on to boil to make coffee, putting the skillet over the fire and cutting rashers of bacon to make sandwiches, as the bacon sizzled Paula woke up.

"Paula go to the stream, wash your face and hands we will have breakfast then move on" Scott informed her.

"Yes, Scott" Paula acknowledged.

Scott did exactly what was said to Paula, at around ten am the pair started riding down Channing main street, coming to a halt outside the sheriff's office.

"Come on Paula let's see the sheriff" Scott said.

"Do we have to; can't I stay with you" Paula asked.

"Paula, I have been paid to get some very evil men, and it is very dangerous and therefore I cannot take you with me it is impossible, and I must finish the job."

Scott put his arm around her and directed her into the sheriff's office.

"Morning sheriff" Scott greeted.

"Morning, how can I be of service to you"" the sheriff inquired.

"About twenty-four hours south of here, a young couple and their daughter lived near the Canadian, well yesterday I found them the couple are dead the man shot, and the woman tortured and killed" Scott informed him.

"Murdered" the sheriff asked.

"Definitely" came the reply.

"Thank you, mister, how can I know you had nothing to do with the crime" the sheriff asked.

"The name is Scott sheriff, and this is Paula the young people's daughter"

"Hello Paula, did you see the men who killed your mother and father" the sheriff asked.

"Yes, Mammy told me to hide in the bushes, but I did see the four men" Paula said.

"If I show you some pictures, could you tell me if they were there" the sheriff asked.

"Yes" she replied.

The sheriff took the sheaf of wanted dodgers from the hook behind his desk and went through them with her, she picked out three pictures.

"Thank you, Paula," the sheriff said.

"Paula was this man with them" Scott asked pulling 'Duchy's' picture from his pocket.

"Yes! Yes! He was their leader and hurt my mammy" Paula cried.

"Just like in the cave" Scott muttered.

"What do you mean" the sheriff asked.

"Oh! Nothing sheriff I'll explain later, but do you know of someone who could look after Paula" Scott asked.

"Paula, I know of a family who would be happy to take you in they are very good people and a nice family" the sheriff said.

"Sheriff I will look after the office for you if you could get the lady of this family you are talking about" Scott asked.

"OK Scott I won't be long" the sheriff left the office.

"Scott where are you going" Paula asked.

"Paula, the picture I showed you is a very evil man and has committed crime after crime and it is my job to stop him, if you were with me, I would not be able to do my job" Scott explained.

"What are you doing after the job" Paula enquired.

"Back in Jayton, my fiancée Danny is waiting for me, when the job is over, we are going to get married leave this type of work and settle down" Scott told her,

Even though Paula was young she saw the love he had for Danny so said no more. The sheriff arrived back at the office with Mr. and Mrs. Mason who said they would be happy to look after Paula. Paula turned and cuddled Scott.

"Thank you, Scott," Paula said then left with the Mason's.

"Now Scott suppose you tell me what is going on and how I can help" the sheriff asked.

"You received a wire from the sheriff of VEGA about the four men mentioned, I am Scott Burrows and have been after these men, in particular 'Dutchy' for nearly a month, let me bring you up to date" Scott said.

For the next hour over a cup of coffee, Scott told the sheriff the whole story about the robbery to the present day.

"So how can I help you" the sheriff asked.

"All I require is for you to tell me everything the four men did while they were here, but as you know the simplest item of information could give me a clue and help me with the task I have" Scott explained.

"To give you the truth if I had not been on the street at the time, I would have missed them, they were so quiet, riding into town stopped at the café to eat bought things from the general store then rode on" the sheriff told him.

"We have talked for quite a while I think it is time for lunch, and I will do a bit of investigating while at the café, before going to the general store" Scott said

"OK good luck" the sheriff said.

Leaving the office, Scott walked along the street to the café called (The Honey Pot) like most towns the café is a busy place normally but as midday meals are nearly over he had no problem in getting a table, the café was clean and each table had clothes and condiments on them, the waitresses all wore the same type of apron.

"Good day sir, what can I get you" the waitress asked.

"Steak pie, beans and potatoes –please and coffee miss" Scott ordered.

"Yes sir"

"The name is Scott"

"I won't be long Scott" she moved to the kitchen.

She was right it did not take her long, only a few moments, she came back with a plate laden with food, and an extra-large mug of coffee.

"That looks great, why is the café called the honey pot" Scott asked.

"The owner is called Honey" the waitress said.

"Miss, do you have a few moments to spare, I'd like to ask a few questions" Scott asked.

She looked around the café it was quiet, and no one was calling for a waitress.

"Scott my name is Norma, if a customer comes in, I will have to serve them, what do you want to know" she asked.

"A few days ago, four men stopped for a meal, one of them was a big Dutchman called 'Dutchy' were you here and what can you tell me about them" Scott asked.

"Why are you asking" Norma asked.

"This man killed a friend of mine, and I want to avenge my friend" Scott had decided to tell Norma, and by the look on her face she did not like the four men.

"Scott the four men came in and sat at the corner table and ordered there food as normal and ate there food without any incident, I approached there table to ask if they would like anything else, one of them a short man going bald said (I want you), I told him he could not have me, this man moved so fast I could not avoid him, he grabbed me and threw me face down across the table, he grabbed my breast, and when I say grab I mean it, it hurt so much I screamed, his other hand started to raise my dress, two of the towns men who sat at another table came to their feet with guns in their hands, another member of the group said to Alf, (Stop it we don't have time for that) this man called Alf dragged me of the table and dropped me on my face onto the floor, the four men left the two customers helped me to my feet, I thanked them, Scott I believe if those two men had not stopped them I could have been raped" Norma explained.

"Can you tell me anything about these men" Scott asked.

"As you can tell, I remember that night very well, I can tell you the big man and leader is called Dutchy but you know that, the small man slightly shorter than me is called Alf he moves quickly, the next man was younger with thick long dark hair they called him Steve, the fourth man I did not get his name, but he smoked continues he had a fancy gunbelt with a white handled revolver, I'm afraid that is all I can remember, there is one thing I can tell you these men are dangerous so take care" Norma warned Scott.

"Thank you, Norma, believe it or not you have given me some good points to start with, a few things I can look for, I'll have to say goodbye now" Scott said.

"Goodbye Scott" Norma excused herself.

Stopping on the street, leaning against a post he pulled out the makings, rolled a cigarette lit it and drew deeply, before proceeding to the general store, stepping from the boardwalk Scott crossed the dusty street to the store.

Walking into the general store he went to the counter where a young man asked if he could help him.

"I'd like to see the manager please" Scott requested.

"Mr. Stevens" the young man yelled.

A middle-aged man the sides of his hair greying came through from the rear of the shop calling sharply.

"What"

"This gentleman has asked to see you" the young man said

"Hello, my name is Stan Stevens store manager how can I assist you."

"A few days ago, four men came through this town, the sheriff said one of the places they stopped at was this store, I wonder if you and your staff can recall it and anything you could remember about them and their visit that may help my cause" Scott told him.

"The one thing I can tell you is the gang headed north out of town, I know that does not really help as there is to directions you can go to either Hartley and Dalhart and Stratford" Stan told Scott.

"You two come here" Mr. Stevens called to his two assistants,

"You want us boss" the young man asked.

"Yes, I want you, I called didn't I" Stevens growled at the young man.

"What is wrong boss" the young lady assistant asked.

"Nothing is wrong, a few days ago four men came into the store, and made some purchases can you remember what they bought" Stan asked.

"I remember them, two of the men bought tobacco" the young lady said.

"Do you know which brand" Scott asked.

"Yes, they smelt the tobacco before buying" she replied.

"Which one miss" Scott said.

"This one sir" as she lifted the pack of the shelf and handed it to him,

Scott excepted the pack, opened it and smelt it.

"I will buy this pack" Scott told them.

Buying a pack of his favourite brand, the type of tobacco the two men bought was very strong, the smell of the pack he bought will help to track the men as he compared it to bits on the trail showing which direction the gang went.

"One of the men, bought a blue checked shirt and a leather band for his Stetson" the young man said.

"I don't think they bought anything else if I remember right, but I do remember one of them saying (he cannot wait to get to the ranch)" the young lady said.

"Thank you all, you have been an immense help, the tobacco most of all will help as cigarette ends take time to decompose, which gives me something to look for" Scott explained.

Now his investigations are complete, Scott started walking towards the sheriff's office but did not get there as he met the sheriff in the street doing his rounds.

"Evening sheriff"

"Howdy Scott, I guess you will be leaving soon" the sheriff stated.

"Yes, sheriff I have been lucky to be able to get enough details and sign to enable me to follow, Dutchy and is a gang, thanks for your help" Scott held out his hand.

Scott returned to his hotel room, checked his weapons making sure he had enough shells in his saddle bags, collected a bag of food from the café, proceeded to the livery stable and picked up Blacky who was happy to see him, an hour after meeting the sheriff Scott rode out of town, a couple of miles out of town, dismounting he surveyed the trail, due to the fact that he smoked himself an how addictive it can be, so started to scan the trail more stringently, with patience Scott searched every inch of the ground until he found crunched into the trail the remains of a cigarette but it was old, picking it up and smelling the strands of tobacco with enough Oder to identify it to the brand of tobacco bought at the store, he smiled but could not relax, it is not certain as it could have been dropped by anyone using the trail into town.

Climbing back into the saddle, riding up the trail for a few miles until arriving at a junction in the trail and two signs one to Dalhart the other to Stratford, dismounting Scott started a detailed search of the two branches for clues, it means finding something to indicate which branch the gang took.

This is where searching and investigating begins the odd fag butt is one thing but there is lots of other signs to look for hoof prints, broken twigs and branches miscellaneous things that may be dropped, but then there was luck.

Scott carefully walked along the left branch for about two hundred yards found no sign so marked the position and retraced his steps back to Blacky who stood waiting for him, taking the right trail, Scott carried out the same routine with the same result, going back to Blacky climbing into the saddle he rode up to the marker on the left trail dismounted and walked the next two hundred yards and once more found nothing, whistling he called Blacky, rode back to the junction and the first two hundred yards to the right and continued with his search, this is where a tracker earns his money. Scott painstakingly hunted for any sign that could be found he found what was needed to know but from an unexpected source, walking up the trail his head down scanning the trail, when he heard a young boys voice.

"Have you lost something mister" a young boy asked.

"Hi boys where you going" as he talked to the four young boys facing him.

"We have been fishing, and on our way home" one boy said.

"I see about four days ago four friends of mine rode through town, I don't know which way they went I have lost their sign, I am trying to find them" Scott told them.

"You said four nights ago mister" one boy asked

"Yes"

"That was the last night we went fishing and we had a swim" another boy said.

"Yeh! I remember four men did ride by" the first boy said.

"If it helps a big man was with them" one of the boys stated.

The boys had pointed to the route to Stratford.

"Thanks boys now I know they rode this way you have saved me a lot of time, I'll find them" Scott said.

"That's OK mister" a boy said

Scott found in his pocket a handful of change and gave the boys two dollars each.

"Thanks again boys" saying as mounting up.

Riding on Scott took the branch to Stratford, and found the place the four men stopped to let their horses blow, that is why it had been hard to find their sign the four men had rode hard from the town as it was over four days since they rode through all sign had been rubbed out and the smokers did not have a chance to roll a smoke until now.

It was now possible to track them easier, the horses were one black, two brown and a piebald, there was numinous fag (cigarettes) ends around the area, it turned out to be a hard search, but he was successful the weather helped by being good for the last few days.

By following the signs, the quartet avoided every town on route, they skirted around Huntley heading towards Stratford this put three more days on his journey he had not accounted for but it did not really bother him as he could make his supplies last, but he also noticed there was an abundance of wild life if it became necessary to hunt.

With two of the four men smoking they made it a lot easier to follow, not that it matters he was now certain that their destination is Stratford, even though he was now certain their destination is Stratford, it being a habit he still looked for sign.

By the amount of territory he had travelled, estimating Stratford would be roughly five maybe six miles away Scott came upon a ranch boundary post it had not been attended to for quite some time weeds and long grass almost covered it but the brand was visible which told him he was on the rolling B ranch, the rolling B brand is a B inside a circle, Scott also noticed there was no one around and at this time of day there should be hands foraging for stray's, a lot goes on at a ranch but when he did work for a while on a ranch a good foreman has everything covered from past experience the signs are not right.

Scott was a little puzzled as he had not seen or heard of this brand before, he will enquire about it in Stratford, with this in mind he carried on to Stratford he was surprised at not seeing a soul until arriving in Stratford in the late afternoon, of course his first act was to see to Blacky, so he rode to the livery stable.

"Hi! Sir, can I help you" a young man asked.

"I would like a clean stall a bucket of clean water and a bag of oats, we have travelled a while and he needs some rest, son he is a one-man horse so don't go near him, he does not like strangers" Scott informed the boy.

"Yes sir, the end stall on the right is empty and clean and here is the bag of oats you require" the young man stated.

"The name is Scott" and sat talking to the young man while Blacky ate this gave him the chance to ask a few questions as stable hands new everything that went on about town.

"My name is Matt" the boy informed him.

"Happy to know you Matt, who owns the stable" Scott enquired.

"The boss is called Dutchy, but he only comes to check on me once a day the stable is mainly left to me or my friend Andy" the young man explained.

"Make sure you tell Andy about Blacky" Scott reminded him.

"Oh, I will Scott"

"Where would I find this man Dutchy" Scott asked.

"He spends most of his time in the saloon" Matt said.

"I see you have a horse in the next stall with a rolling B brand, I haven't heard of that brand before who does it belong to" Scott enquired.

"The horse belongs to Dutchy butt the brand is mister Bates ranch"

"Mister Ronald Bates" Scott said

"Yes" Matt replied.

"Thank you, Matt," as he headed for the hotel.

Walking down the main street he was deep in thought and in a way relieved to see that the last two men he was hunting were here in the same place, but he must tread carefully, Scott was beginning to feel as if everything was not right, if word gets out about his task, he could have one hell of a problem so has come to the conclusion it will be best to say nothing to anyone that includes the sheriff.

It might be possible to pump Matt for more information later when he goes back to see Blacky but he must not over do it as Matt might smell a rat, as he carried on walking down Main street he paused to admire the new Winchester rifle displayed in the gunsmith's window, as he looked there was a reflection in the window of Dutchy as he walked towards the livery stables.

On his arrival in his room at the hotel, because he had been riding for some distance knew a good wash was necessary so stripping he washed himself all over with a bowl of water and a hand towel and dressed in a clean set of clothes, leaving the hotel his next stop is the local café 'SANDIES STOP' walking in the first person he spotted was the bald headed man called Alf, and another man sitting at a table in front of him.

Scott sat at the table opposite the table the two men were sitting, a pretty young lady a waitress approached Scott's table, she quickly avoided the grabbing hands of Alf to come to Scott's table.

"Hello sir, what would you like" she asked.

"I know what I would like" Alf sneered at her, she looked a little scared.

"Steak and Ale pie, mashed potatoes and veg please plus a large mug of coffee please miss.

"Yes sir" she acknowledged, then walked behind Scott up the side of the café so she can avoid Alf.

A few moments later the young lady walked towards him with a mug of coffee for Scott, she almost reached the table when the man with Alf took the coffee out of her hands as Alf grabbed the girl.

Scott stood up his revolver in his hand thumb holding back the hammer.

"Let her go now" Scott ordered; Alf let her go

"Now miss the gentleman seems to like my coffee, he can keep it I will pay for it could you get me another please" Scott ordered loudly.

The girl nodded and left the room, looking around the room he saw the customers leaving the room some leaving incomplete meals on the table, lowering the hammer he holstered the pistol but left the loop of the hammer.

After a few moments, the waitress returned carrying a tray with Scott's dinner and coffee, Alf once again grabbed the waitress again, the tray of food went flying across the room, Alf threw the girl face down across the table, the other man taking her dress up, there intensions to Scott were obvious, standing up pushing the chair behind him.

"Right, you two" Scott called.

Both men turned going for their guns, Scott drew and fired at Alf the bullet hit Alf in the face which turned to a red blotch as the back of his head open spewing blood and brains all over the next table, but not before Alf got off a shot which missed Scott's head by a fraction of an inch, Scott quickly sat down on the chair levelled his pistol with both hands, resting his arms on the table, but the second man did get of two shots one going through his left arm, the other man fell back two, holes in his chest the blue shirt turning red, colt in hand he checked the two men were dead.

The sheriff burst through the door gun in hand.

"What happened here" the sheriff asked.

"Sheriff I am a stranger to your town, I came into the café ordered a meal, as the waitress came out with my order, the man with the bald head pushed the tray out of the ladies hands, I stood up and told the man that he owed me a dinner, I don't know these men and I don't know why they reached for their guns, I shot it out with them" Scott explained.

"Mister you are under arrest"

"NO, I am not"

"What do you mean NO" the sheriff blurted out.

"Sheriff I am a lawyer and under the constitution of the state of Texas a man is allowed to defend himself if attacked, I was certainly attacked by these two men, they drew first I had to fight two men, I have a hole in my arm to prove it, plus you only have to ask these ladies, who can confirm I tell the truth, so you have no grounds for murder" Scott explained.

"Misters get out of town" the sheriff demanded.

"Sheriff, I'm hungry, I intend to have my dinner, go to the doctors and get my arm seen to, then I will consider whether I should leave town, but it will be my decision not yours" Scott told him.

The sheriff glared at Scott, growled turned around and slammed the door. Not being stupid Scott read the signs and now knew the sheriff is bent; after eating and seeing the doctors he has decided to leave town butt not go far, find a place to camp and do his investigations from there.

"Excuse me miss, could I have the meal I ordered" the waitresses face lit up and spoke.

"Yes sir" the girl smiled.

As Scott ripped the sleeve of his shirt a middle-aged woman approached the table.

"Can I help you with that" she asked.

"It's OK I'm only stemming the flow of blood until I see the doctor" Scott said.

"May I sit" she asked.

"Sure"

"My name is Sandie, I own this café, I'd like to thank you for stopping those men from raping my daughter" she said

"That's OK, I don't like animals like them"

"The meal is on the house, and any other time you eat here, is there anything else I can help you with" she asked.

"I know by our encounter that the sheriff of this town is bent do you know of anyone I can trust" Scott asked.

"I never said this, the doctor and the newspaper editor, thanks again" Sandie told him.

Sandie moved off as her daughter arrived with a tray topped up with food the dinner was so large you could not see the plate, a large steaming mug of coffee and a desert of apple pie and cream.

"Thank you, mister, here is your dinner"

"The name is Scott"

"Well thanks again Scott.

As Sandie supervised the removal of the bodies and her girls cleared up the miss Scott left it to them, he ate his dinner with relish, then left with praises ringing in his ear as he proceeded to the doctors house, Scott notice the man tailing him straight away but kept on walking pretending he had not spotted him, the man was not very good he stood out like a sore thumb, on purpose he banged loudly on the doctors door

"Who's there" a voice rang out.

"Doc, I have a hole in my arm that needs fixing" Scott replied. The door opened.

"OK come in" the doctor said.

"Doc, I need your advice" Scott told him.

"One thing at a time, lets sort this wound first, how did you come by it" Doc asked.

Scott smiled, that is not the type of question you would ask a stranger, but because he had asked the doctor for advice, the doctor was fishing, seeing if he could trust Scott.

"I'm afraid two men at the café Sandie's Stop tried to take me out and failed".

"What did they look like" Doc asked.

Scott told the doc what happened and gave a good description of the two men.

"Ah! Bates henchmen" Doc said sarcastically and nodded his head.

"Look Doc, I am one of your patients, and you will not repeat to anyone what I have to say, I know the sheriff is bent and I need someone I can trust, and I have been told I can trust you, is that true.

"Yes mister, from what you have told me, you can trust me anything we say will not leave this office".

"OK Doc, the name is Scott, can you tell me who else I can trust in this town" he asked the Doc.

"Whoa! Hold it there I said you can trust me, but I am not giving the names to anyone, particular a stranger". Doc announced.

"OK Doc, I understand to gain any confidence one of us will have to open up and since you have told me nothing will be repeated outside this room I will explain I'll put my cards on the table, I am Scott Burrows bounty hunter, (Scott told the Doc everything from the robbery in Jayton until the present day) so I need to take Bates and Dutchy it's been six weeks since I started this job after taking these last two out the job will be complete" Scott explained.

"Scott thank you for trusting me, you have come to the right person, there is a few of us in town that will be happy to see the back of Bates and Dutchy, I will speak to them on your behalf" Doc replied.

"I take it Sandie is one she told me about you" Scott told him the Doc nodded.

"OK Scott this is the situation, just over a month ago Ron Bates arrived in town went to the bank and bought the deed for a rundown ranch just out of town and called it the Rolling B ranch, most of the residents of the town thought it was a good thing new blood, new custom, being a small town we were all happy about new investment in the area, but the only person he associated with was Dutchy who had recently purchased the towns livery stable, around the same time three men arrived at the ranch, we were told they were ranch hands but anyone could see they were gunmen and undesirable men, then the sheriff we all know is crooked joined forces with Bates, now the three men Bates recruited whenever they came to town caused trouble and the sheriff backed them up, the town's population became scared and terrorised no one would talk to each other mistrust was everywhere, mainly because of the two men you took out tonight women would stay indoors every time the two were about few men ventured out also, Ha! Ha! Ha! believe it or not you have taken out half the opposition tonight" the Doc ended.

"Now I need to know of Bates and Duchy's movements"

"What do you want to know" Doc asked.

"There daily routines I have to capture them at roughly the same time so I have to work out how I can do it" Scott explained.

"I see, I will make a few checks" Doc said.

"What now Scott" Doc asked.

"A trip to the general store to stock up with supplies, then I will mount up and ride out of town this will make the sheriff relax, but don't worry I am not going far I will, camp outside town then I will scout the rolling B see what I can pick up, I am going to sneak back to see you from time to time" Scott explained.

"OK Scott see you soon" Doc said.

"Doc, you have a stall out back, I will knock on your rear door tomorrow night after dark" Scott informed him.

Leaving the Doc's house, he walked towards the livery stable deep in thought thinking of the information he had gathered, suddenly the scream of an angry horse shattered the night air, Scott ran the rest of the way but heard voices as he arrived.

"Sir you should leave the horse alone" young Matt said.

"Shut up you little brat" Dutchy said.

"He's not your horse"

"He will be or dead"

"You cannot do that "young Matt said.

"Yes, I can" Dutchy drew his revolver pointing it at Blacky

The night was shattered by a single shot as it echoed through the stable the shot from Scott's .45 tore the pistol from Dutchy's grip.

"Mister if you had shot my pal, you would be dead also" Scott warned him.

"I'm going to kill you" Dutchy said.

"OK pick up your gun" Scott said there was a pregnant pause.

"No" Dutchy yelled as he rushed at Scott arms ready to grab Scott

Quickly side-stepping Scott brought his pistol down on the side of Dutchy's head Dutchy stumbled, climbed to his feet shook his head then charged again, seeing the affect the pistol did Scott decided to disguard it, so when Dutchy charged again Scott moved in to meet him, grabbing Dutchy's shirt going back onto his back using his legs he propelled him across the stable. Most men would have been finished after that throw, butt Dutchy was built like a buffalo, and acted like a raging bull, Scott knew the most important thing to do is to keep out of the way of Dutchy's outstretched arms and the bear hug, Scott could see that Dutchy was getting madder and madder and now being very angry, did not think and charged again, Scott waited until Dutchy came close, then quickly side stepped, using his leg swept Dutchy's legs from under him, with the momentum of speed Dutchy's body flew in a dive through the air his head came in contact with a solid gate post at the entrance of the stable which knocked him out, walking over to Dutchy Scott made sure he was still alive, picking up his pistol, checked it was loaded holstered it and put the thong on the hammer as he crouched gasping for breath,

"You alright Scott" Matt asked.

"Sure" Scott croaked trying to get his breath back.

Going to the horse trough, stuck his head under the water, dried himself of and patted Blacky's neck, then started saddling up, he rode to the hotel picked up his gear, rode out of town, the sheriff saw him go and was elated not knowing that he was not going far,

Riding out of town for about three miles, leaving the main trail he rode on until finding a good place to make camp, as it was dark now there was no way he could build a fire so had a cold camp until morning.

Scott had a lot to think about with both of the men he has hunted being in the same vicinity his mind was on how to be able to capture both men taking them alive, then there is the trip back to Jayton, which is about ten days ride from Stratford, being able to manage to get both men will be quite a fete getting them to the destination, wanting to avoid other town's on route, also the supplies needed for three men for ten days, he could maybe make one stop about half way through the journey.

Just before dawn the next morning Scott's eyes opened but lying still his ears listening to the sounds around him, a few seconds listening a smile came to his face, the sound of the dawn chorus plus Blacky chomping away at the lush green grass, Scott was not in any hurry as it is his intension to do a couple of tasks before seeing the doctor so took his time.

Making a fire, placing a pot of water on it to make coffee, while waiting for the water to boil, pulled out the skillet and started slicing bacon, before the water boiled Scott poured a little out of the pot to wash and shave, once the water boiled he made the coffee put the pot with the remaining water over the fire and threw a handful of beans in the pot, by the time Scott had finished his ablutions (washing and shaving), the coffee had settled in the pot, the beans almost ready and the bacon sizzled away.

Scott took his time over breakfast, the bacon sandwich was great, the beans tasty, but the best part of breakfast was sitting back relaxing with a mug of coffee in his hands.

"Ah! Blacky this is great" he said and relaxed.

Scott sighed, his moment of pleasure came to an end, he broke up camp and saddled up, when ready to ride, having a quick look around to check everything had been done before riding out.

"Come on boy, back to work" talking to the big horse as he always did.

The destination that was on his mind is the rolling B ranch, which is going to take a little time as his present position is north of town and the rolling B is south of the town, and it will take time as he must make a big circle to totally miss the town, not wanting to go through the town, once south of the town Scott became more alert checking everything as he travelled, coming across a ranch boundary marker, or should he say what is left of a boundary marker, it has had no attention, by rubbing the top of the post he could just make out the rolling B brand, a little further he spotted an abandoned line shack and decided to check it out, once again there was signs of complete neglect.

This once more started Scott thinking, asking himself questions, why did Bates buy this ranch, it is not being operated as a ranch and from what he could see the men Bates has hired so far are not cowhands, in fact from what he could understand none of the men Bates has employed would not know one end of a cow to the other.

Scott new that the line shack could come in handy, he had an idea but put his idea to the back of his mind for the time being, another sign of neglect was the state of the cattle that roamed about, Scott reflected to himself if the ranch had been ran properly it could be successful and make a prophit.

Seeing the thin trail of smoke up ahead, he knew that the ranch house was not far ahead, moving forward slowly, stopping pulling Blacky back as he saw the ranch house about a mile away, dismounting he took his glasses (binoculars) from his saddle bag.

Scott did not want to be seen and there was less chance now he had taken out half of Bates employees in the café in town, but Bates still has two men left, there is Lenny the man with the thick dark hair and one other.

Crawling onto the small mound in front of him Scott started looking down on the ranch, scanning every inch the stables, bunkhouse, ranch house and corrals apart from a few horses in the corral there was no movement on the ranch to be seen. Turning his attention to the surrounding area, on the opposite side of the ranch house he noticed that trees and brush came almost right down to the house if he rode around he would have deep cover and enable him to get a lot nearer, maybe be able to get near the ranch house itself.

Scott returned to Blacky, mounted up and started riding in a large circle keeping well out of sight of the ranch house which made him lose a bit of time, but he did eventually make it into the forest of trees behind the house, checking it out he found that he was able to creep right up to the ranch house being happy about that, going back up the way he had arrived reaching the top of the slope at the top he rode about two miles away from the ranch. Scott found a safe place to set up camp.

CHAPTER ELEVEN

THAT'S WHAT IT IS ALL ABOUT

It was dusk as Scott started for town, it was still quite warm because of the sun during the day, he had timed his departure at this time as it would be just after dark when he hits town, when reaching Stratford instead of going down the main street guiding Blacky down the rear of the buildings until reaching the doctors house, Scott put Blacky into a stall behind the Doctors house and rapped at the rear door of the Doc's house.

"Hi! Doc" Scott greeted.

"Evening Scott the Doc replied.

"Doc, I'd like to get from you a list of those I can trust in town, being a stranger, I need to know who I can trust, I have already found the sheriff is bent and untrust worthy" Scott admitted.

"The people you can definitely trust are; – Sandie at the café, Henry the newspaper editor and Smithy the Gunsmith" Doc informed him.

"It's important I find out how Mr. Turner the bank manager stands" Scott said.

"To tell you the truth few people know where Mr, Turner stands he is a very quiet conservative person and keeps mainly to himself" Doc explained.

"Doc, who do you think is the best person to ask about Mr. Turner the bank manager" he enquired

"Sandie" Doc said

"Sandie"

"Yes, I suppose most of the business use the bank including Wells Fargo, but I know Sandie is trustworthy and I would ask her". Doc told him.

"You said Wells Fargo, do you know if they are friendly with the sheriff, also do you know of any of the Wells Fargo staff" Scott asked.

"No Scott"

"What about the rest of the town" Scott asked.

"Look Scott, the people of this town have been terrorised and are frightened to speak to themselves they will avoid telling the truth, most of the people in the town do not like Bates, Dutchy or the sheriff, these three and the people who work for them are vicious, and the towns folk will avoid coming into contact with these men, basically the town is scared" Doc explained.

"What's the Wells Fargo managers name Doc"

"Adams why"

"I am officially working for Wells Fargo, I guess I will have to have a friendly talk to him, I've got to have a talk with Sandie first, see you Doc," Scott said.

"OK Scott"

"Doc, can you get the people you have talked about together tomorrow night here at your house "Scott asked.

"I'll see what I can do"

"By Doc" Scott slipped out of the door.

Pulling his Stetson down over his face he nipped across the street, down the alley turned left stopped at the rear door of the café, tapping on the door, Sandie's daughter opened the door, Scott put a finger over his lips.

"I want to talk to your mum" he said in a muffled voice.

"OK" she whispered. A moment later Sandie emerged

"Hi! Scott" Sandie greeted

"Shhh Sandie I'm trying to keep away from the sheriff

Sandie's daughter came out stuck a large steak sandwich and a cup of coffee into his hands.

"Scott eat we will talk when you are finished" Sandie said.

Scott relished the sandwich because he realised, he had not eaten all day.

"How can I help you Scott" Sandie enquired

"Sandie how well do you know Adam's the Wells Fargo manager, do you know how he gets on with the sheriff" Scott asked.

"I don't know much about him, I have never seen him with the sheriff, the man does say hello when he comes in and is polite, a gentleman" Sandie said.

"Mmmm I suppose I will have to take a chance, see him and ask him and find out where he stands" Scott murmured.

"Scott the Wells Fargo office closes at ten and it is ten to ten now"

"Thanks Sandie" Scott said and keeping under cover left and walked towards the Wells Fargo office.

When he arrived at the rear entrance to the office, he could see the light was still on sneaking a peak through the window and saw the manager locking up, Scott waited for Mr, Adams to leave the building and lock the door before he spoke.

"Good evening, Mr, Adams" Scott said.

"Who are you" Adams asked.

"My name is Scott Burrows"

"What do you want" Adams asked. Scott putt his cards on the table.

"I work for Wells Fargo, and I need to talk to you" Scott told him.

"Then let's go to the saloon and talk" Adams suggested.

"No Mr. Adams, I cannot do that, I am an undercover agent, I am working and must not be seen" Scott explained.

"How can I help you" Adams asked.

"First, how is your relationship with the sheriff"

"I don't have anything to do with that man, he is not fit to be sheriff" Adam's replied.

"Mr. Adam's the sheriff works for, or should I say is paid by Ron Bates where do you stand with Bates" Scott asked.

"I have done no business with Bates, I do not now him, why" Adams asked.

"Did you hear about the robbery and murders in Jayton" Scott asked.

"Yes of course I did"

"Ron Bates was the leader of the gang who pulled of the robbery" Scott told him.

"You're kidding"

"I'm afraid not, Bates is a murderer, a robber and rapist and I want him" Scott" said.

"I see" Adam saw the look on Scott's face.

"How well do you know the bank manager" Scott asked.

"Quite well really I am courting his daughter" Adams said.

"He's not in cahoots with Bates or the sheriff" Scott asked

"No Scott"

"Good, you can tell him, about me and that I will be coming to see him but do it discreetly I don't want anyone to know about me" Scott informed him.

"OK I will let him know" Adams said.

Going back to Sandie's he knocked on the rear door again.

"Sandie, have you met the Bank Manager" Scott asked.

"Yes" she said.

"Do you trust him"

"Scott, I have met him a few times, as far as I am concerned, he is an honest man and yes I think you can trust him" Sandie told him.

"Thank you, Sandie," then Scott disappeared back to the Doc's house to pick up Blacky. The doctor came to the door.

"Well Doc, I have my answers, I hope to see you tomorrow night" Scott climbed into the saddle and rode into the night.

The next morning after the usual start he found a good position in the woods to be able to observe anything that goes on down below on the ranch, this part of the job takes a lot of patience as you must sit and watch the ranch for hours, After his breakfast Scott started watching with a canteen of water and some jerky meat, he stayed there all morning and just after lunch he spotted a man riding towards the ranch, picking up his glasses (Binoculars).

"What the hell is he doing here" Scott said to himself.

Scott carried on watching the approaching figure of the sheriff, about half an hour later the second man arrived, Scott was not surprised to see this man 'Dutchy' but Scott realised he must get nearer to enable him to hear what is going on, creeping down the tree covered hillside facing the rear of the house, assuming all the men were gathered in the lounge at the front of the house he ran the last twenty yards from the trees to the side of the ranchouse, flattening himself alongside the building he inched around silently step by step, as it was a warm day most of the windows were open to allow air to flow through the building, this was good and meant Scott could crawl near enough to enable him to hear what was going on.

What Scott heard cleared up many things that had been puzzling him, like why Bates did the robbery, to raise the money to buy the ranch, and the reason for doing it, plus the reason Bates had hired criminals in place of cowmen and why the sheriff is aiding Bates.

As the meeting comes to an end they all settled down to having a beer, Scott retraced his steps, ran across the gap between the building and the bushes and trees up through the trees to where Blacky waited then rode to his camp, making a cup of coffee then sat and mulled over what he had heard, before working out what his actions must be to stop the events the group planned to do, one of the items talked about was to take out the six homesteads around the ranch.

Now near dusk, Scott broke camp, saddled Blacky getting under way in the direction of the town as he had previously done to the Docs house, timing his arrival for just after dark, tapped on the door.

"Evening Doc" Scott greeted.

"Hi! Scott".

Walking into the living room, there was three men Adams and two others.

"Scott, you know Mr. Adams" Doc said.

"Jim" Adams said.

"This is Mr. Turner the bank manager.

"How do you do" Scott said.

"And this is Henry the editor of the newspaper" Doc introduced.

"Howdy" Scott said.

"I heard you wish to see me" Mr. Turner asked.

"Yes I do, but I would have preferred it to be tomorrow or the next day and mainly by yourself, but as long as Henry promises not to print what I say tonight until I say so, I will let you know what I want to see you about and Henry if you do hold of printing the story, I will give you the story of a lifetime" Scott asked Henry.

"I promise I will not write anything that is said tonight or until you tell me I can" Henry promise.

"Doc, Jim." Scott asked.

Doc and Jim give their word also said that what was said in the room tonight would stay there until told otherwise.

"Mr. Turner, have you heard about the robbery and murder in Jayton down south on the Wells Fargo office" Scott enquired.

"Yes, the gang got away with one hundred thousand dollars (100.000)" Turner admitted.

"Well Ron Bates and Dutchy were part of that gang, Bates was the leader, they committed robbery, murder and rape, you all know me just as Scott which officially is true, but my full title is Scott Burrows bounty hunter, Wells Fargo and the sheriff's office tried everything and everybody they could to get this gang and failed, the sheriff and a dying young lady called Laura, asked me if I would take the job, I excepted it, I have spent almost six weeks tracking them I am now down to the last two" Scott explained.

"I see, why do you not capture and take them now" Jim asked.

"The main reason is the sheriff, yes he is bent, but he is the law wears the badge It would be against the law, if I caught them now the sheriff would have them out on some reason, no I have to make it permanent and I will" Scott explained.

"Henry when I am ready, I have a fantastic story for your readers" Scott informed him.

"Now Mr. Turner the reason I wanted to see you and Jim together is when I am finished here the Bates RANCH (The Rolling B) and Dutchy's livery stable will have to be sold and Bates and Dutchy's assets will have to be sent to the bank in Jayton to be returned to Wells Fargo, that's why Jim is here, the money is a Wells Fargo payroll, obviously you will take your normal payment for work done, also Mr Turner what I have to tell Henry will benefit not only the town but yourself" Scott told them.

"By the way you are talking it will improve my business in town" Turner said.

"Yes"

"Well Scott will I see you tomorrow" Doc asked.

"As of yet I do not know, but I may see you I will knock as usual" Scott said.

Scott left the Doc's office climbed in the saddle and rode out of town, looked for a place to camp for the night it had to be a cold camp as he needed to be up early the next morning, because of what Scott had heard through the open window the day before, after breakfast Scott rode back to the observation point he had the day before above the ranchouse and waited.

A short while later, spotting movement he raised his glasses (binoculars) two riders, the sheriff and Dutchy surprisingly rode together towards the ranch, riding into the yard where they were greeted by Bates, where they paused to have a cup of coffee before, they started saddling up, Scott climbed into the saddle ready to follow the gang.

Scott knew what the gang were about to do, but did not know where they will go to first , so Scott had to follow them, following at a discreet distance, the gang rode for around five miles to the north of the ranch after going over a small ridge there laying in a vale was a cabin with gardens front and rear flowers in the front, vegetables at the rear it was a pleasant setting as the five men rode to the cabin and spread themselves in a line in front of the cabin as Scott dismounted and lay on the ridge his rifle in his hands, one of the five, it looked like Bates, called out the owner, after a few words the owner started to raise his rifle, the sheriff drew and fired this took everyone by surprise, no one expected the sheriff to react that way.

Scott's rifle came to his shoulder, his idea was to shoot close to scare the sheriff, but his horse bucked the bullet hit him square in the chest, the shot killed him his body fell from the horse. The remaining four members of the gang yelled then rode of, in a hurry.

Making sure the gang had rode off, Scott mounted up and rode down towards the cabin, the first job was to check the sheriff, the soggy red coloured shirt and the glazed eyes looking into the sky gave him the answer before ,he checked the pulse the sheriff is dead, moving to the man the sheriff shot Scott found the man was badly wounded but still lived, picking him up Scott walked to the cabin, where just inside the door he found a woman and two children, checking the man's wounds he found the man was lucky in the fact the bullet had passed straight through him missing all main organs so needed patched up quickly to prevent blood loss.

"Marm water, clothes and bandages, your man is still alive" Scott stated.

"Thank you Mister I can look after him" she said

"OK Marm I'll get rid of the other body outside" Scott said, looking at the kids.

"OK yes please" she replied.

"Just look after your man and kids I'll get rid of the body" Scott said.

Putting the sheriff's body over his horse Scott took them about three hundred yards from the house picking a very secluded spot, buried the sheriff and did not mark it, taking the horse back unsaddled it and let him into the homestead corral.

"Are you OK Marm" Scott asked.

"We will be alright thank you, if you had not shot that man, we would possibly all be dead thanks again mister" the lady said.

"If there is nothing I can do, I will carry on Marm" Scott said.

"My man is alive and will live and recover I will see to that I can manage thank you" the lady told him.

Scott started following sign left by the four men to find out where the four men were going, the next time Scott saw the men they were riding away from a cabin, riding up to the cabin he found two dead men, he checked the bodies to make sure they were dead, but had to leave the men to be able to keep up with the four man gang, when catching up to the killers they were approaching the third cabin, Scott dismounted finding a large rock he used to steady his aim he lined the Winchester, seeing one of the gunmen draw and level his pistol, Scott squeezed the trigger the rifle bark was loud the heavy bullet hit the gunman's shoulder the man reeled but stayed in the saddle as once again the gang rode off.

"Are you OK" Scott asked.

"Yeh! Thanks mister" the homesteader answered.

"Good" Scott said then rode in the direction the raiders went.

Once more Scott followed the sign left by the four men, Scott knew by previous studying a ruff map knew there was six homesteaders in the area and Bates at his meeting had told the raiders that the whole six were to be wiped out, that was his intentions, At the fourth cabin, there was woman hanging up clothes and three children played games in the yard, the four men advanced once again, Scott could see there was no chance of him getting to the ranch before the raiders, so again he dismounted and picked a spot where he could settled down with his rifle.

Bates had decided to change tactics and ride in with guns blazing as they charged the cabin, Scott raised the rifle squinted along the barrel drew in his breath and held it then squeezed the trigger, the bullet hit the man with the long dark hair called Steve, he arched his back slumped forward over the horses neck but remained in the saddle, the horse veered away from the cabin, Bates was not stupid he now realised that his plan had failed due to the man with a rifle and ordered the raiders back to the ranch.

On their arrival, back at the ranch Bates and Dutchy washed, cleaned and wrapped the two men wounds as they could not take them to the doctors which is where they went wrong, because of not getting the proper attention Steve the man with the bullet in his back by nightfall was paralysed from the waist down and jeb the other man had a heavy rifle bullet lodged in his shoulder making his arm useless putting both men out of action.

Scott found a good spot where he could keep his eyes on the ranch he saw Bates and Dutchy leave the bunkhouse, the two men with a beer in their hands sat on the veranda and talked for a while Scott could not hear what they talked about but could guess, half an hour later Dutchy mounted up and rode towards town, It was now time for him to ride to town also, now the sheriff has gone, with no sheriff there was no reason why Scott cannot openly ride into town but he still put Blacky in the stall behind the doctors.

"Hi! Doc" Scott greeted.

"Scott what you doing here" Doc said in amazement.

"It's Ok Doc relax" Scott assured him.

"How" the Doc asked

"Not many people know about it, but the sheriff is dead" Scott said.

"What now Scott" Doc asked.

"Well, I am starving it's time for dinner, Doc I want you to get all the folk we can trust together, I'll leave that to you while I eat" Scott asked him.

"OK Scott I'll see to that and get them together" Doc said.

Going out back of Doc's house Scott made sure Blacky had something to eat and water in the trough before going to Sandie's Shack to eat, Sandie's Daughter came to the table a smile on her face.

"Hello Scott, what can I get you" she asked.

"Steak well done potatoes, vegetables and gravy, followed by a large slab of apple pie with ice cream and a coffee please, also could you ask your mother if I can see her please" Scott asked.

"OK Scott" she acknowledged. Moments later Sandie came to the table.

"Sandie, do you have about half an hour to spare" Scott asked.

"Sure, my eldest daughter can do the cooking" Sandie said.

"Good, as soon as I finish dinner we will leave" Scott told her.

"Scott what is it all about" Sandie asked.

"Sandie all I will tell you it will be beneficial to you" Scott declared.

Scott finished his dinner and Sandie's daughter refused to take payment, then Scott with Sandie on his arm walked to the doctor's house, on their arrival the Doc's lounge was full of people, Sandie was given a seat and Scott wasted no time explaining why he had asked them there.

"Lady and Gentlemen I am hoping to complete the reason I came here but things have escalated here since I arrived and the outcome will affect you all, this all started for me around six weeks ago, you all know me as Scott, well I am Scott Burrows, bounty hunter, yes I can see by the look on your faces when I said bounty hunter, I feel I must give you an explanation, around six months ago the Wells Fargo office was robbed in the town of Jayton by a gang of five men they stole $100.000 dollars and killed three men, the law failed to capture these men, they could evade justice and get away with not only the money but a stream of terrorism, murder and rape they left behind them, they kidnaped a seventeen year old virgin and raped her to death, the sheriff and Wells Fargo approached me plus a dying young lady called Laura persuaded me to get these animals, I am happy to say I have taken three of them out, now the two remaining men are here in this area Ron Bates and Dutchy I found it hard to take these men because of the situation in town as they had a bent sheriff, Bates instead of employing cowhands took on criminals to protect him.

Today everything has changed the sheriff is dead, Bates two henchmen are very badly wounded so I intend to complete my job tonight now the main reason I have asked you here, I knew Ron Bates intended to buy a ranch but when I came here found it was not being ran as a ranch, WHY? I said and why employ criminals found out yesterday he not only wanted the ranch but all the land around the town, today these men tried to drive the homesteaders out, I managed to stop them, now this gives me the chance to complete the job I came here to do.

"What has this got to do with us" Mr. Turner asked

"All of what I have told you is because Bates has a friend who works for the railway and told Bates that the intended track was going through that ranch and a station will be built in Stratford, the land around here will be worth a lot and each of your businesses will increase the town will grow you still have time to think about it, until Henry puts it in his paper you are the only people who know" Scott explained.

"What now Scott" Jim asked.

"OK Sandie, you have time to think about what you are going to do, you will first have engineers coming to town then linesmen, stevedores and your business will grow you may need bigger premises, Henry I do not want you to print anything until I finish this job, Mr. Turner when Henry prints the story about the railway coming property will be worth more that means the rolling B and the livery stable, sell them and send the money Wells Fargo Jayton care off the bank Jim are you busy tonight" Scot asked.

"What time" Jim asked.

"Anytime you are free" Scott said.

"How about ten pm" Jim said

"Alright Jim meet me here at the doctors" Scott asked.

"I will be there" Jim said.

"Right folk that's all, I have told you because I have had help from each of you good luck to you" Scott informed them.

After everyone had departed Scott and Doc sat and talked over a cup of coffee Scott wanted to pick the doctors brains.

"Doc, I want to get both these men tonight, my intension is to get Dutchy first when I put him out, I want him to stay out for a while, long enough for me to be able to get Bates I know because Dutchy is built solidly if I knock him out, either with my fist or pistol whip him he will be back on his feet in ten to fifteen minutes I needs some way to knock him out for a longer period so I can at least get Bates, means putting Dutchy out for a couple of hours at least.

"I have a sedative that is only used when doing operations this potion can knock a person out for a prolonged period" Doc informed him.

"How much do you need to give someone" Scott asked.

"A capful will do" Doc said.

"In what way can it be administered" Scott inquired.

"Anyway, as long as it is swallowed" Doc told him.

"Would it work if given to a sleeping or unconscious person" Scott asked.

"Yes"

"Doc, I believe you have solved my problem this is the last piece of the way I will be able to complete capturing both men thanks" Scott said.

"Scott here is a bottle of the potion if you get it in someone's mouth either poured in, with food or drink he will have to swallow, and it will knock them out" the Doc informed him. Scott put the bottle in his pocket.

"Thanks Doc let's have a coffee" Scott and the Doc sat and talked over the coffee until Jim turned up at just after ten pm.

"Well, I'm here Scott how can I help you" Jim asked.

"Jim, it will mean you losing a few hours' sleep" Scott said.

"OK I'm up for that" Jim replied

"I want you to help me capture Dutchy and Bates" Scott explained.

"OK where do we start" Jim asked.

"I have heard from a reliable source that Dutchy gets drunk most nights and sleeps in the top tier of the livery stable, I hope to render him unconscious I then need you to help me to load him on his horse, then help me to kidnap Bates, once I have them you can return to town sleep for the rest of the night, tomorrow you can tell the rest of the folk of our success" Scott informed him.

"OK I'd like that" Jim said enthusiastically.

"Great let's get started" Scott said.

Scott and Jim moved slowly into the livery stable; Scott was surprised as Matt was there.

"Matt it's a bit late for you to be here" Scott said

"We do shift's tonight I am on the late shift" Matt explained.

"Matt, I know that you and your friends don't like Dutchy I want you to help me take him OK" Scott said.

"Yes Scott" Matt replied.

"I understand Dutchy sleeps here at night" Scott asked.

"He is here, drunk up there" Matt pointed aloft.

"OK where is his horse" Scott asked.

"Second stall on the right" Matt told them.

"Saddle it for me"

Scott paused below the ladder, pulled from his shirt a pair of moccasins praising of his boots, putting on the moccasins he crept slowly a rung at a time up the ladder at the top the floor squeaked, Scott paused then edged slowly towards the sleeping, snoring Dutchy, opening the bottle and fill the cap, creeping to the head of the sleeping man the next time he snored his mouth opened Scott poured the liquid into his mouth, this caused him to partially choke, open his mouth and start to wake up, drawing his pistol he lifted it ready to clip Dutchy over the head, but he coughed rolled over and fell asleep.

While giving time for the potion to work, he had Matt bring Dutchy's horse just below the ladder, then from the rafter just above the horse Scott rigged a block and tackle putting a rope on his upper torso he lowered the unconscious body down onto the horse, Scott and Jim lashed Dutchy to the horse, making sure he could not move his hands or legs.

"Matt thanks for your help, when we leave go to sleep you did not see anything, now does Dutchy have another horse" Scott asked.

"Yes, Scott the brown horse in the second last stall on the left" Matt informed them.

"Matt put some reins on it and bring it here" Scott told him.

"Jim get your horse, I'll see you at the Doc's house" Scott said.

Leading the two horses Scott lead them to the back of the Doctors house and saddled Blacky, as he collected his bags and attached them to the spare horse Jim arrived.

"Well Doc it is goodbye I very much think we will not be seeing each other again so thanks again for your help, Jim will pop in tomorrow and let you know how things went" Scott informed.

"Bye Scott and good luck" Doc replied.

Scott, Jim and their burdens rode away from the town heading for the rolling B ranch, there was no need to hurry Scott had a long journey ahead and did not want to tire the houses, so they had the horses walk the distance to the ranch, as they rode Scott gave Jim some instructions.

"Jim, I do not expect any problems from the bunkhouse but just in case watch out, go to the barn and saddle a horse for Bates, while I am here, I intend to raid the larder for food and look around for anything else I can use" Scott informed him. with the aid of the moon and lovely clear sky, there was no trouble as they approached the ranchouse, Scott slipped from the saddle and once more donned his moccasins moving slowly through the main door of the ranchouse he made for the staircase, as he wore moccasins a slight pressure on the step tells him if the step is loose and could squeak, with stealth he slowly moved through the house until when outside one door he heard snoring, slowly opening the door the moon shone through the flimsy curtain on the window to give him enough light to be able to see, this caused Scott to pause, before going forward because Bates was not alone there was the shape of a female in the bed with him, his first move was to remove the gunbelt that lay beside the bed within the reach of the sleeping man, next he fully opened the curtain, this unfortunately caused Bates to wake up Scott moved quickly to the bed and bring his pistol down hard on Bates head who moaned his head collapsing on to the pillow, Scott immediately putting a finger to his lips looking at the girl, she nodded, it was at that moment Scott saw she was bound she was tied to the bed.

At this time Bates moaned as he began to revive, Scott took out the bottle given to him by the Doc filled the cap rolled Bates on his back and poured the liquid into his mouth, putting his hand over his mouth pinched the nose until Bates swallowed, giving the sedative time to work he untied the young lady.

"Get dressed miss"

"Thank you, mister,"

"That OK, we now have to get out of here"

"OK mister I understand"

"Now help me to dress our friend"

"I'll kill him"

"No, you won't the law wants him alive if possible and that's what I want, this man is going to be tried for his crimes and hung" Scott assured her.

"In that case OK" she agreed.

"Right, give me a hand"

Taking the blankets from the bed, Scott ripped them into strips, tied them together to make a rope out of them and between them lowered Bates body through the window to the ground to where Jim waited.

"Now miss take hold of the rope and climb down, I have a friend down there, then go quietly and saddle a horse for yourself" Scott instructed her.

"Right mister thanks"

On completion of the task of lowering the young lady to the ground Scott started going back to the staircase creeping down to the pantry, finding a gummy bag (Kit bag) taking two sides of salted bacon, a large bag of beans, a couple of loaf's of bread, on top of that a dozen cans of fruit peaches, before leaving Scott opened the cupboard next to the pantry and found ammunition for both pistol and rifle taking it also.

They rode from the ranch towards the town, just under a mile and a half from the ranch the trail split one going to the town the other heading south, Scott brought them to a halt

"Right Jim this is where we part, please take the lady to town, then I would get myself to bed, and tell Mr. Turner in the morning, telling him he could start the sales of ranch and livery stable, you can also pass the word onto, the Doc, Henry, Sandie and others, I intend to ride hard , long as far and as fast as I can," Scott told them.

"Scott. I will send word to Wells Fargo in Jayton that you are on the way" Jim said.

"Good luck mister" the young lady said.

"Bye" Scott said, turned and rode south.

CHAPTER TWELVE

SEND SOMEONE TO ASSIST HIM

Scott did exactly what he told Jim he would do; he rode south and apart from the occasional break for the horses to blow and have a smoke he carried on moving eating and drinking as he rode on through the night and all the following day.

The drug the Doctor supplied was strong just as the doctor prescribed, it lasted for a little more than twenty-four hours, it was late into the next night, when Dutchy started coming out of it first which was expected as he was drugged a few hours before Bates, as Scott expected Dutchy growled like a wild animal.

"Grrr Grrr Hey! You what is happening" he growled.

Scott ignored him and stayed silent, just carried on riding which angered Dutchy and made him yell louder about being tied up, he tried brute force to free himself but to no avail, Scott was not stupid he knew because of his brute strength that he would have to be secured properly and he is, and as much as the big man strained and fought to get free, after trying for over an hour came to the understanding that it was futile and excepted the fact and settled down. Three hours later Bates started to revive, he also strained to get free butt Dutchy told him it was not possible so he stopped he knew if Dutchy could not get free then he would have little chance.

At sundown the next day Scott found a place to make camp, it was a clearing in front of a cave with enough grass for the horses, everyone by this time was very tired even the horses heads were down, but the site he had picked was perfect with a lovely pool of water the ideal place to build a fire, make no mistake Scott knew he had his job cut out because of the prisoners and the four horses.

His first task was the prisoners as the other jobs could not be done, so going to Dutchy untying his legs Scott pulled him out of the saddle dropping him to the ground, drawing his pistol marched him to a tree he tied him tightly to it, then repeated the routine with Bates, now the two men had been seen to Scott could get on setting up camp, first relieving the horses of their loads and tethering them, second building a fire putting water on for coffee, getting out the skillet he cut thick large rashers of bacon for quickness making thick bacon sandwiches.

With the sandwich on a plate and a mug of coffee he moved over to Dutchy put the food where he could reach it then untied one of Dutchy's hands.

"Bates when Dutchy is finished I will give you yours" Scott told him.

"What is this all about anyway" Bates asked.

"We are all going to eat, after that I have a little story to tell you" Scott said.

"Why not now" Bates asked.

"Patience".

As Dutchy finished eating Scott retied him before allowing Bates to have his food and coffee as Bates ate Scott made his own sandwich and sat with a cup of coffee when Bates was finished Scott retied him, then threw each man a blanket, on completion of having his own food he checked the horses getting everything done so it is possible to have a good night's rest, now all the tasks have been done Scott sat facing the two men as he rolled a cigarette lit it took a deep drag (draw).

"Well gentlemen the first thing I must tell you I was sent by Laura" Scott pronounced then let it sink into their heads.

"Laura" Bates said.

"Yes, the Laura you left in the cave" Scott said.

"You're a liar she is dead" Dutchy said loudly.

"Dutchy is right Laura is dead" Bates said.

"Let me tell you a little story before you go to bed, while in a cave committing murder and rape, by a man who said he loved her then told two of his criminal gang (ordering) them to kill her, by the man she thought she loved (yes Bates Laura), she was shot in the back, but she still lived (Ah! Wait before you say anything hear me out), this young lady had guts even though you dynamited the entrance to the cave, Laura because of her hate for you she spent seven days, just with her hands she dug her way out, she managed to make a hole big enough to drag her slender body through, after finally getting out she collapsed and new she was dying, but her luck was there as two teamsters spotted her body and looked after her, the doctor said she should be dead the doctor nursed her back to life, Laura admitted the only reason she lived was the hate for five evil men and their leader Ronald Bates, you did kill her in the end but not before she told her story" Scott paused threw his fag end into the fire.

"What do you mean we killed her" Dutchy growled.

"Because she had no water, during the seven days she dug herself out, it helped her to suck on a smooth stone, but she had no water and was unable to tend to her wounds in her back, so dust and bugs and beetles got into her wounds, getting her to the doctors found the wound in her shoulder had turned green it was gangrene which was travelling to her heart, she was told and knew she was dying" Scott told them.

"So, what have you got to do about this case" Bates asked.

"Laura told her story to the sheriff and Wells Fargo, the sheriff has boundaries and lost your sign, Wells Fargo are not a law agency and the best they could do was to get there agents to keep an eye out for these killers, then Laura heard I was in town and asked for my assistance, now if it had been about retrieving money I would not be interested but when she told me about killing three guards, shooting down in cold blood a young man of eighteen years old who was unarmed, but the thing that sealed it for me was the story of a seventeen year old virgin being raped to death and how the five men laughed about their actions, the last words that Laura said to me was (GET THESE ANIMALS) She was very pleased when I excepted the job" Scott explained.

"And who are you" Dutchy asked.

"I am Scott Burrows bounty hunter"

"Bounty hunter" Bates exclaimed.

"Yes"

"So, what is next, you are going after the other three" Dutchy sneered.

"Ha!! Ha! Ha!!! Scott had a fit of laughter.

"What's so funny" Bates inquired.

"You two are the last the others are dead" Scott informed them.

"Wes would not be taken easy" Bates said.

"No, he didn't we shot it out and he lost" Scott told them.

"You beat Wes Arnold" Dutchy said in disbelief, Bates was quiet for a moment.

"Now, you know why you are here, let me tell you how it is going to be, It will take us around a week to get to Jayton, and you are going to be good boys, even the slightest problem from any of you, I will shoot you, I have in my pocket wanted dodgers for both of you, it says on those dodgers Dead or Alive, any troubles I only have to shoot you" Scott told them.

"Yeh!" Dutchy sneered.

"Yeh! When you eat, have a pee, wash your face, anything you do will only be done by one of you at any time and you will only have one hand to do it, next we are going to ride as much as we can stopping only for the horses to blow, each of you will have a handful of jerky meat and a canteen of water, within your reach to keep you going as I do not intend to stop unless necessary do you understand." Scott asked.

"We understand" Bates said in a subdued voice.

"I hope you do, it will not bother me if I have to kill you, I will still get paid, If I was you, I would be good, it's up to you" Scott explained.

Scott lay down gun in hand, turned over and went to sleep.

As a ribbon of light showed on the horizon, Scott's eyes opened, he lay for few seconds digesting the sounds of dawn, a smile came to his face the only sound that spoilt the dawn chorus was the loud snores coming from Dutchy and Bates still tied to the tree, Scott knew he had to get up as there is lots to do, he first checked the horses then had a wash to wake himself up built up the fire put the Billie on to boil water for coffee and carried out his normal routine before waking his prisoners.

After feeding the prisoners making sure they were ready to ride, his attention went to loading the horses getting the prisoners one at a time onto the horses making them secure he checked the camp area then moved out.

Scott and the cavalcade rode out, as Alex Morrison opened his office in Jayton, getting a cup of coffee he was relaxed the normal start of a normal day, the office door opened and the boy from the telegraph office stood at the desk he handed a wire then left, Alex opened it and yelled.

"Yes! Yes!! Yippee.

Leaving the office locking the office door he made his way to the hotel knocked on Danny's door, Danny opened the door.

"Morning miss Danny" Alex said.

"You have news Alex"

"Yes, I have just received this wire from the Wells Fargo agent in Stratford Scott has captured the last two and is on his way back" Alex said excitedly as he handed Danny the wire.

"How long will it take him" Danny asked.

"At least a week" Alex said.

"Is there any way we can help him" Danny asked.

"I will see what I can do" Alex replied.

"Look Alex, couldn't we (SEND SOMEONE TO ASSIST HIM) maybe send a couple of men to help for the last couple of days, the men would have to have identification and he might be getting short of food" Danny told him firmly, Alex noted the look on her face.

"Miss Danny, I know you are worried about him, but if any man can do it, Scott can" Alex assured her.

"Thank you, Alex,".

Alex left the hotel deep in thought with a red face not for embarrassments but in anger as he had not thought of sending help, (she is right why did I not think of that) were his thought's.

Arriving back at his office, he called all his present free agents together there was six of them in all.

"Right men I have just received a wire from Stratford, Scott Burrows has captured the last two men who robbed us and killed our agents" Alex said the men cheered.

"Now boys you all know it will take Scott about a week I want two volunteers to go and meet him, help him and take him some supplies, now who wants to go" Alex asked.

The whole six men stepped forward.

"Thank you, boys we will have to cut cards, the two who draws the highest cards will go, I expect you to be on your way in two hours" Alex told them.

Scott carried on being strict, he watched every move, making sure the two men were not given any chance of attempting something stupid like trying to overcome him and escape, he still had the bottle of knockout drops, but reframed from using it and as long as they don't cause trouble, he is determined not to use the bottle.

As it happened because he was careful and made sure they were securely tied, Scott pushed himself and his two captives to the limit, with a meal in the morning, and a meal in the evening, but every day they had Jerky and water, stopped for the horses to blow and roll a cigarette and have a smoke, his main problem is the supplies, they have already ran out of bread, getting very short of bean's and he was thinking that he may have to go hunting for food.

At the end of the fifth day, the estimate was that Scott and the prisoners would take about three days to get to Jayton, straight away his thoughts went to Danny The nearer he got to his destination the more and more Danny came to mind.

"Burrows, when do we get to Jayton" Dutchy growled.

"Why are you in a hurry" Scott asked.

"I just want to know how long I am going to be tied up like this"

"If we are lucky three days"

The two prisoners suddenly saw Scott's face go straight and he came to his feet picked up his rifle and levered a bullet into the barrel ready to shoot as Scott heard the noise of approaching horses.

"Hello, the camp" a man's voice called

"Come ahead friend" Scott replied, his rifle ready

"Howdy, smelt your coffee" two men stepped into the fire light.

"Welcome take a cup" Scott offered.

"You are Scott Burrows" the first man asked.

"I am"

"Good we thought we had missed you" the second man said.

"Missed me"

"Sure, we have been sent to assist you" the second man said.

"Alex Morrison received a wire from Stratford" the first man told him.

"Alex took the wire to show a lovely young lady called Danny, she persuaded Alex to send someone to assist you and bring you some supplies so here we are there is bread, bacon and some eggs" the second man said.

"She did that" Scott smiled.

"Oh! Yes, she really told him, I am John Jorden Wells Fargo agent and my partner is Ben Albright" John explained as they flashed their badges.

Scott relaxed lowered the rifle, he knew they were genuine when they mentioned Danny, few people know about him and Danny, they only had one night together.

"Boys, let me introduce you, this pair are the leaders of the gang who robbed Jayton Wells Fargo office and killed the guards this big fat ugly looking bastard is Dutchy and this smooth womaniser is Ronald Bates and no you cannot shoot them I want them to hang" Scott said.

"I will admit it would be a pleasure to cut them down, one of the agents they killed was my stepbrother, but with the work you have done and the fact I will be happy to see them swing" John informed them.

"John, Ben I am happy you are here because doing things together we can get on faster, but I still intend to push on as fast and far as I can, if we do we should reach town midday on the third day, anyway if you two look after your horses I'll start with the bacon we will have bacon sandwiches before turning in" Scott said.

"OK Scott" they chorused.

Due to the fact that John and Ben was with him time did seem to go faster as they now had vittles' (FOOD) but most of all he had someone to be able to talk to plus Scott was right they made back to Jayton On the third day around midday Scott leading the cavalcade turned into Jayton main street heading for the sheriff's office going past the hotel behind Scott the prisoners heads down lashed to their horses John and Ben were at the rear their rifles across their knees.

As it was lunch time most people were already on the street the word carried around the small-town fast people in shops stuck there heads out of windows and doors and a crowd started to gather outside the sheriff's office, Danny heard the commotion in the street though the open window so peeped out and yelled.

"Ben! Ben he's back, he's back, It's Scott" she put on her bonnet and left the hotel quickly.

"Howdy Scott" the sheriff greeted.

"Hi! Sheriff meet Dutchy and Bates the last of the five" Scott said

Alex Morrison walked through the crowd.

"Excellent job Scott" Alex came forward hand out.

Meanwhile John and Ben dragged Dutchy and Bates out of the saddle and marched them through the office to the cells.

"Well the horses have to be attended to" Scott announced.

"Don't worry about the horses I'll get them attended to" Alex told him.

"I have to see Blacky is OK"

"OK see you later Scott" the sheriff said.

Scott replaced his Stetson and walked out of the door and received the biggest surprise in his life a beautiful female form, dived into his body the crowd that had gathered cheered as he was almost knocked of his feet putting his arms around her and whispered in her ear.

"I love you"

"I love you too"

"Now would you walk with me, I must take Blacky to the livery stable he has done a lot of work lately, I will then freshen up, before going to lunch" Scott said.

"OK Darling"

"Is Ben going to eat with us" Scott asked.

"Sh! Sh!! My brother can look after himself, I want us to spend some time together, and I know Ben will understand, you will see to Blacky, if it is quiet and there is no one around we will kiss, we will go to the hotel and get you a room I will help you to freshen up, then we will go to lunch" Danny told him.

"Come on then" Scott smiled and put his arm around her.

With his arm around Danny's waist, they walked up the street talking and laughing all the way to the livery stable, Scott found an empty stall that had been mucked out, he made sure Blacky had a nose bag and fresh water, while Blacky ate the oats Scott putt his arm around her waist drew her two him, two pairs of hungry lips searched for each other, the kiss was long and passionate.

"Oh! Danny, I have missed you" Scott whispered in her ear.

"Scott the month away from you was terrible, I missed you, I love you" Danny said breathing heavy.

"Darling it will take another week to clear up this job" Scott informed her.

"As long as we are together it will be OK" she assured him in a husky voice.

The two of them kissed and cuddled until Blacky snorted indicating he had finished with the nosebag; Scott removed the nosebag patted his neck talked to him soothingly for a few moments.

Scott and Danny walked arm in arm down the Main street in the direction of the hotel, a few people recognised him and congratulated him, entering the hotel they approached the desk straight away Danny spotted the room next to her was vacant so booked it, Scout allowed Danny to enter the room walked in behind her and kicked the door closed behind them, as the door clicked shut , a second later they were in each other's arms lips welded together, as they kissed passionately Scott automatically placed his hand on her breast.

"Yes Scott" Danny whispered.

As they hurriedly undressed Scott turned the key in the lock, two pile of clothes dropped to the floor, Danny noticed Scott's rampant, throbbing erection, their lips stilled joined, Scott's felt the stream of juices flowing between Danny's legs there was no need for foreplay they were obviously both turned on Danny gasped as the erection invaded her body , leaving only the noises of two people making love, after being apart for so long lust had taken over the satisfaction and release came as Scott's seed transferred to Danny they relaxed slightly.

"–Danny that was fantastic, I love you" Scott breathing heavily said, then kissed her.

"Thank you Scott, I love you" Danny replied.

Now having their breath back Scott pulled her body to him his lips searched for hers as the pair caressed Scott's finger ran slowly up and down her spine she giggled, 'Yes, darling she whisper' in his ear as their lips came together once more, he kissed her lips, neck and shoulders as his hand enveloped the already swollen breasts the nipples protruding and sensitive.

"Oooo Arr Yes" As his lips sucked her right breast the vibrating tongue tantalizing and teasing the proud sensitive nipples, with his hand caressing her left breast his thumb brushing the proud nipples, combined with the actions of his mouth on her right breast the feeling was sensational you could tell the by her action of extending her breasts and the wonderful sounds coming through her beautiful lips, Ohhh Oooo Ohh! Arrrrr, more, lovely she muttered.

Her body tensed as she experienced a tickling feeling as the fingers of his right hand walked down her body to pause at her belly button, as the fingers continued their journey south she sucked in held her breath his hand proceeded to glide over the smooth silky skin heading for the forbidden forest of lovely black curly triangle of pubic hair combing the hair caused her legs to open enough to allowing the finger in so it can brush the lips to the private entrance to her body causing more sounds of love to come from her lips Ahhhhh! Arrrr Ooo Oooooo Ahh!

Danny's legs opened automatically to allow the finger to invade and advanced, she gasped as the probing finger moved in and out, swirled around inside her and increased the sensation as it brushed the clitoris, giving more sensation Ahhhh yes Ooooo Arrr yes, the noises of love louder and louder as she experienced a higher level of pleasure.

The sounds of love were now coming continues from both their lips as they found it impossible to stop Danny feeling the erection prod her tummy murmured yes, yes now Scott, Scott held off as long as he could to build up tension until it was unbearable, Danny gasped loudly as the erection pushed through her lips and entered her body, Arrrrr! Arrrrr yes, she cried.

Scott and Danny had now disappeared into a world of their own as the erection probed deeper and faster this put them into a world of their own as they experienced an organism when his seed transferred into her body, Danny felt as if she had been taken apart and lovingly put back together again, Scott withdrew they lay together two sweat covered bodies getting their breath back. Scott getting his breath back first whispered.

"Thank you darling I love you" reaching over he kissed her tenderly.

"I love you Scott" she smiled happily as she excepted the compliment, he gave her.

"Danny darling when the court case is over, the job is over and I will be free, I never did this job for money but I will be getting a large sum of money, Danny darling I want us to travel south where Scott Burrows the bounty hunter is not known, find and buy a ranch, we can settle down and have a family what do you think" Scott asked.

"As long as we are married, and we can do a lot of what we have just done, I will go anywhere with you darling, now I am hungry, let's get up and dressed and go to lunch" Danny told him.

"I love you" Scott whispered.

They both rose Scott could not help the feeling between his legs as Danny's naked body was displayed in front of him, butt grabbing a towel dipped in cold water relieved his wanting for the moment, with the towels they washed and dressed Scott had a quick shave, Scott sighed at the sight of Danny in the blue suit that did not hide her curves.

"Come on you let's go" Scott said quickly.

Scott knew that the town was in a good mood due to the capture of the five men who had carried out the biggest crime ever carried out in this town, but he did not realise that he is now a celebrity and as he walked to the café with Danny on his arm was surprised at the number of people who congratulated him, he did not know that the story of how he beat each member of the Bates gang became public, a few of the men of the town were taking bets that he could not complete the job, a lot of people patted him on the back.

With a few people stopping him they did eventually arrive at the café, even in the café a few people put their thumbs up as he passed, as usual the food was great they both ate the today's special consisting of a steak, French fries and garden peas, the sweet was a slab of thick apple pie and cream followed by coffee. They did linger at the table for a while and talked about their future like, love, sex, marriage, ranching and lots of things they would like to do in the future, catching the waitress's eye he asked for the bill.

"It has already been paid sir" she told him.

"How"

"I don't know, the boss said it has been paid for".

"Could you ask your boss to come out here please"

"Yes sir" she replied.

After a few moments, the waitress returned with the lady who owns the café who came straight to the table.

"I understand someone has paid my bill, who" Scott asked.

"Yes, Alex Morrison of Wells Fargo came in and told me all your meals are free bill to go to Wells Fargo" she informed him.

"Thank you, come on Danny darling" Scott said.

Scott and Danny arm in arm walked down Main street their destination the Wells Fargo office, the short journey took a lot longer than Scott planned due to Danny's excitement as she passed every display in the shop windows, but they did eventually arrive outside the Wells Fargo office.

"Could I see Alex please" asking the young man behind the counter.

"MR. MORRISON" the young man yelled. Alex came through from the back office his hand stuck out as he spotted Scott and Danny.

"Hi Scott, lovely to see you, Danny,"

"Howdy Alex you are keeping well" Scott asked

"I'm fine now how can I help you" Alex queried.

"Alex, we have just been to the café for lunch, and they told me that you paid the bill" Scott asked,

"Sorry Scott, I thought I had already told you, I must be getting old the way I keep forgetting things" Alex said. "Told me what"

"Yours and Danny's rooms plus your meals are on Wells Fargo while you are in town" Alex told them.

"OK that is great, but the question is still why" Scott asked.

"Look Scott, The day we stood by Laura's bedside and she asked you, if you would get those five men, we all knew by reputation that you are the best bounty hunter and that you have up to that time, always got the people you went after, when you left that room, Laura was elated she said (he will get them) the sheriff told her if any man can bring these evil men to justice you could, but while talking we agreed that it would be impossible to retrieve the money, we expected the five men to go on a spending spree and spend a good part of the $100,000 so we did not expect to be able to retrieve the money, but when we counted the money you had returned taking it from all five men the money came to well over the $100.000."

"I immediately sent a message to Wells Fargo Central office telling them of your success and the amount of money that has been returned, they told me that you must be rewarded, they suggested to me that you deserve a bonus and that I was to make your time in Jayton as cash free as possible."

"Look Scott before you turned up we had tried everything to get these evil men and the money, there is quite a lot of people who thought you could not do it, some of them making bets you would fail, the money you recovered was substantial we have been able to look after the dead guards family's, Scott don't knock it, you did a job everyone thought was impossible you deserve what you are getting and more thank you" Alex explained.

Danny stood looking at Scott proudly, Alex waited for his reply as Scott stood silently thinking deep in thought.

"OK Alex thanks, now I have a question for you, I notice there is no preacher in this town could you tell me when the circuit preacher is due, I want him to marry me and Danny" Scott asked.

"Yippee" Danny yelled and jumped into Scott's arms.

"Mmmm that is a problem he should have been here yesterday I do not know why he has been delayed" Alex told him.

"He is a circuit preacher so where does he stop before coming here" Scott asked.

"Claremont" Alex said.

"According to this map Claremont is half a day's ride and it does not get dark until nine pm, we could make it tonight and stay overnight, Danny go to the hotel get into riding gear I'll go saddle up the horses and meet you outside the hotel, there is enough time to get there" Scout said

"Yes darling" Danny replied.

Scott did as he said saddled the horses and was waiting for Danny.

"If we get to the priest, we can get married, are you happy about that".

"Oh! Scott that would be wonderful" Danny told him.

"I can then make love to you all the time legally" Scott said

"Darling, I love you and I want to marry you, you can make love to me anytime married or not" Danny said in a muffled voice.

"Your fantastic, I love you"

They rode out of town at a cantor, which is a fast pace that eats up the distance it does of course mean they could not sit together and kiss. After riding for about an hour and a half, only getting a quarter of the way, they rode over a small hill, there was a wagon hanging over the side of a deep gorge right on the edge.

"Danny stay here"

Scott dismounted and moved slowly towards the wagon, when he was near, he called out.

"Hello anyone in the wagon"

"Yes, came a weak voice"

"Are you alone" Scott asked.

"No, my wife is here unconscious, Mister the slightest move and the wagon moves, I have been here for hours unable to move"

"Hold on a little longer" Scott said. Then retreated to his horse Blacky where he collected the rope from the saddle horn.

"Danny there are two people in the wagon, but it is unstable, I am going to tie this rope to the chassis of the wagon, then lash it to that tree ten feet away from the wagon, when secure I will get the people out" Scott told her.

"Are you sure darling" a worried Danny asked.

"Yes, it is the only way I must get the people out first"

Scott once more advanced on the wagon, attaching the rope to the chassis high on the right side of the wagon, wrapping the rope around a large thick tree pulling it tight then swung around the tree and tied it before returning to the wagon.

"Sir the wagon will move a bit but it is secure could you drag your wife so I can reach her" Scott asked.

"I will give it a try" the man said.

The lady was big, and it took all their strength to get her out and up the hill to where Danny was, she was out but alive, Scott left Danny to look after the lady.

"Right sir I am Scott this is Danny"

"I am the Revenant Ashley the circuit preacher, thank you".

"Now sir, is the horse dead"

"I don't know"

"OK sir" Scott picked up a broken branch approached the wagon and prodded the horse first then whacked it hard and found the horse was dead, releasing the harness the horse fell allowing the wagon to rise a little.

"Sir do you have anything in the wagon that is heavy" Scott asked.

"Yes, Scott an organ"

"Don't tell me the organ is on the left side of the wagon"

"I'm afraid so".

"The idea was to put Danny's rope on the wagon and pull it out but with a heavyweight hanging on the side hanging over the side it will not be possible to do so."

"Do you have a rope in the wagon" Scott asked.

"Only the rope holding the organ in place".

Scott thought about the situation and came to the answer, walking over to Blacky he praised his boots of and from his saddlebags extracted a pair of moccasins then removed his gunbelt and Stetson, Danny had been watching Scott's actions.

"What are you up to" Danny asked.

"Danny, I have thought about the situation the only way I can solve the problem is to climb into the wagon unlash the organ using the rope by tying it to the organ then with Blacky's help drag it to the right side of the wagon, this should straighten the wagon we can pull it upright" he told her.

"Scott that is dangerous if that wagon goes while you're in there" Danny exclaimed.

"Shhh! It's the only way" Danny watched eagerly as he walked to the wagon.

Walking along the wagon testing it before taking the step onto the wagon which moved he had to steady himself, slowly bending his knees so he could reach the straps that tied down wagon cover, lifting the canopy a little he climbed inside the wagon it swayed sweat was running down his face and back, every step he took there was movement, carefully Scott took the rope of the organ, tied the rope end to the organ, slipped the rest of the rope through the canopy and followed it by climbing back through the gap, holding the end of the rope he jumped lightly onto the grass covered slope.

"What now darling" Danny said happy he had got of the wagon,

"I'm glad you asked that" she looked at his face

"Now why did you say that" she asked

"Because for the next part of this recovery I need your help"

"what" she stopped as Scott stopped her.

"Right darling this is what we have to do, first we attach your rope to the front of the wagon the other end to your saddle horn, next I attach this rope to my saddlehorn, if I have it right the wagon is a light vehicle and the organ is a solid heavy object, I will move Blacky forward which will pull the organ from the left side of the wagon to the right side, if I am right this will bring the wagon upright on two wheels then you move forward on my command until you have the strain then hold it while I release my rope from the tree, slowly you will pull forward and I will edge Blacky back, when you have moved the wagon forward about four feet three wheels of the wagon will be on solid ground and it will move more easily, after another six feet all four wheels will be on solid ground, I will release my rope you will pull the wagon forward a few yards, we put the wagon brake on remove all the ropes then harness your horse to the wagon" Scott explained.

"OK Scott" Danny replied.

They carried out Scott's routine and to their delight everything worked perfectly exactly as he said it would.

"Well done darling your plan worked" Danny called out.

"Are you two married, the preacher asked,

"No, we want to be, but there is never a preacher around when you want one" Danny told him.

"Danny how is the lady" Scott called.

"I am OK" the lady spoke up.

"Good your OK darling" the preacher said.

"When the wagon went over, so fast I hit my head on the organ, it must have knocked me out" she said.

"OK Listen up, we are going to rest for half an hour we have canteens of water to drink, there is jerky meat in my saddle bags, Sir you and your wife can use the wagon with Danny's horse harnessed up and Danny can ride with me" Scott told them.

After half an hour, Danny was all smiles as Scott bent down grabbed her under the arms lifted her up to sit across his knees, she giggled happily and kissed him as they set of for town. It was dusk, not far of dark when they arrived outside the doctor's office the sheriff and Alex Morrison saw them arrived and could see it was not normal so walked over to them to find out what had happened.

The story of what happened and making Scott a hero soon went around mainly because the preacher's wife would not stop talking about what had happened, as the preacher followed his wife into the doctors, Scott followed them Danny on his heels.

Scott waited for the preacher to finish talking to the doctor.

"Sir, when you are feeling better, could you marry Danny and I" Scott asked.

"Yes, my boy get things ready let me know and I will arrange the time and date." The preacher agreed.

Scott and Danny were all smiles as they came together their lips met.

"Come on Danny, dinner I am starving" the café was still open over dinner they made plans.

"Tomorrow I will spend some time on my own, I intend to ask Ben to give me away, then I will have to look for a dress which may take some time" Danny told him.

Scott took $200,00 dollars from his pocket and gave it to her, Danny put it in her purse then lent over and kissed him.

"I'm going to ask Alex to be my best man" Scott informed her.

"Oh! Scott I'm looking forward to getting married" Danny said.

"If we get everything ready tomorrow we can go and see the preacher with a time and date to get married, we will be married but remember I may have to attend court any day now, that is another thing I will have to check on tomorrow, but whatever happens we will be married before heading south" Scott explained.

"We are still going to bed together tonight" Danny asked.

"Of course, we are going to bed every night" Scott assured her.

"I'm happy about that darling, but it will be even better when we marry" Danny admitted.

"Danny darling, over the next few days we are going to be very busy, with the court case, marriage, planning the trip south but we will leave all that until tomorrow, it's getting late" Scott said. Danny smiled.

The pair of lovers headed for the hotel, where they did spend the night together and did make love.

The next morning Danny woke up in Scott's arms, she sighed, felt happy and secure, she had enjoyed the night before, making love, also they talked of love, plus talked of plans for the future, as far as she was concerned the night was perfect, as the two of them lay contented the morning sun started lighting up the room, Scott's arm went around her his erection touched her tummy her hand held it.

"Yes" she whispered. Scott and Danny gave into their desires.

"Danny, I love you, thank you" Scott whispered to her tenderly.

"I love you darling" Danny said in a husky voice, she was elated at his complement.

"Now my darling, the morning is getting on and we have lots to do" Scott said.

"Yes, there is lots to do" Danny agreed. Scott gave her a tender kiss.

"Come on darling, get up get dressed, we will go to breakfast" Scott said.

"OK darling" she threw the bed clothes off, Scott sighed at the sight of the beautiful naked body teasing him.

"Scott" she teased.

"Danny" he replied turned his back, went to the wash basin poured water from the jug and started washing, a lovely naked body came alongside him, a hand went around her then gave her bottom a sound slap, she scowled for a moment, seeing the smile on Scott's face she smiled rubbing her bum.

After getting dressed but before leaving the room, Scott caught her arm pulled her round to face him taking her into his arms he kissed her tenderly.

"I love you, my little trouble maker" Scott said in a faint voice.

"I love you darling" she whispered in a husky voice.

Scott and Danny, left the hotel Danny slipped her arm through his as they walked through the town to the café, it did not take long for them to get there and as they were late getting up this morning found it easy to get a table at the café, sitting down at a table in a quiet place at the rear of the room, as it was quiet the waitress arrived at the table before the pair had taken their seats.

"What can I get you Mr. Burrows" the waitress asked.

"You know my name" Scott asked in surprise.

"Everyone in this town knows you, your famous" she replied.

"Could we have two full breakfasts please"

"Coming right up sir" the waitress said.

As the waitress left a nice looking slightly older lady came to the table.

"Mr. Burrows" she said Scott stood up.

"Thank you" she said, "could I sit here" she asked.

"Yes of course please do" Scott said.

"I am Cat and I own this café, when one of my waitresses told me you were out here, I had to come out to meet you, one of the Wells Fargo guards killed in the robbery was my fiancée, we were going to be married two weeks after the date of the robbery" she explained.

"Oh! I am sorry" Danny exclaimed.

"No don't be, I have had time to get over it, but I had to come out and thank you for getting the five men, it could not have been easy, but you succeeded in catching those criminals I had to come out and thank you" Cat said.

"That's OK Cat, I am sorry for your loss, yes we have the men in jail who committed the crime one of them is Bates the leader" Scott told her.

"Are you married" Cat asked

"No, not yet" Danny revealed.

"Not yet" Cat looked at her question Ly.

"Today is preparation day I'm looking for a dress, Scott is seeing Alex to see if he will be his best man, if we get all the arrangements done the preacher says he will marry us, we have a lot to do we have no witnesses, yet we have a lot to organise, after breakfast we have to get started." Danny told her.

"Enjoy your breakfast" Cat said as she left.

"Thank you, Cat," Scott said.

On completion of their breakfast Scott and Danny made for the door, they kissed lightly then parted Danny turned right Scott paused, took out the makings and rolled and lit a cigarette before proceeding to the Wells Fargo office, on his arrival at the office Alex spotted him coming through the door came forward his hand held out.

"Hi! Scott its great seeing you".

"Hello Alex, you know my fiancée Danny" Scott asked.

"Yes, she is a lovely girl you're a lucky man" Alex told him.

"Well Danny and I are going to get married, I would like to ask you if you would be my best man." Scott asked.

"Scott, it would be a privilege yes I will" Alex agreed.

"Now the second question, is when does the circuit judge get here and what day am, I required to be in court" Scott enquired.

"Oh! I am sorry Scott. I should have got word to you, the judge has been delayed, but is expected to be here in three days, the court will convene the next day so it will be four days at least" Alex explained.

"Don't be sorry Alex, if we can get things sorted over the next twenty-four hours we can maybe get married before the trial" Scott said.

Meanwhile, when leaving Scott Danny sundered (strolled) down Main street, arriving at the milliners (ladies' cloth shop), she entered a middle aged lady approached.

"Hello, how can I help you" she asked,

"Hello, my name is Danny and I am getting married in a couple of days and I wonder if you would have a dress, I could buy " Danny asked.

"We only take orders for wedding dresses and they are made to measure so that is out of the question, but we could maybe find an alternative, there is party dresses, or a suit, or possibly a blouse and skirt, let's see what we have in stock" the assistant advised.

Danny tried a few item's, after trying a few party dresses she ruled party dresses out, she liked a couple of the dresses but they were not appropriated for a wedding, it took her time but Danny did settle for a white frilly blouse, a slightly white long skirt, white slippers and a white bonnet with a band of flowers around it, not a wedding dress but after looking in the long mirror she liked what she saw, after paying for her purchases her next task was at the hotel.

"Ben! Ben!" She called excitedly as she entered the room,

Ben emerged from his room rubbing his eyes.

"OK What is the problem" he demanded.

"Ohh! Ben, I am sorry I did not know you were asleep" she held her hand to her mouth.

"Alright what is the problem" Ben asked.

"Sorry" she said sheepishly "Scott and I intend to marry in a couple of days' time, as Dad is gone, will you give me away" she asked.

"Sis of course I will" Ben smiling replied.

"Thank you, Ben."

"Danny, you should have known I would say yes" Ben said.

"Ben, it is only right I ask you, now Ben, Scott and I after we are married are travelling south, we intend to buy a ranch, would you like to come along with us" Danny told him.

"I'll have to think about that, I will let you know before you set out, don't worry I am not certain if I want to leave this town, I like it here" Ben admitted.

"The offer is open, if you stay and decide to come down at a later day you can that will be OK, we are family you will be welcome at any time" Danny explained.

"As I said I like it here I am looking for a job, I have recovered from the wound, I will let you know" Ben replied.

"OK I will see you later, I'm meeting Scott, so I will be off" Danny left.

Leaving the hotel Danny made her way to 'Cats house' and was the first to arrive so picked a table and ordered coffee and asked if she could see Cat.

"Hi Danny, you want to see me" Cat asked.

"I want to ask if you would consider being my bridesmaid and witness" she asked

"I will be your witness, but (JENNY Cat yelled) I think my daughter would be best as your bridesmaid" a young lady approached the table.

"This is your daughter." Danny asked.

"Yes, Danny this is Jenny" Cat admitted.

"Jenny this is Danny" Cat said

"I know" Jenny admitted.

"Jenny, Danny wants to know if you would be her bridesmaid" Cat asked her.

"Oh! Yes, yes I'd love to when" Jenny asked.

"I'm waiting here for Scott, who should have some idea, I will let you know when I find out, we hopefully will be able to tell you before the day is out" Danny stated.

"Did you get the dress" Cat asked.

"The shop does not keep any of the shelf dresses, but I have chosen a skirt and blouse that I like and will service" Danny explained.

"Jenny get three coffee's" Cat said.

"Three mam"

"Yes three" nodding towards the door as Scott entered.

"OK mam" Jenny said.

"Hi darling" Scott greeted Danny and kissed her on the cheek.

"Hi sweetheart" Danny replied.

"Hello Cat" Scott greeted.

"Well how did it go" Danny asked.

"OK, Alex has agreed to be my best man, plus I found out that the judge has been delayed for another three days, so the trial cannot convene for four days at least, the preacher is only here for three days, so we must get married within the next two days, after lunch Danny we will go see the preacher to organise the wedding" Scott explained to her.

"Alright let's have lunch, then make our first stop seeing the preacher as most things have been done, we still need a second witness, but if we arrange the date and time of the wedding, we can do any patching up afterwards" Danny said.

"If we are pushed for a witness, Alex could be our witness" Scott suggested.

"I think it would be better to have someone who is not from the wedding party Danny said.

"I don't think that will be a problem I could get either the sheriff or the doctor" Scott said.

"OK Scott as you said the important thing to do is sort the day and time" Danny agreed.

Scott and Danny continued with their lunch there was no need to rush, but on completion they left the café and made their way to the hotel, finding out from the reception the preacher's room, where they knocked on the door.

"Scott, Danny come in" the preacher invited them in.

"Thank you, sir," Scott said as he allowed Danny to enter first.

"I can guess why you two are here" the preacher's wife pronounced.

"We want to thank you two for coming to our rescue, if you had not come across us, I don't know how long I could stay calm, and could have been out there for a long time so thank you again" the preacher said

"Now how can we help you" the preacher's wife asked.

"We would like to be married and the only day available is the day after tomorrow could you please do that sir" Scott asked.

"Yes" the preacher replied.

"Would eleven am be OK" Scott asked.

"Yes, it will be OK, it gives us time to set up in the council office, which is designated to us, yes that would be great" the preacher said.

"Yippee" Danny cried. She kissed Scott.

"Thank you, sir, that's fantastic" Scott told him.

"Scott, Danny you make a good couple"

"How are you keeping now Marm" Danny asked the preachers wife.

"Thank you for asking, I feel fine Danny" she replied.

"That is good news" Scott said.

"Thanks again sir, we must get going now we have the time and date we have a few people to inform" Scott informed them.

Scott and Danny spent the next hour and a half going around the town informing all their friends, including the Sheriff, Doctor and their wives plus they asked the doctor to be their witness, when they told Cat she surprised them.

"Danny, Scott come back here straight after you are married, the wedding reception lunch is on me" Cat informed them.

"Thank you, Cat," Scott said.

"Yes, thank you" Danny acknowledged.

Now everything was ready to go ahead with the wedding it was only a time to wait, even though two days was not long, to Danny and Scott time dragged by ever so slowly butt eventually the big day arrived as they slept apart the night before the wedding the next day could not come faster.

At eight am the next morning, Danny had just woke up when there was a knock on the door of her room wrapping her dressing gown around her she answered the door and was surprised to see Cat and Jenny standing there, the next surprise was when her brother Ben came in the room and heard him exclaim.

"Jenny".

"Ben" she said in a surprised voice.

"Oh! That answers a few questions" Danny said.

"Danny" Cat looked at her.

"Over the last twenty-four hour I have asked Ben, if he would like to travel with us after the wedding as we intend to leave, he said he likes it here and is looking for a job, I know see why" Danny explained.

"Jenny, Danny is my sister" Ben explained.

"Oh! I see, I wondered why you are here" Jenny said.

"Jenny what are you doing here" Ben asked.

"I am Danny's bridesmaid" she replied.

"Ben, we have come here to get Danny ready for the wedding, we need you to disappear" Cat told him.

"I have all my clothes for the wedding ready" Ben said.

"Ben, pick up everything you require and knock on Scott's door" Danny suggested.

"OK Danny" Ben picked up his neatly folded clothes, walked to the next door up and knocked on Scott's door.

"What's up Ben" Scott asked.

"I have been kicked out of the room, by Cat and Jenny" Ben explained.

"OK come on in" Scott understood.

Cat and Jenny helped Danny to get ready for her wedding, when satisfied Cat, Jenny and Danny left the room at around ten thirty, on leaving the hotel Danny received another surprise, standing in the street was a white four seated buggy with two white horses.

In the counsel office, the preacher had made up an alter his wife sat at the organ playing hymn's as Scott and Alex came forward and stood in front of the alter, after a few moments the organ burst out loudly playing 'Here comes the bride' as Danny and Jenny walked towards them.

Scott looked around, a lump came in his throat as he saw Danny his beautiful bride came towards him, "Oh! Danny" he whispered.

The rest of the wedding proceeded as normal and after the preacher said they were man and wife Scott kissed Danny and everyone there cheered. Outside the buggy and horses waited for them which took them to Cat's house the café, where the reception is going to be, being a small town quite a few people stopped and cheered as they arrived at the café Cat's waitresses were waiting for them ushered them to a seat and delivered their lunch to them. Cat had really gone out of the way for the reception by having a band with music and dancing as dusk approached then it started to get dark Scott and Danny made their excuses and returned to the hotel, Danny collected a change of clothing in a bag before going into Scott's room, now their room closed the door and locked it.

"Come here Mrs. Burrows" Danny smiled then walked straight into Scott's arms, two pairs of hungry lips searched and joined in a passionate kiss, holding her in his arms was wonderful it felt good her body close to him and the smell of the perfume she was wearing smelt great, kissing her lips was smashing, she began to purr as his lips kissed her neck and he nibbled her ears, then squealed and giggled as his hands caressed her, his fingers moved all over her body.

"My darling you are beautiful" Scott spoke softly in her ears.

"Thank you darling" Danny replied, her lips searched for his.

Scott hands played patterns on Danny's back his hands holding the cheeks of her arse as he pulled her body into him, still kissing her lips, neck and ears and whispering word of love, his hand moved to her breasts feeling the wonderful smooth balls of flesh under the silk blouse which made him start undoing the buttons of the blouse, Danny returned the favour by unfastening the buttons of Scott's shirt, as the blouse opened he kissed her shoulders as it gave him access to her beautiful body, unfastening the last button on the blouse he pushed it over her shoulders and let it flutter to the floor.

The hands caressing her body made her feel good, the sighs the sounds of enjoyments showed the feelings she was having.

"Ahh! Scott, I love you" she whispered, "Ohhh yes lovely" she cried.

Undoing her bra and letting it drop, Scott sighed at the sight of the beautiful pair of breasts, "beautiful my darling" omitted from his lips as his hand held and caressed the lovely mounds of flesh, as Scott's right hand caressed her left breast the thumb teasing the nipple his mouth covered her right breast his vibrating tongue exciting the nipple, (Ohhh! Arr! Yes, yes lovely) Danny cried.

"I love you darling" Scott said lovingly.

As the right hand and mouth tantalized her breasts his left hand released the skirt pushed it over her hips and let it drop to the floor, Danny's breast had swelled the nipples protruded and were now so sensitive the slightest touch caused her to cry out, (Arrrr! Ahhh! Ohh more) Scott could see the pleasure it gave her, turning her body so her back was to the bed Scott's hands moved down her back entering her pants for a second held the cheeks of her arse, then with a gentle push, as her body went back onto the bed Scott relieved her of her pants, she now lay naked on the bed as Scott quickly removed the remaining clothes, Danny said a silent yes as Scott's erection was released.

The two naked bodies came together on the bed, Scott's lips kissed her lips, neck, shoulders and the sensitive breasts, Danny tensed as she felt the hand travelling down her body to pause briefly at her belly button, his dancing fingers continued over her tummy Danny breathed in her belly flattened as the hand moved over the smooth silky skin, until it reached the beautiful triangle of black pubic hair hiding the lips to the private entrance to her body, it felt good as the fingers combed the lovely forest of hair, (Arrr yes) she sighed as she let out the air and the invading finger rubbed the lips of her crotch, Danny's legs opened allowing the finger to enter her body she gasped (My angel) Scott whispered as Danny made more and more sounds of love. As the finger teased her crotch by swirling his fingers Danny's crotch rubbing her clitiuos as it moved around sending Danny into a higher level of pleasure and arousal, the sounds of love came constantly from Danny's lips, each time the revolving finger brushed her clitiuos, she could not suppress the enjoyment she was enduring Scott smiled seeing the pleasure of love Danny was experiencing (Oh! My beautiful baby).

The sounds of love continued as the juices of love began to flow, lubricating the lips to her private entrance to her body, her body writhed more as her body pushed up her arse leaving the bed, (now Scott now) she pleaded, Scott's erection was throbbing itching to enter but Scott knew the longer he held off there is more chance of an organism, so held of a few seconds until it was impossible to hold off any longer, Danny gasped as the erection entered her body through the wet lips to probe deeply, at first moving slowly to give her more pleasure as he increased the speed and penetration building up the speed until not being able to go faster this put them into a world of their own as the theruos of love took over, Scott's body jerked as his seed transferred into Danny. Danny felt as if her body had been taken apart and lovingly put back together as they both experienced organisms as they climaxed bringing their love actions to a halt the two sweat covered bodies held together as they struggled to get their breath back, Scott's erection still in Danny, Scott slowly began to get his breath back first, as he struggled to talk.

"Danny, Danny I I I love you, that was fantastic" struggling to talk.

"Thank you darling" Danny whispered thrilled at her husband's compliments.

Scott leaned towards her, two pairs of lips came together as Scott kissed her tenderly, she snuggled into him, after getting their breath back, Scott's erection started probing again, (Yes, darling yes) Danny whispered.

Scott and Danny made love a few times during the night until knackered and fell asleep tangled in each other's arms, in the morning they made love again, after making love again, being hungry they rose for a late breakfast, then going to the hotel the pair went back to bed where the lovers spent most of their time together.

"Darling now we are married wouldn't it be good if you have made me pregnant, we can now start a family" Danny spoke softly.

"Yes, darling we can have a couple of kids"

"WHAT only a couple" Danny exclaimed.

"OK we will have as many you want" Scott assured her.

"That's better" Danny said happily.

"Come on darling time to get up for dinner" Scott told her.

"Oh! OK can we try for a baby after dinner" Danny asked, he smiled and kissed her.

"Yes"

The next day Scott was told, he was required to go to court at eleven am, Scott and Danny arrived at the courthouse at ten forty-five. Sitting beside each other Scott took hold od Danny's hands.

"Danny some of the story that is in this case is quite unsavoury, I don't know if it is a good idea for you to be here" Scott said.

"Scott thank you for wanting to protect me, but I know the world is not always right in fact remember when you found and saved me I was naked and about to be raped, you saved me, thank you darling but I am an adult and married and I must face up to the good and the terrible things in this world" Danny explained.

"I love you" Scott whispered.

"I know" she whispered back.

For the next thirty minutes while the courtroom filled, they sat and talked, until the judge was in place and the sheriff and the prisoners were in the dock and the clerk of the court opened the trial by rapping his gavel to get the courts attention.

The clerk opened the proceeding then called the sheriff to the stand who outlined the reason for the trial against the two men in the dock.

The clerk next called Alex Morrison manager of Wells Fargo who gave the details of the raid on the Wells Fargo office, the theft of the payroll and the unwanted killing of the three Wells Fargo guards.

The clerk was advised by the sheriff to call Scott.

"Could I please call Mr. Scott Burrows to the stand". Scott took the stand.

"Mr Burrows please give your account of the case" the judge said.

"Ladies and Gentlemen, if this story was only about money being stolen, I would not have any interest in the case, and would not be here, but I was asked to do the job and given the true facts by a very brave dying young lady. Miss Laura Gibbs told me how she was seduced to help with the robbery by the man who told her he loved her, when I talked to her she was on her death bed and she told me she was the one that made the robbery happen and that she deserved to die, so let me tell you the true facts of the case". Scott paused to have a drink of water.

First, we know their target is $100,000 payroll,

Second, the gang shot three guards in cold blood,

Third, they kidnaped and murdered a young man and woman.

"All three are against the law, they did not have to kill the guards the gang could have tied and gagged them, It was also not necessary to kidnap the young couple, What happened in the cave should not have happened, the young lady I talked about earlier had two bullets in her back, she informed me of what happened, the man she thought she loved ordered his men to shoot her, then these men dynamited the cave entrance, thinking she was dead, but she was not and with her bare hands she dug herself out, it took her seven days, she told me the crimes that were committed in the cave".

One, Laura was shot in the back twice.

Two, the young man was unarmed, they shot him as he tried to protect the girl.

Three, these animals raped a seventeen-year-old virgin until she was dead.

There was loud gasps and angry faces all around the courtroom.

"This gang of five men if you can call them men, terrorised the town called 'Turkey' and raped a saloon girl and shot two men who tried to stop them, I am happy to say that with these two men the leaders of the gang, Ronald Bates and Dutchy all five men have been brought to justice your honour", Scott stopped talking as some of the people cheered.

"While following clues which turned out to belong to Dutchy and four other men took me to the Canadian river, picking up the sign on the other side of the river, I followed them to a cabin in a grove of trees, and straight away I saw the body of a dead man he had been shot down in cold blood, but the terrible sight that was left inside the cabin made my blood boil, the young lady had been raped but the worst thing these evil men had done was to torture the lady to death, you in the court may be thinking how do I know it was Dutchy, before riding of I heard crying following the sound I found a young eleven year old girl who witnessed what went on at the cabin, she picked out a dodger on Dutchy. When I reached the town of Vega, I dropped the young lady of at the sheriff's office, where the sheriff told me about another attempt to rape another girl in town, but they were stopped".

"After taking the first three of this evil gang, I followed sign and arrived at Stratford and was happy to see the last two men (Bates and Dutchy) were in Stratford".

"Now Ladies and Gentlemen the next part tells you what it is all about and why Bates and his gang carried out the robbery in the first place, Laura before she died told me that Bates had told her he was going to buy a ranch and he carried out the robbery to get the money to buy it, the thing that did puzzle me the ranch was workable but Bates did not hire cowhands but criminals instead, Bates had Dutchy and the four gunmen then also recruited the local sheriff who was crooked, what I found is with their help he intends to take all the land around the ranch and there is six homesteaders he wants the land and is going to get it full stop, I did not know my way around so decided to follow this gang, at the first homestead they shot the man and would have shot the woman and two children if I had not fired at them from the hill in front of the shack, I stopped to help the family and because I stopped to assist the woman and children I arrived too late at the second homestead the owners had been slaughtered learning from the first homestead I knew I had to carry on so left them, When I arrived at the third homestead one of the gang had shot one of the children who were playing in the yard, I shot and hit one of the men in the shoulder so the gang once more rode off, the folk at the homestead told me the boy was alive and they would look after him and for me to carry on with my pursuit, when getting to the fourth homestead they had shot the homesteader just before I arrived I raised my rifle and shot instinctively the other criminal cried out as my bullet hit this man in the back with my chasing them Bates decided to give up as he had not succeeded in his plan instead of going to the next homestead the remainder of the gang returned to the ranch, with the sheriff gone and his two remaining crooks wounded– Dutchy returned to the town leaving Bates alone, I couldn't be more elated this was the ideal chance to capture these two men and finish the job I had been sent to do".

"That night with the aid of the doctor and the Wells Fargo agent in Stratford I was able to capture the last two members of the gang, Dutchy and their leader Ronald Bates." Scott paused to have a sip of water.

"I know some of you are wondering what it was all about, the robbery in town and a ranch miles away near Texas northern border, well it's like this Bates has a friend that works for the railway, who told him in confidence that the railway was coming through Stratford in a few months' time and that the railroad would pay a lot of money to buy the land to lay the tracks on., folk I have to admit if I had not been given the information Laura gave me it would have been a lot harder. Your honour that is the end of my statement" Scott completed his evidence.

The sheriff was asked by the court to contact the town Scott mentioned as one man's word was not enough to hang a man, information gathered sealed the fate of the two men as they told the same story, Bates and Dutchy were sentenced to hang the punishment was carried out the next day.

As it was now the end of the case and they started to get ready to leave town Scott received a message to come down to the Wells Fargo office to see Alex.

At the counter, a young man asked.

"How can I help you sir".

"Could you tell Mr. Morrison, that Mr. Burrows is here as requested" Scott said.

"Yes sir Mr. Burrows" the young man replied. The young man went through to the office a moment later he returned with Alex Morrison who came through the counter his hand held out.

"Scott, Danny hello please come through to the office" Alex invited.

The three of them went into the office Alex closed the door and made sure the blinds on the windows were down.

"Right Scott I have asked you down here, so I can pay you for the job you have done, and to once more thank you on behalf of Wells Fargo for you retrieving the money stolen" Alex informed him.

"OK Thanks Alex" Scott replied.

"Right Scott, the amount you earned for doing the job is $10.000, but you recovered more than the money stolen, so Wells Fargo has instructed me to pay you a bonus of $5.000, you are also entitled to expenses of $1.000 a total of $16.000 and you earned every cent, thank you" Alex said.

"Thank you, we will say goodbye now as Danny and I intend to leave early in the morning" Scott told him.

"I'm sorry to see you go but it has been great knowing you both" Alex said.

Scott and Danny her arm through his strolled along the main street of the town.

"Where to now darling" Danny asked.

"The bank sweetheart "Scott returned.

"Hi! Miss, I would like to put some money in my account" Scott told the teller.

"Yes, sir fill this deposit slip in" Scott filled in the slip.

The teller looked at the slip then called the manager. Who came to the teller straight away?

"Is there a problem" Scott asked.

"Oh! No sir you wish to deposit $14.000 anything over $1.000 the cashier must tell a senior member of staff" the manager explained.

"OK. Thank you. You will only be looking after the money for me, me and my wife are going to travel, when we get to the town of our destination, I will be wanting the money to be transferred there" Scott explained

"OK sir can do" the manager

"Now darling let's have lunch" Scott said

"OK Scott, after lunch we will make the rounds and say goodbye to all our friends then get back and start packing" Danny suggested.

"Yes, you are right darling" Scott replied. Scott and Danny did exactly what they agreed. Scott and Danny spent quite some time going around town with the frequent stops and cups of coffee.

Going back to the hotel for the last night, as they wanted to get away early the pair of them spent the next hour packing getting everything ready to go.

"Danny, we are going to be together just the two of us-, we are not going to be in any hurry, I want us to enjoy the time together treat it like a honeymoon we will not go to any town's unless we need supplies, it will possibly take around two weeks

I am hoping we can swim most nights, also we will only use one bedroll to sleep in".

"Sleep "Danny broke in.

"Sometimes" Scott stated with a smile.

"OK" she said sullenly.

"Danny, we will make love every night" Scott told her.

"That's better, I love you" Danny said in a husky voice as they both undressed and slipped into bed.

Scott reached over and kissed her tenderly, Danny sighed, her eyes closed, and, in her head, she said (Yes please) as the hand stroked her crotch.

THE END

THE PREFACE.

A gang of ruthless men robbed the Wells Fargo office in the town of Jayton because a large payroll had been delivered there, as they did so they murdered three guards, as they left the gang kidnaped a young couple, who they also murdered, the Sheriff and Wells Fargo tried everything possible to track and catch these evil men but to no avail and were on the verge of admitting defeat.

At this time Scott Burrows bounty hunter rode into town, with a dead killer over his horse, you could ask who is Scott Burrows but his reputation is that he is the best and always gets who he goes after. The sheriff and the Wells Fargo agent decided to approach him and ask him if he would take the job and if he would hear the story from a lady who has all the details, Scott listened to the dying Laura and immediately excepted the job.

THE AUTHOR

My name is J.G.Thompson, but write under the name of J.G.Tee, I am seventy eight years old / young, I have been writing about my favourite subject and passion (the American old west), for many years during my twenty five years at sea, twenty two in the Royal Navy, I read every western I could get my hands on, my favourite author is Louis Lamour my interest in writing continued after I left the Royal Navy thirty years ago, I have since spent twenty years as a AA patrolman, during this time I was able to accumulate a lot of knowledge and experience, It has taken a long time to write this novel I enjoy reading it. I am therefore certain other people will enjoy it also.

I am also proud to admit have been decorated by Her Majesty the Queen herself who presented me with the (BEM) the British Empire Medal.

Notes of Interest

When writing its best to write as realistic as possible so the violence and sex parts of this book are as realistic as can be made, I do not class the sex parts as pornographic I have written about two people who fall in love so also make love, because of this call my books (Pocket erotic westerns).

Yours faithfully.
J.G. Tee